# Kingz of the Game 6

Lock Down Publications and Ca$h
Presents

# Kingz of the Game 6

A Novel by *Playa Ray*

# Lock Down Publications

P.O. Box 944
Stockbridge, Ga 30281

**Visit our website @**
www.lockdownpublications.com

Copyright 2021 by Playa Ray
Kingz of the Game 6

First Edition October 2021
Printed in the United States of America

*This is a work of fiction. Names, characters, places, and incidents either are products of the author's imagination or are used ficti-tiously. Any similarity to actual events or locales or persons, living or dead, is entirely coincidental.*

**Lock Down Publications**
**Like our page on Facebook: Lock Down Publications @**
www.facebook.com/lockdownpublications.ldp

Book interior design by: **Shawn Walker**
Edited by: **Lashonda Johnson**

Playa Ray

# Stay Connected with Us!

Text **LOCKDOWN** to 22828 to stay up-to-date with
new releases, sneak peaks, contests and more...
Thank you.

# Submission Guideline.

Submit the first three chapters of your completed manuscript to ldpsubmissions@gmail.com, subject line: Your book's title. The manuscript must be in a .doc file and sent as an attachment. Document should be in Times New Roman, double spaced and in size 12 font. Also, provide your synopsis and full contact information. If sending multiple submissions, they must each be in a separate email.

Have a story but no way to send it electronically? You can still submit to LDP/Ca$h Presents. Send in the first three chapters, written or typed, of your completed manuscript to:

LDP: Submissions Dept
P.O. Box 944
Stockbridge, Ga 30281

*DO NOT send original manuscript. Must be a duplicate.*

Provide your synopsis and a cover letter containing your full contact information.

Thanks for considering LDP and Ca$h Presents.

Playa Ray

*"There's no harm in hoping for the best, as long as you're prepared for the worst."*

*~Stephen King~*
*Author*

*THE INVESTIGATION* continues! After the Kingz investigation takes a turn for the worse, FBI's Special Agent Brian Bishop finds himself in the same dilemma after pursuing the Queenz.

Still hell-bent on finishing what he'd started, the dedicated agent continues stalking the sole survivors of each organization, and refuses to hand up his badge, until they are both sentenced to death for the crimes they committed or buried alongside their fallen comrades.

On the night that a pregnant Sheila is abducted by a killer who's only interested in the death of her boyfriend, Ray agrees to trade his life for hers and their unborn child.

What really happened to the Last King standing whose body has yet to surface?

Did the murderer do a good job of disposing of the corpse or did Agent Bishop play a part in the King's disappearance?

Playa Ray

# Chapter 1

*Wednesday*

*June 8, 2005*

It was 8:17 p.m., when Special Agent Rhonda Thomas pulled the gray, 2004 Mercedes Benz into the lot of the warehouse building that produced no kind of light, which gave the place an ominous look. Plus, the sole dimlit lamp in the parking lot was as worthless as one of those plugin night lights most children felt safe sleeping with.

Just like on our last three visits, Thomas and I were casually dressed. She was clad in an orange Donna Karen dress, and matching metallic Casadei heels. I had on a burgundy three-piece suit by Sean Jean with black Italian loafers designed by somebody whose name I couldn't pronounce, which were all provided by the bureau for this investigation, including the Benz. They'd even draped us in expensive pieces of jewelry, to make sure we looked the part of a well-to-do married couple, who had the means to pay for illegal sexual services, that may comprise having group sex with under aged children of either gender, and heritage.

Okay, I think now's the time to put you up to speed on what's going on. Well, a little over a year ago, the missing child rate in Georgia, gradually increased, placing the crime at number two, right up under murder. The mass abductions sparked an epidemic that eventually caught the attention of the Department of Justice, who subsequently applied pressure to the Federal Bureau of Investigation, to bring somebody-anybody-to justice.

Therefore, with the aegis of the GBI, agents had been persistently beating up the streets for months which finally yielded an anonymous tip that a possible illegal prostitution ring containing under aged children was taking place somewhere in Sandy Springs, Georgia. For the record, we've received numerous tips, considering the reward that was put in place by the governor, and although most tips we received were bogus, the situation made it imperative that we entertain them all.

However, when the tip came in about the prostitution ring in Sandy Springs, the director sent Thomas and I out to investigate. We didn't go around questioning people, instead, we hung out at bars, lounges, and a few night clubs, just mingling with ordinary people which brought us a break. The director had given us a week, and on our sixth day, while having drinks at a daytime bar, Thomas and I were approached by a forty-year-old Caucasian female with long, dark hair, and high cheekbones. She was a bit swanky, with the excessive jewelry and make-up.

She introduced herself as, Phoenix and inquired about our marriage, apparently taking notice of Thomas' wedding ring, and my engagement band. Being two astute, and well-trained agents, we went along with the unceremonious play expertly improvising, though most of Phoenix's questions were aimed at Thomas.

Maintaining my belief that women are much better actors than men, I pretty much deferred, and let the women take over the conversation, while evaluating Phoenix who was visibly flirting with Thomas. I mean, she was actually touching and rubbing her in places that clearly suggested sexual intercourse.

Then, she started asking questions, "Have you and Thomas ever participated in an orgy?"

"No."

"Have you ever fantasized about inviting a third party into your bed?"

"We've joked about it, but never gave it any serious thought."

Would you guys like to experience that in my hotel room tonight?"

"Um, can you give us a minute to discuss?"

"Of course!"

Phoenix excused herself and made for the restroom to give us some time to *discuss* her sexual proposal which we used to call our director. A fast talker, Thomas hurriedly explained everything in small details, hoping to be off the phone by the time the older woman returned, but failed. Before the women came into earshot,

Thomas was able to mention the proposal, and where it could possibly lead. When Phoenix rejoined us, Thomas pretended to be talking to her sister, telling her to meet our daughters at their bus stop after school, and to stay with them until we got home.

To make a long story short, we followed Phoenix's Aston Martin to her hotel room, where she insisted that we all take a shower together, before initiating intercourse, which pretty much started in the shower. Phoenix had all kinds of sex toys that she was quite fond of using on Thomas. Hell, that was the first time I'd ever seen anal beads outside of porn movies.

After our sexual romp that lasted for almost two hours, Phoenix informed us that she had friends who specialize in fulfilling people's sexual fantasies no matter how bizarre. You know just in case we were interested in *exploring new heights*, as she put it. Considering the case, we were investigating of course we were interested. Phoenix logged her contact number into Thomas' cell phone, and insisted we call her once we conjured up a sexual fantasy that would befit us.

She didn't receive a call from us until a month later, which is how long it took to get the investigation approved. Plus, the bureau had to furnish us with new identities, just in case we were dealing with professionals, who were capable, and willing to conduct background checks on whomever they were willing to provide services for.

Our call to Phoenix was conducted at the James P. Russell building, and being monitored, recorded and traced. Agent Rhonda Thomas and I insisted that our sexual fantasy was to have another orgy with a much younger female, preferably African-American. The older woman claimed she'd call us back, and quickly hung up seconds before the trace was complete.

Another week had gone by, when Phoenix called Thomas' cell phone from a pay phone, insisting that we meet her at the same bar we encountered her. There, she had us sign confidentiality agreement forms, basically claiming knowledge of purchasing, and indulging in illegal sexual activities, and to write her a check for five hundred dollars. Rhonda Thomas, as Trina Shaw wrote her the five-hundred-dollar check from the checkbook attached to the banking account that was also set up by the bureau.

That following Wednesday, four days later, Phoenix called from another pay phone, requesting another rendezvous at the same place, at 8:00 p.m. She told us that we should dress casually. However, we did as requested and that time, followed her silver Range Rover to the nondescript warehouse building we're now parked at, and ready to make our fourth and final visit.

"Are you ready, Mr. Shaw?" Thomas now asked, upon shutting off the engine.

"Yeah, I guess so," I answered, glad that this would be my last night as Mr. Patrick Shaw. "You're gonna make the call?"

Pulling her cellular from one of the cupholders, Thomas selected the appropriate phone number, and opted for speakerphone.

"We have eyes on you," answered Agent Powell, who was on point. "Everybody's in position. You can proceed when ready."

"We're moving," she told him.

"Roger that. You guys be careful."

Being that we weren't allowed to bring cell phones inside, Thomas put hers back into the cupholder, and we dismounted. There were about twelve vehicles present, mostly expensive. I find it sickening what people with money would pay to appease their twisted sexual appetites. Especially when it included under aged children, which is something these people seemed to specialize in.

As always, under the notion that we were being watched, Thomas and I put our arms around each other, and made the short walk toward the building. We reached the rust-covered steel door that looked like it once had a decent red paint job back in the 70s. There was no door handle, or knob, but a rectangular cutout in the door that acted as a peephole whenever a metal plate is slid to the side. As always, I took the initiative and pressed the button on the side of the door, it yielded no sounds inside, though we were certain it worked.

Seconds later, the plate slid aside, allowing us to see nothing but a pair of eyes, surrounded by darkness.

"Who sent you?" the same baritone voice resounded from the dark hole.

"Farouk," I answered. "King of Egypt."

"From whence have thou cometh?" he inquired

"Bari delle Puglie," Thomas concluded our code of passage.

Instantly, the plate slammed shut. Then, there was the loud clunk of a large bolt shifting from one side to the other, before the rusty steel door creaked open to a well-dressed, white male and female, who resembled butlers, with their dark suits and white gloves. The man held a clipboard, and the woman was holding a hand-held metal detector down by her side. Once we entered, the man closed and secured the door.

"Welcome back, Mr. and Mrs. Shaw!" he greeted, checking our names off on his roster, before placing it atop the small table sitting off to the side. "Shall we get this part over with, so we can get you to your room?"

Already knowing what *this part* consisted of, I assumed the position, allowing him to frisk me. Thomas let the woman rummage through her purse, before running the wand over her body. When this was complete, the woman insisted we follow her.

About twenty yards from the entrance, a walled concrete structure began, stopping midway from the ceiling, and stretched out for another fifty yards. It was topped with tin, which made up the roof for the several rooms that were partitioned by concrete walls and finished with plywood doors that had black numbers spray painted on them. The one we were led to, had the number seven on it.

"You guys can go ahead and settle in," said the woman, who I could barely hear over the multiple industrial fans spread throughout the large building that had just a tad bit more lighting than the parking lot. "The host will be with you shortly."

"Thank you, sweetheart!" Thomas said, handing her a fifty-dollar bill. "And this is for you."

When we entered the room, our escort flipped the sign on the doorknob, to indicate that it was occupied, before closing the door behind her. Our small, temporary quarters only contained a small

13

table, air conditioner, lamp, and a queen-size bed. The air conditioner sat atop the table, along with the lamp that illuminated the room through a red-light bulb. The bed was made and decorated with posts and privacy curtains. Wires for the electronic items were plugged into an extension cord that ran between the concrete and tin roof, providing electricity for the makeshift compound.

Immediately after the woman left us alone, Thomas and I searched the room for any kind of recording devices that may have been planted for the pleasure of some sick individual. Once we saw that everything was clear as always, we joined each other on the bed, sitting extremely close, to maintain our play as husband and wife.

"I'm glad this is about to be over," Thomas admitted in a low tone. "I feel sorry for that little girl."

"We have to remain clinical, Thomas," I chided, knowing damn well I was just as emotionally attached as she was. "Plus, there are other children held captive here, who are suffering the same abuse. We're doing this for them, also. Just keep—" I stopped short at the sound of someone tapping on the door.

"Mr. and Mrs. Shaw?" the familiar voice of the host inquired from beyond the wooden door.

"Come on in," I answered, taking hold of one of Thomas' hands in mine.

The host sagely stuck his head in, before entering, carrying his ever-present clipboard, and clad in a suit that may have been gray, though I really couldn't tell for the red lighting. The white man, whose name we've never known was in his early fifties, about 5'7, and 155 pounds. Plus, he was a bit feminine. Of course, this was something Thomas had pointed out to me on our first visit.

"How's my favorite couple, tonight?" he asked, revealing perfectly straight teeth that I was highly in favor of knocking down his throat for running such a sadistic operation.

"We're fine," Thomas answered, sweetly. "How are you tonight?"

"I'm wonderful, doll!" he replied, with a slight roll of the neck. "Just trying to meet everybody's needs. So, what kind of mischievous acts are you guys trying to participate in this evening? Please, tell me you're interested in trying another one of my beauties."

"Is there a problem with our regular request?" Thomas inquired, anger and disappointment lacing her tone.

"Not the request, darling," the host answered, one hand poised on his hip. "But the girl. She's occupied at the moment."

Rhonda Thomas lunged from the bed with her hands balled into fists, as though she was going to assail the man. "What do you mean she's occupied at the moment?" she hissed.

Of course, Thomas knew what he meant. Hell, I knew what the fucker meant, but the very thought of some grown-ass man having his way with the fourteen-year-old girl, made me want to choke this son of a bitch right now.

The host let out a sharp breath, then asserted: "Look, why don't you guys let me pick a fruit from the basket. At the conclusion of your session, if you're not satisfied, I'll grant you a full refund."

"That's mighty generous of you," said Thomas. "Thank you, but no thank you! We want our same girl."

"But she's with another client."

"We'll wait," she insisted, flopping back down onto the bed, and folding her arms over her chest.

"Well, that's a first," said the host, with raised eyebrows." I've never had a client come back for the same piece of ass before. Everyone's always into trying something new, but you guys struck me as an odd pair from the moment I laid eyes on you. Even Phoenix thinks you two are strange." After a moment's pause, he shrugged and said, "Very well, if you get tired of waiting, and feel the urge to try a different flavor, have one of my employees ring for me."

"Will do," Thomas said, handing him the sealed envelope containing five, one-hundred-dollar bills. When he left, she turned to me. "Did I play it right? I mean, what if she's not with us when the time comes?"

"She'll still be rescued," I assured, still thinking about what the host said about us being an odd pair, clearly stating that he was suspicious of us from the beginning. Could he have already made us? "Did you send out our location?"

"Not yet," she answered, a worried expression on her face.

"The plan was to send it out the moment we found out what room we were in," I reminded. "The T.O.E is already set. When that time arrives, wherever the girl is, she'll be safe. The thing is to secure *our* safety."

"You're right."

Thomas received her set of keys from her purse. The black alarm box attached to the keyring wasn't an alarm box at all. It was a transmitter used for sending out Morse codes, but in this case, it was used to pinpoint which room we're occupying, to prevent being harmed in the impending raid. Thomas pressed the button seven times, then waited. Once the device chirruped twice, indicating that our location had been confirmed, she placed the keys back into her purse, and began nervously wringing her hands. Twenty-four minutes had gone by, when there was another rap at the door.

"Are you guys decent?" the host asked.

"Come on," Thomas answered.

The host pushed the door open but didn't enter. Instead, he stepped aside, and allowed one of his butler-dressed men to usher in the little girl we'd been colluding with since our first visit. She was dark-complexioned, 5'6, and 140 pounds. Plus, as the company's custom, she was outfitted in a black, snug-fitted, patent leather skirt, matching heels, and a burgundy, crop-styled wig that made her look twenty-four, instead of fourteen. The make-up and red lipstick were a bit too much if you ask me.

When her handler removed his white gloved hands from her shoulders, April slowly staggered forward, with her eyes downcast. Thomas got up to help her to the bed, while the two men looked on stoically. Just as they were watching the scene, I was watching them. You know how you get that feeling in your gut that something's not right? Well, this is that point where I experienced that feeling.

Yeah, I really believe the host is on to the three of us. He'd probably uncovered our true identities and realized April had come up with a way to prevent digesting the ecstasy pills they administer to their captive minors.

However, if this was the case, the big question was: what did he intend to do about it?

"Thank you, gentlemen!" Thomas said, dismissively, after placing April beside me on the edge of the bed.

There was a brief second of hesitation, then a quick exchange, before the employee backed out of the room, and the host closed the door behind them. I don't even think Thomas noticed any of this, while she was visibly displaying the affection of a mama bear over its cub. Or maybe it was just me. I've been wrong on several occasions.

"I want my mama!" said April, who smelled of fresh soap, and too much perfume. The stoned look she had on her face upon entering, had quickly evaporated.

"Shh!" I said, as Thomas took a seat on the other side of her.

Upon my signal, she took the girl's wig off, and checked it for a listening device. Finding nothing, she strategically replaced the hair piece.

"Y'all promised—"

"Yes, we did," I cut her off, still hearing those warning bells going off inside my head.

My watch was showing 8:54 p.m., which meant we had approximately six minutes before the breach. I looked at Thomas.

"We have less than six minutes," I informed her.

She glanced down at her own watch. "Good! I'll be glad when—"

*Boom!*

Her words were cut off, when our door was forced open, crashing into the inner wall. In walked three of the butler-dressed employees, followed by the host who had his hands stuffed into his pockets, while his men held us at gunpoint with handguns. At this time, April clinged to Thomas out of fear. I was thinking about my twenty-one-month-old son, Brian Bishop Jr., wondering if this would be the day I failed him as a father by getting myself murdered, and not being there to teach him how to be a man.

"I can't quite put my finger on it," the host started. "But there's something going on between the three of you. I can only surmise that you two have known the girl, prior to her abduction, and are plotting a way to get her out of here. Perhaps she's a relative, or something. I mean, I don't see any other reason why you chose to deal only with her."

"If all this was so," I endeavored. "We would've contacted the authorities after our *first* visit."

"Maybe you did," he said. "Maybe they're already outside, waiting to kick the doors down any minute now."

I swallowed. This fucker already knows!

"That's one of the cons of running this kind of operation," he went on. "You let the johns in, running the risk of them being familiar with some of the merchandise, which could be a huge problem. Well, that's unless you identify it, and neutralize it *before* it becomes a problem—" He paused for effect. Perhaps to let those words sink in. "Now," he resumed. "If you lovely people don't mind, I'm gonna need you off the bed, and facing the rear wall."

April still clung to Thomas as we all got up, and faced the concrete wall. Considering the width of it, I found myself standing protectively behind them. One of the men ordered me to place my hands behind my back, then bind them with a plastic zip-tie. Thrusting me to the side, he performed the same maneuver on Thomas. April cried uncontrollably now, but she didn't put up a fight as the man took hold of her frail limbs, and seemed to snap the manacle on rather tight, causing her to wince.

"Somebody grab that purse," the host instructed, backing out of the room." Once we take out the trash, I want this room wiped down."

Of course, I was the first to be shoved through the threshold by one of the men, followed by Thomas and April bringing up the rear with her handler and the host. As I figured, we were being herded in the opposite direction from whence we'd come, which was certainly toward the rear of the building.

Then, all of a sudden, there was a loud, explosive sound, followed by another one by a quarter of a second. The sound of glass shattering from above caused me to stop in my tracks, and look up in time to see four, tactical-clad figures, spring down from the ceiling on rope. Yes! The fucking cavalry is here!

Just then, the goon escorting me, raised his gun as if taking aim at one of the men dropping from above. On instinct, I leaned forward, and drove my shoulder into his chest, knocking him into the wall. Making a quick recovery, he swung the gun toward my temple. The last thing I heard was the report from the weapon, before darkness befell me.

# Playa Ray

# Chapter 2

"What's the status of his condition?"

I heard Special Agent Dan Powell's voice, but couldn't see him because of the surrounding darkness. Besides feeling numb all over, I was cold, and my head was throbbing with pain which was probably symptoms associated with dying a slow death. If that's the case, I would gladly rest in peace. I just wanted the pain in my head to go away.

"He's stable," this was a female's voice. "He didn't lose a large amount of blood, but the gash was almost an inch wide, and required seven stitches. Perhaps he'll come around once the anesthesia wears off."

"Thanks, ma'am!"

"You're welcome, sir!"

I forced my eyes open, just in time to see a blurred, curly-haired figure strut out of the room. The masculine figure of Powell who stood a few feet from where I laid, watched her leave. It took several tries to blink the filmy curtains from my eyes. When they were ninety-eight percent clear, I saw that Powell had traded in his field attire for a dark-blue dress suit and red necktie.

Noticing me awake, he spun on his heels, and made for the exit, where he looked out into the corridor, before closing the door. Then, retracing his steps, he approached and stood beside the bed, looking down at me with uncertainty. Or was it pity?

"I know this is not a good time to be standing over you like the grim reaper," he started. "But the mission log needs to be completed, and a few affidavits are missing. That would be mine, yours, and Thomas. Considering your current condition, I've given you a forty-eight-hour continuance. However, as point, I can't complete mine and go home, until you explain what happened back there."

*"What happened?"* I asked voice groggy beyond recognition.

Clearly, recognizing it, Powell rounded the bed, and poured me a cup of water from the canteen on the portable table, making sure to electronically elevate the head part of the bed, before handing me the small, paper cup. Despite the throbbing pain in my temple, I downed the cool water in two gulps, and handed the cup back, closing my eyes.

"Now—" Powell resumed, "—unless this was some kind of sexual play you and Thomas came up with to dally until the breach. I really need to know how you two *and* the little girl, ended up bound with zipties?"

That's when the horror came back to me unabated. My eyes shot open. "April!" I uttered. "Did y'all get her out of there?"

"We rescued *all* the children that were held captive there," he pointed out. "By now, the GBI and locals should have gotten statements, and reunited the children with their families. Speaking of which, I notified your fiance of your condition, or whatnot."

"Is she on the way?"

"Negative!" the lead investigator replied. "I have you under strict observation. No visits."

*"No visits?"*

"This investigation is still ongoing, Bishop."

"But how? Didn't you just tell me—"

"I'll explain later," he cut me off. "Zipties, explain!"

I took a deep breath, before saying, "I think the host made us."

"You think?"

"I don't think he made us as FBI agents," I went on to explain. "He assumed Thomas and I were familiar with the girl and were plotting to help her escape."

"Did he actually say this?"

"Those were his words."

"Okay, go on."

"That's when he ordered his men to bind us," I said, seeing the scene play out in my mind.

"Fast forward it a bit," said Powell. "One of the men discharged his weapon which resulted in you being injured. Take me there."

"They were escorting us to the rear of the warehouse," I explained.

"That's when the team breached. The man escorting me, raised his gun to secure an aim on one of the agents dropping from the ceiling. I drove my body into him, forcing him into the wall. That's when he recovered, and shot me, but I'm assuming the bullet only grazed my skull."

"*Shot you?*" Powell asked, furrowing his eyebrows.

"Yeah." Now I was giving *him* a suspicious look. Did he think I was lying? Would I be laying up in Grady Memorial Hospital, with my head bandaged, if I wasn't shot? *I saw the guy aim his gun at me! I heard the fucking shot!*

"I see," Powell muttered, clearing his throat. "Before the gun went off, do you remember exactly where Thomas was standing?"

"She was behind me," I answered, now confused at his line of questioning.

"Directly behind you?"

"Directly behind the man escorting me," I clarified, sensing something was amiss. "Why is that so important? I mean, why can't you just ask Thomas to verify her own location?" He gave me a knowing look. "Was there a shootout?" I inquired, not liking the look.

"A little," he answered, casting a glance at the closed door. "The three gunmen put up some resistance but were subdued by rubber bullets. No casualties on their end."

"And our end?" For some reason, I felt I already knew the answer.

"I guess you were immediately rendered unconscious when you were struck," he asserted with a pensive look on his face. "And, by the way, you were not shot. When the goon struck you with his gun, it accidentally discharged. Thomas was the recipient of the bullet. She didn't make it."

\*\*\*

### *Saturday*

"From the dirt, we were created. To the dirt, we shall return."

While the Reverend conducted his final eulogy, prior to the casket of Rhonda Thomas being lowered into the earth. I couldn't help but look over at Rhonda Thomas' husband, Michale Thomas who seemed impassive behind his dark sunglasses, even though I knew better. I couldn't say the same for their son and daughter, who were standing on each side of him, bawling their little hearts out throughout the whole service.

Two older women had been doing their best to console the children all day and were still endeavoring to do so at this point. Their emotional disorders played on the strings of my mental, because there was no way I could not accept the blame for their mother's death. Had I not thrown myself into the gunman in an attempt to save another agent, maybe Thomas would still be alive.

I promised Monique I would come straight home after the funeral service, but I found myself breaking that promise when I pulled into the parking lot of a nearby pub. I was hungry though I had no appetite. All I wanted was to have a couple of drinks and be alone for a few hours which is why I left my phone in the car.

The aroma of various cooked foods reached my nostrils before I'd made it through the entrance of the establishment that wasn't at all crowded. Some hip hop song played low from speakers. I didn't care to look around for, while people ate, drank, and just had a grand old time, as though Rhonda Thomas hadn't just been lowered into the ground, never to be seen again. That goes to show how much the world cares about you, I guess.

"What'll it be, my man?" the bartender inquired upon my approach.

I took a good sixty seconds to half scan the posted menu, before asking, "How are the red links cooked?"

"However, you want them cooked," he told me. "Is that what you want?"

"Yeah, I guess so," I replied, now regarding the alcohol section of the menu. "I want two links cut down the middle, fried, and laid on toasted light bread with cheese, onions, and mustard. For my beverage, I want two Miller Lites."

"Will you be eating in?"

"Of course."

"Okay." He retrieved two bottles of Miller Lites, popped their caps, then set them on the bar before me. "There you go, sir. You can wait here for your order, or you can find a table, and it will be brought out to you."

Of course, I chose to find myself a table, glad to find one in a corner, and extremely glad that the place was built like a nightclub, with no window which seemed more suitable for my gloomy mood. Now, sitting with my back facing the corner, I started on one of my beers while surveying the mid-day crowd through the mirror-tinted lenses of my sunglasses.

About eight minutes later, I saw a rather slim woman round the counter carrying a plate in one hand, and cellular in the other. She was wearing blue leggings and a red tank top beneath her stained, white apron. As she neared my table with a broad smile on her face, I pulled out my band of bills, peeling a five-dollar bill from it.

"Fried links, right?" she asked.

"That's me."

She placed the plate down in front of me.

I handed her the bill. "This is for you."

"Thank you, sir!" she beamed. "If you need anything else, just holler for Patrice."

"Will do."

Just as she walked away, two men sat down at the table close to mine. Having only a mere glance in their direction, I swallowed the remainder of my first beer, and decided to try one of my sandwiches.

"I don't know why you're procrastinating," I heard one of the men say as I bit into my sandwich that was pretty good. "These girls might be the move," he went on. "Especially if they're anything like the Kingz."

I almost choked on my meal at the mention of the late Kingz who were all murdered almost two years ago, on the same night I was set to arrest them on a gang of charges, following an interesting investigation. Since then, I hadn't taken on any investigations of that caliber, until this recent child abduction case, although I had become something of a technical advisor to some of my fellow agents working the interstate BMF case.

"Man, those girls are not the Kingz' widows," the second guy spoke. "They're just using that as a means to come up."

"Who gives a fuck!" the first guy shot back. "Whether they were married to the Kingz or not. I don't think motherfuckers really care. They came into the game as *The Queenz*. If that's what they want the streets to know them by, so be it. I'm fucking with their campaign."

"So, you're going to the birthday bash they're throwing on the twenty-fifth?"

"Hell yeah!" said the first man. "Who knows? I may end up fucking one of 'em."

By the time they were ready to order, I had consumed my second sandwich, downed my last beer, and was ready to leave. I stuck around for another minute or so, to see if they would reveal anything else about this group of women known as *The Queenz*, especially the name of the club the birthday bash would be at, but they didn't. After seven minutes of listening to them brag about the women they'd slept with. I ordered two more beers to go, then made my exit.

However, I still wasn't interested in heading home, so I just drove around, enjoying my beer, and losing myself in my thoughts. Of course, I was thinking about this female group, and wondering if I should pursue them as I'd done the Kingz, which would probably be futile, being that they're women, and I'd never seen, or heard of any women prospering in the drug game. Especially without the backing of at least one male figure.

It was after 7:00 p.m., when I finally pulled into the driveway of the three-bedroom home that I share with Monique and our two children, parking beside Monique's gray Lexus truck. By this time, I was a bit tipsy from the beers, though I managed to dispose of the bottles before coming home. It's not that Monique was against me drinking. I just didn't want her thinking I was drinking from emotions fueled by Thomas' death, which was sure to bring on another one of her jealous, accusatory tantrums.

Speaking of the devil, as soon as I killed the engine, Monique emerged from the house, clad in the same blue jean shorts, and green shirt she had on when I left this morning. Upon sliding in beside me, she took hold of and began massaging my right hand. The look on her face was impassive with a hint of compassion.

"I'm sorry, baby," she said in almost a whisper.

"For what?" I asked, truly confused.

"For going on and on about you having sex with Rhonda Thomas," she said. "I know it was something you had to do for the sake of the investigation. I should've been more open-minded about it."

"It's okay, Monique," I told her. "How are the kids?"

# Playa Ray

# Chapter 3

## *Monday*

This was my first day back to work since the night Thomas was murdered, and I still wasn't all that enthused about it which is why I took my sweet time getting there. Plus, when I got off the elevator, it seemed like everybody was rubbernecking me from their cubicles as I made for my own, though no one made any attempts to greet me.

Yes, we now have cubicles, thanks to the overhaul done on the building to make room for new recruits fresh out of the academy. Even though we'd also received agents from other branches, some being swapped out with some of our agents. At first, I was against the non-privacy set-up, but it slowly grew on me. It's okay, I guess.

One thing I still didn't like about the arrangement was the accessibility people had to my private space, offering them the liberty to leave post-its smack dab in the center of my monitor, as though I wouldn't see them if they were posted anywhere else. However, the message for the morning was from Agent Dan Powell telling me to meet with him as soon as I got in.

Now, I was wondering what he could possibly want with me. The investigation was over. I'd made out my statement the day I was released from the hospital. Surely, the case wasn't ready to go before a court this early. Ah, fuck it! Whatever it is, I might as well had gotten it over with but first, I had to get my caffeine fix for the morning.

As a late-comer, one can expect the breakroom to be empty, and the coffee and pastries to be gone. The room was empty and there was one jelly roll, and a little more than half of coffee for my thermos. No complaints here, I gladly scooped the sweet bread into a napkin, poured the last of the steaming liquid, then made for the elevators, thankful that no one endeavored to speak to me.

Just as I was still located on the sixth floor, Powell was still located on the fourth. I had already consumed a greater portion of my sweet roll by the time I stepped off the elevator, so to avoid looking unprofessional, I stopped by the trash bin, finished it off, wiped my mouth, then proceeded to Powell's cubicle, where he was jotting something down. I stood over him for a good thirty seconds, before he looked up from his work.

"Have a seat, Bishop!" he said, gesturing toward the second chair.

I sat and took a sip from my thermos. Since that Saturday night at his home, two years ago, I still didn't feel comfortable around him.

"Are you well?" he inquired. "I had you scheduled to see Dr. Shoob last week, but he said you never showed."

"What else is new?" I sassed. Surely, he didn't think I was going to waste my time being dissected by our residential shrink. "Is this why you summoned me down here?"

"Part of it," Powell admitted, now visibly analyzing me. "I also wanted to put you up to speed on the child abduction case."

"That case is closed," I insisted.

"Trust me, I wish it was."

"How is it not?"

"According to the GBI—" he started. "—when they began taking down pictures of the rescued children, six remained attached to their board."

"So, six children are still missing?"

"Exactly," answered Powell. "Expecting the worst, we assembled a search party, and canvassed the grounds surrounding the warehouse at about a five-mile radius but turned up nothing. There's speculation that these people also operated at another undisclosed location. So far, nobody's talking."

"What about Phoenix?" I inquired, remembering that Thomas and I had never actually seen the older woman on any of our visits to the place.

"That's the thing," Powell let out. "She wasn't there that night. Maybe she's just a scout. Or maybe she clocks in at their other location. Wherever it is, we're hoping to get a proximity on its location by setting up a perimeter around the payphones she used to contact you from."

"I don't think it'll be wise for me to continue posing as a customer," I told him. "Especially-"

"I've already considered that, Bishop," he cut me off. "We've confiscated their logbook, and a file cabinet full of signed consent forms from people they'd offered services to."

"So, the johns will be rounded up and charged with rape." This was not a question.

"Multiple counts of rape," said Powell, who looked at his desk phone that started ringing but didn't bother to answer it. "Right now," he resumed, "The techies are running profiles. I just wanted to see if you were up for it. I mean, we're pretty much gonna need all hands on deck."

"Count me in," I said, getting to my feet.

"Great! I'll call Dr. Shoob and let him know you're fine."

"Yeah, you do that."

I was hoping the elevator shaft took me straight to the sixth floor, but it stopped on the fifth, and on stepped Agent Christopher Count, to whom I'd been a technical advisor for on the Flenory investigation. A couple of years younger than me, the white guy was clad in dark-brown slacks, and a matching Izod shirt. Plus, he was carrying that green folder of his.

"I was just on my way up to see you," he announced. "How are you feeling?"

"I'm good, Count," I said, nodding toward the folders. "I see you brought your homework."

"Um, yeah," the agent stammered, a bashful look on his face. "I mean, if you're not up for it..."

"It's fine."

The doors opened and we stepped off.

"I think we're about to wrap this investigation up," Count went on as we made for my cubicle. "The guys and I missed you when you were out last week. Especially when we had to meet up with the DEA this past Saturday."

"You mean to tell me y'all actually had a sit-down with Bob Bell?" I asked, upon approaching my area, where I powered up my computer as we sat.

"Did we!" he exclaimed, smiling. "That damned Bob Bell is one tenacious son of a bitch, too! However, he's fair. Although he kept reminding us that he's the lead investigator, he still took time to solicit our opinions and you better believe while we were bouncing ideas off each other, your name came up. Bell said it would be a pleasure to work with you."

"I'm assuming you're here to put me up to speed," I said, hoping to expedite the process, so I could make the phone call I'd been dying to make since Saturday.

"Sure." He opened the folder on my desk, and compiled three stacks of paperwork, one being of digitally enhanced photos. "You remember how it all starts, right?"

"Yeah," I answered, taking a large gulp of coffee. "Demetrius Flenory was arrested in November last year for double homicide, resulting from a shootout at Club Chaos, leaving the bodyguard of a rap artist dead and Flenory wounded. Subsequently, the charges were dropped."

"Right." Count referred to one of his stacks. "Demetrius Flenory, who goes by *Big Meech*, started a movement, dubbing it *BMF—Black Mafia Family*. Latching *Entertainment* onto it, he started a record company, signing a Detroit rapper by the name of *Blu Da Vinci*. Flenory's brother, Terry Flenory, who goes by *Southwest T* is still funneling his drug money through his limousine company back in Detroit."

Count and I went over the facts in the case up until eleven-twenty. By this time, I was hungry and exhausted, so I went ahead and took my break, opting to leave the premises. Hardees was my choice of eatery. After receiving my order at the drive-thru I found a spot in the parking lot, grabbed my cellular, and was finally able to make the call I'd been anticipating since this weekend.

"McCoy," Detective Kowanda McCoy announced through the device.

"Are you busy? I asked.

"Always," she shot back. "How are you holding up?"

"I'm making it. Thanks for asking."

"So, to what do I owe this phone call?"

"I wanted to ask you about a female group."

"A female group?" she asked. "I hope you're talking about a female gospel group."

I smiled, knowing she was serious. "Not that kind of group, Lieutenant. I'm looking into a group of female drug dealers, who call themselves The Queenz, or The Kingz Widows for that matter."

"You can't be serious," said McCoy. "A group of female drug dealers? And I'm assuming they're supposed to be widows of that group you were investigating a couple of years ago that would make them Queen dowagers, right?"

"Neither of the Kingz were married," I pointed out, feeling myself becoming defensive. "These women are using the Kingz' notoriety for self-gain."

"So, they really exist?"

"Of course," I answered, figuring the two guys at the bar had no apparent reason to fabricate their conversation. It's not like they knew who I was, or if I could hear them. "I just need you to keep your ear to the streets," I told her. "I need to know about any and every crime committed with their name attached to it."

"Aye aye, Captain!" she jested. "Would this be an appropriate time to discuss my raise?"

"Very funny!" I told her. "How's your husband's movie doing?"

"It made over eight hundred thousand on its first weekend out."

I let out a low whistle. "That's pretty decent for a first project! If I had that kind of money, I definitely wouldn't be out here playing Cops and Robbers."

"I am a *homicide* detective," McCoy rectified. "So, the correct term would be Cops and Murderers."

"Well, I wouldn't be playing that, either," I joked. "However, congratulations to the both of you!"

"Thanks, Bishop!"

There really wasn't much to do back at the office which is why I ended up leaving early, making it home a quarter till five. Monique hadn't started cooking dinner. Melody was awaiting my arrival. So,

I could help her with her homework, and Junior was being his regular hyper self, flitting from person to person, demanding attention.

"Daddy, will we get a chance to go to Six Flags before the summer is out?" Melody asked over dinner with a mouthful of spaghetti.

I looked over at Monique. "I don't know why you're looking at *me*!" she protested. "I'm not her daddy."

After wiping my mouth, I finally regarded Melody who was seated across the table, beside her brother. "I know I promised to take y'all to Six Flags," I told her. "Your mom and I just haven't set an exact date yet."

# Chapter 4

## *Saturday*

## *June 18, 2005*

"You're all done, my friend," said my barber, Jake as he removed the barber's tarp from over me.

Ever since Tyrone informed me that my identity had been compromised at his shop, I'd been getting my hair cut at another place not too far from my home.

Today's the day that Monique and I promised to take the kids to the movie theater saving the Six Flags voyage for next week. Monique had taken the day off for this matter and chose to pick up D.J. my father's recent creation while I set out to get groomed.

After paying my barber I exited the building, and stood out front for a few minutes, taking in the warm breeze that was a bit of a relief from the high-powered air condition unit inside the shop. Plus, I was furtively surveying the parking lot of the small plaza, through the lenses of my sunglasses, which is like a cautionary first nature for me. Not registering any potential danger, I crossed the lot to my car, activating the remote start. After climbing in, my eyes dropped to my business cell phone sitting in a cup holder between the front seats.

I'm off today, so there was no reason for me to check it for messages, but the agent in me wouldn't allow me to proceed without doing so. Retrieving it, I typed in my four-digit passcode, and immediately saw that there was one missed call from Detective McCoy. According to the time, it was seven minutes ago. Of course, I called her back.

"McCoy," she answered.

"Sorry I missed your call!" I told her. "I was getting my haircut. I assume it was important?"

"All of my cases are important, Bishop," said the lieutenant. "However, I was calling to inform you of the scene I'm currently standing on in the Kroger's plaza on Howell Mill Road."

"I'm all ears."

McCoy resumed, "A black male was found with a gunshot wound to his temple while seated behind the wheel of his car parked farther away from those of the employees and shoppers. Upon my viewing of the video that was too far for facial recognition, I saw the victim when he pulled into the lot. A little over ten minutes later, another vehicle arrived, parking at about fifteen yards of his. The driver got out and climbed into the front-passenger seat of the victim's car.

"Then, from the direction of Howell Mill Road, came two men on foot, approaching the driver's side of the vic's car. That's when the shot was fired. Rounding the car, the two perps snatched the passenger from the car, and assaulted the passenger with their feet for a brief moment before tearing off in the direction from which they'd approached." She cleared her throat. "Are you ready for my theory?"

"You know I am," I replied, finally pulling out of my parking spot, knowing I needed to get going.

"Our victim was in the middle of a drug transaction when he was murdered," McCoy let on. "I deduced that from the drugs found on the floorboard of the driver's side. Bloodied bills were scattered abroad on the passenger's side of the car, when the passenger was extracted from it."

"Is there an exit wound?" I inquired.

"Yes, there is."

"So, if blood ended up on the bills, it had to have splashed on the passenger who was probably counting them out after making the sale."

"Exactly!" exclaimed the detective. "And, it wasn't robbery, because, although there was nothing but a couple of half ounces, they didn't take the drugs, the victim's jewelry, or the car with its pretty wheels."

"Just killed the driver and assaulted the passenger," I summarized. Then, it dawned on me. "By the way, where is the passenger?"

"I wish I knew," she answered. "After being assaulted, they fled the scene, also."

"And why would you think I'd be interested in this case?"

"Because, the passenger was the drug dealer," she replied, "Who just so happened to be a woman."

"A woman!" I let out. "Are you saying—"

"I'm not saying anything, Bishop," she cut me off. "I was just sharing this bit of information with you. What you do with it is totally up to you. And, of course, I may need your help to solve this case."

"Do you think you could get hold of that surveillance for me?" I asked, mind now racing.

"Not without a warrant," McCoy responded. "And you know all the mess us *little* people have to go through to obtain one of those."

"Yeah, I guess it's too late to convince them you're FBI," I said, knowing damn well she wouldn't attempt such a stunt. "How long have you been on the scene?"

"Are you asking me how long I will be here?"

"Pretty much."

"That depends on how far you are."

"I'm on my way," I told her, then concluded the call, thinking about how Monique was gonna have a fit when I relay this. However, I still had to make the call.

"I hope you're on your way!" Monique hissed through the phone.

*Damn! This is not how this day was supposed to go,* I thought.

"Something came up, baby," I plunged right in, mentally bracing myself for her retort.

"No, Brian!" She voiced. "You promised to take these kids to see a movie and you're gonna honor that fucking promise! I'm not going for that shit, today!"

"Would you calm down!" I said, mind moving in overdrive to come up with a way to assuage the situation. "I didn't say we are not going. I just have to make another stop, and don't know how long it's gonna take."

"So, we have to sit here until you—"

"No, Monique," I cut her off. "Drive on out to the theater. I'll meet y'all there. Just text me the name of the movie y'all choose."

She let out an exaggerating breath. "Alright, Brian. You just make sure you show up. Don't disappoint these kids! If you do, you might as well make yourself comfortable on the couch tonight!"

Of course, I knew not to take her threat lightly, but I didn't plan on lingering too long at the scene that took me a good thirty-eight minutes to reach. Parking outside the perimeter set up by the locals, I killed the engine, dismounted, and instantly realized I didn't have my credentials on me. Therefore, I sent a text to McCoy's phone, letting her know I'd arrived, but needed her assistance with crossing into the hot zone.

I spotted her talking to the two paramedics at the rear of the ambulance. After viewing my message, she looked around for me. I threw a hand up, so she could spot me amongst the small crowd of spectators. Acknowledging me, she shared a few more words with the paramedical personnel, then started in my direction, looking more like a runaway model in her purple dress pants, and matching vest over a red, short-sleeve shirt, while the warm breeze teased her dark, below-shoulder length hair.

"Let him in, Jameson!" she told one of the young policemen standing sentry at the police line that was made up of a circle of wooden horses, and emergency vehicles.

The young man adjusted one of the wooden figures to allow me passage. Detective McCoy spun on her heels as I approached, then started back in the opposite direction with me flanking her.

"We're pretty much done here," she told me. "But I assume you're here to view the footage."

"Yeah, I am," I answered, surveying the scene.

"Well, I guess I have a few minutes to waste on you," she offered with a smile.

However, I didn't respond. My eyes shifted over to the black Acura being loaded onto the bed of a wrecker. McCoy mentioned bloodied bills scattered about but there were no signs of them thanks to the crime scene investigators, who were packing their things into their utility vehicle. At this time, the ambulance drove off, switching off their emergency lights, being that there was no emergency, due to the fact that their package had already expired.

"Have you identified the vic?" I finally asked.

"Twenty-four-year old Clarence Mikah," Lieutenant McCoy answered

"I'll dig into his background once I get back to the office." She looked over her shoulder. "I'm glad we wrapped it up before *they* got here."

The comment caused me to look over my own shoulder, to see the van of one of our famous news stations, though I couldn't make out the logo on the side as it neared the scene that was no longer active.

"Have you no love for the press?" I teased, remembering how uncomfortable she'd always looked in front of the cameras.

"Not today," she answered. "Once I get rid of you, I have a ton of paperwork to do back at the office."

Upon entering Kroger, McCoy located the manager in the Deli section, and asked if she could see the surveillance footage again, after introducing me as her *F.B.I friend*. More than happy to comply, the manager led us to her office, and obligingly relinquished control of her surveillance system to me.

Working my magic, I pulled the footage back to the moment the black Acura pulled into the lot, and watched the scene play out just the way Lieutenant McCoy described over the phone. However, considering the distance, it was hard to identify the woman, who'd exited the familiar-looking red Ford Mustang with its shiny wheels, and climbed into the passenger side of the Acura.

Looking beyond them, I spotted two male figures moving in their direction, at a quick pace. I'm quite sure the woman had seen them before joining Mikah, but this is a public place, so she probably figured they were on their way to any of the stores that made up the plaza.

So it went, the two men approached the driver's side of the Acura. Seeing no indications of a weapon being fired, I imagined it in my mind, then watched them round the car. One of the men pulled the passenger door open, yanked the woman out, and threw her to the ground. Immediately, both of them assaulted her with their feet which lasted for a good thirteen seconds. Then, the assailants took off back in the direction they'd come.

I felt sorry for the woman, as I watched her grab what appeared to be her pocketbook, and willed her aching body off the ground, staggering back to her own car. After watching her speed off, I set the surveillance footage back to real-time, thanked the manager, then McCoy and I were on our way.

"So, I take it there were no potential witnesses?" I inquired once we exited the building.

"None," she answered.

"Did you view Arby's surveillance for the suspects?"

"And Taco Bell's."

I shot her an inquisitive look.

"Zilch," she replied. "Neither restaurant's exterior surveillance picked them up. Right now, my main focus is to find the woman, and see if she can identify the assailants. Without her, I have nothing."

Of course, my main focus is to also find the woman. That would help my friends out, but if I locate this woman, and she turns out to be one of the Queenz or whatever the hell they go by, then Detective Kowanda McCoy may have to place this one in her cold case files with the other thousands of unsolved mysteries."

***

*Monday*

The background information I asked Detective McCoy to send me on Clarence Mikah was sticking out of my fax machine when I got to my cubicle this morning. So was a message from the director, requesting my presence at once. Knowing I had to honor the request, I postponed my early morning caffeine fix, figuring there'd be some left after my meeting, then made for the director's office, and knocked on the door that always seemed to be closed.

"Come on!" the all-business feminine tone reached my ears.

Turning the knob, I pushed the door open to find Director Amy Hall seated behind her desk, looking ever so professional in her dark dress suit and blonde hair pulled into a ponytail. Oh! I forgot to mention that Manny Hopkins along with Agent North and several other agents, has been transferred to another branch.

"Have a seat, Mr. Bishop!"

Closing the door, I approached and took a seat in one of the two chairs across from her. Besides the family photos and feminine items atop the desk, the office was pretty much the same as it was when Hopkins presided.

"How are you this morning?" Hall inquired, visibly analyzing me with her ocean-blue eyes.

"I'm good, Director. How are you this morning?"

"That's not important," she told me. "Dr. Shoob's report came across my desk with a permission to pardon from Agent Powell. Now, Powell may have a degree in psychology, as I do myself, but he doesn't have the authority to psychoanalyze any agent at this branch. And you better believe I'll be paying him an unpleasant visit later today."

"So, you're insisting that I make the appointment with Dr. Shoob?" I asked, knowing it was protocol after sustaining an ordeal such as the one I'd just went through with Agent Thomas.

"I'm just trying to make sure you're mentally stable enough to carry out your duties."

"And my word is not good enough?" I challenged. "I'll tell the psychiatrist I'm good, and he'll relay it to you. I guess it holds more weight coming from him, huh?"

Amy Hall narrowed her eyes, and studied me for a moment before asking, "Are you doing okay, Mr. Bishop?"

"Yes, I am."

"Good!" She jotted something down on the piece of paper in front of her, then sat back in her chair. "Are you familiar with DEA Agent Bob Bell?"

"The lead investigator on the BMF case?" I asked.

"Yes, him."

"I'm familiar with his name, but I've never actually met him."

"Well," she started, "He's assembling an interagency Task Force, and wanted me to ask if you would be a part of it."

"Sure."

"Great!" Hall expressed. "I'll make sure to relay that to him. In the meantime, what case are you working on?"

"I was doing some profiling and running prints for the Alpharetta Police Department."

"Okay." She tapped a few keys on her keypad and seemed to become interested in something on her monitor. Without another look in my direction, she said, "Once you're done with that, I want you doing light work for the remainder of the week. Is that understood?"

"Yes, ma'am."

I left the director's office, feeling like a kid leaving the assistant principal's office. Hall called herself looking out for me by not assigning me to any major cases for a while, but I didn't like the idea of being pampered. Yes, I'm affected by Thomas' death, and feel greatly responsible for it, but I don't think I'll go off the deep end and shoot up the damned place.

However, I didn't plan to contend with her advisory, which is why I took my precious time profiling and running prints for Alpharetta, then purposefully waited a whole hour before faxing the results over to them. By that time, it was a quarter to eleven. Instead of sitting around looking like a sad puppy, I put myself down for a lunch break, and left the building with no intention of feeding my face.

Back upon Howell Mill Road and driving in the direction of Kroger's Plaza, I was thinking about the two assailants, and how they appeared and disappeared from the scene of the crime. I'm not doubting Detective McCoy's word that the external surveillance cameras at the two neighboring restaurants didn't pick them up, but I do have a theory that's been eating away at my conscience from the moment she informed me of this. I was now pulling into the small lot of the Jiffy Lube Auto that sat directly across the street from Arby's.

Employees and customers alike were shooting side-long glances at the Ford, so you can pretty much imagine the looks they were giving me. When I dismounted, I thought it was the prominent display of the gun on my hip, and my badge hanging from the black string around my neck like a medallion. Of course, my *Highway Patrol*s may have given my presence a little more eminence. However, accustomed to such ogling, I walked right up to one of the employees down in one of the oil gutters. I found it funny how he regarded me like I was about to read him his rights but dared show it.

"Where's the manager?" I asked, excluding the formal introduction.

"He's out back," the man answered, hooking a thumb over his shoulder. "Old, white guy, long beard."

I had already spotted an exterior camera hanging out front. Upon exiting the rear of the small building, I looked up and immediately spotted a second one, duly noting its angel and condition. Considering its hull, I could tell they were older models. I just hoped they were functional, and not up for decoration.

The older, white man with the long beard was the only somebody out back. His back was to me and he appeared to be siphoning oil from a drum into a plastic gallon container. The whole back of his uniform shirt was matted to his back from profuse sweating, and the stench assaulted my nostrils when I got within a good eight feet of him. By the time, he had filled the container. I stopped in my tracks, and the first thing he saw when he turned around was my government identification.

"Hello, sir!" I spoke with much authority. "I'm Special Agent Bishop from the Federal Bureau of Investigation. Are you the manager?"

"Ah, yes, I am," he stammered.

"Name?"

"Jeff. Jeff McGhee."

"Mr. McGhee, I need to view your surveillance footage from Saturday morning. Can you assist me with that?"

"Does this have anything to do with what happened in the parking lot across yonder?" he inquired.

I narrowed my eyes at him. "Maybe"

"Well, right this way, sir!"

I followed him back into the shop, where he handed the siphoned oil off to one of his employees, then ducked into a small office that I expected to look and smell like a pig sty. Careful not to touch anything, I stood by while he searched out the proper disc, injected it into the drive, and relinquished the controls to me. Of course, I chose to remain standing as I tapped on the oily keys of the ancient old keypad, bringing the timeframe up to 12:14 p.m., six minutes before Clarence Mikah entered the parking lot of Kroger.

Though old, the images on the split screen were pretty clear, as they were both slightly pointed toward the side street to the left of the establishment. If a vehicle entered the street from Howell Mill Road, I would see it from the camera at the front of the building before it passed, then pick it up from the rear camera once it cleared the side of the building, and vice versa.

As I said, I'm moving on theory, so I really didn't know if I was looking in the right place, but I kept my eyes on the split images, watching as vehicles periodically rode by.

It was 12:34 p.m. at the bottom of the screen, when a bright red pick-up caught my attention, before passing the building. I shifted my eyes to the rear camera to get a better look at it, but it didn't appear, which could only mean it stopped on the side of the building. Suddenly, two men came into view, walking toward Howell Mill Road. By the color of their attire, I could tell they were the two culprits from Saturday's ordeal.

I immediately froze the frame, before they were out of view. The time on the screen was a couple of minutes after the unidentified woman entered the parking lot that day, which had me wondering if they actually followed *her* to the drop spot, and murdered Mikah to convey a grave message to her. It's possible that one of the men could've been an ex-lover, who was hell-bent on making sure she didn't find happiness with another man, but I wouldn't bet anything on it in this case.

Now, staring at the left side of these guys' faces, I couldn't help but sense some kind of familiarity, though they were both sporting ball caps. I couldn't place them at the moment, but I knew I didn't have to view the footage any further to find out what they were about to do. I turned to the shop's manager.

"I need this disc!" I told him.

"Fine," he replied, throwing his hands up. "It's yours!"

# Playa Ray

46

## Chapter 5

### Saturday

### June 25, 2005

"Aw, man!" Melody's voice carried across the Bumper Cars rink when the operator shut the system down.

I watched as Melody, Monique, Carmen, and the other nine drivers climbed from their manually deactivated bumper cars and exited the rink. I would've joined them but I knew my father, being confined to a wheelchair was incapable of keeping up with Bishop Jr., Dorian Jr., and Montez my mother's newest addition to the family. My mother and her boyfriend, who used to be my father's best friend, are in Georgia for the weekend, but made a wise choice to not join us.

Montez spent the night at my home, after I picked him up from the hotel his parents stay in. All day, since we've been at the Atlanta theme park, my father hadn't shown the child any affection, nor paid him any attention, outside of periodic cold stares ascribed to the hatred he harbored for his former wife. I wanted to reprimand him for his behavior but decided to do so later, not wanting to put a damper on the fun everyone was having.

"Daddy, can we ride the Cyclone again?" Melody asked approaching.

"No, Mel'!" Monique answered as B.J. ran into her open arms. "It's time for us to head on home."

"She's right, babe." I tugged on one of Melody's pigtails, then handed her the stuffed animal she'd won at the water gun shooting range. "We should be heading on out."

At 5:48 p.m., that's exactly what we did. Monique had our son, Carmen had their son, Melody had taken possession of Montez, and I was piloting my father's wheelchair as we maneuvered through the mass crowd of people of all shapes, sizes, ages, and nationalities, making for the exit. As a law enforcer, and a person with an innate sense of being observant, my eyes were all over the place behind my sunglasses, searching for any sign of danger.

Suddenly, from the right of me, at about eighty yards out, I spotted a familiar Caucasian woman, staring back at me from behind the dark lenses of her own sunglasses. The high cheek bones were a dead giveaway but the hair was different. What used to be dark and long, was now sandy brown and cropped. I found it utterly strange that she was just standing in the midst of the moving crowd, watching me.

A light blow to my left arm caused me to draw my attention from the older woman to Monique who'd struck me. With Our son cradled in her arms, she was giving me an accusatory look as though she'd caught me checking out another woman. Only regarding her for a millisecond, I looked back over my right shoulder to see that the woman was nowhere to be found.

The temperature was in the mid-nineties, but I don't think it was hot enough to spark hallucinations. I know who I saw, and, evidently, she knew who she was looking at. This actually had me wondering if she'd been surveilling me some time after the fall of her employer, or just so happened to be on a family outing and spotted me amongst the hundreds of other people roaming the theme park.

"I'll meet y'all at the car," I told Monique, once we were almost in the center of the parking lot.

Everyone exchanged goodbyes, before Monique and the kids branched off. While trailing behind Carmen, still pushing my father's wheelchair, I slowed my momentum to put a little distance between us, so I could have a few words with the old man.

"Did you enjoy yourself, Pops?" I finally asked, breaking the ice.

*"Pops!"* he let out. "Do I look like Fred Sandford to you?"

"From a certain angle," I answered, smiling.

"Well, that means you look like Lamont Sandford from that same exact angle," he shot back.

I couldn't help but laugh.

"But I did have fun," he admitted. "Hell, I had fun just watching you all have fun. That was enough for me."

"What about Montez?" I got to the point. "Did you enjoy watching *him* have fun?"

"Who?" he played dumb.

"Stop it, Dad!"

"I don't know anybody by that name."

"He's only a child," I explained. "An innocent bystander to the perpetual beef that you *grown* children refuse to let go of, and I think it's unfair to him."

"Who in the hell asked you what you think?"

"You know I'm right, old man," I said, giving his chair a shake.

"Do that shit again!"

"You're gonna kick my ass?" I taunted.

"Just do that bullshit again!"

"Of course, I did it again.

All Dorian Bishop could do was throw a menacing look at me over his shoulder.

"That was a James Bond movie," I told him. "Looks, don't actually kill people."

By this time, we'd made it to their car. I helped my dad into the vehicle, while Carmen strapped their son in. After placing the wheelchair into the trunk, I hugged Carmen, kissed my little brother, then looked in at my father, who was giving me that same look that would kill, if looks actually killed people.

"Don't forget what I said, Fred Sandford!" I told him, then went my way.

While making my way to Monique's car, I tried my best to scan the immense parking lot for two vehicles in particular, to no avail. I knew I would have to circle the entire lot in order to see if one of those automobiles were present. Even if I did have the time to do so, who's to say that the wanted woman was even driving one of those vehicles that she was sure to be picked up in upon being spotted by authorities.

B.J. and Montez were already secured in their car seats in the third row of Monique's Lexus truck, behind Melody, when I climbed in beside Monique. Glad to be reprieved of the heat by the car's A.C., I sighed aloud as I fastened my seat belt, then looked over at my fiance who was giving me an expecting look.

"What's wrong?" I asked.

"Will you have time for dinner?" she asked, a tinge of attitude laced her tone.

"Sure."

Then, she slightly tilted her head to the side, posing another question that needed no words.

"We're wasting time just sitting here," I told her, putting a smile on her dark face, as she snatched the gear into reverse, and backed out of the parking spot.

\*\*\*

It really wasn't hard to find out which club the Queenz were using to throw their birthday bash for one of their members, being that it seemed like the most talked about event in Atlanta. I overheard two women excitedly bickering about it this past Tuesday at Walgreens while purchasing Calamine lotion for a rash my son developed on his left calf and couldn't help myself. Of course, I was going to get around to finding out who these women were, but this was too sweet to pass up.

At 10:09 p.m., I was still stuck in line not too far from the entrance, when a black GMC Denali pulled up and stopped directly in front of Club Strokers. The tinted window on the front passenger's side rolled down, though I was too far back to see any occupant. I didn't notice the reserved sign, until one of the bouncers rushed over to move it, allowing the SUV to park right at the entrance.

Just like every other inquisitive person in line, I had my full attention on the truck, whose occupant received the royal treatment. Perhaps, it's the manager, but I assume the manager would already be inside, especially on such a special occasion. The vehicle had no special effects to it, something I didn't think the Queenz, or any celebrity would attend a birthday bash in.

However, I was wrong. The four doors on the truck simultaneously came open, and four casually dressed women emerged, carrying purses with diamond-encrusted tiaras atop their heads. If the tiaras didn't validate it, then the cheers and applause that erupted from the outside crowd definitely let me know that the Queenz had arrived. While the women were smiling and waving in response to the affection of their admirers, I was trying to get a look at their faces, before they ducked off in the club, but they were immediately escorted in by one of the security members, hindering my chance to do so.

"Ahh shit!" I heard the D.J.'s voice boom over the music inside. "The Birthday Girl has finally arrived. I repeat the Birthday Girl has finally arrived! That can only mean one thing. The Queenz are in the building! Y'all give it up for the lovely, and beautiful Queenz!"

I wasn't surprised to hear what sounded like an arena-size crowd greeting the Queenz in the same manner as the outside crowd. About seven minutes later, I reached the entrance, where I had to pay the thirty-dollar admittance fee, that I was told covered the food and drinks. I've never been inside the club before, but I assumed the multiple buffet tables that made a perimeter around the bar were not originally part of the establishment, but were set up by a catering service, conjuring the uniform-clad servers, who tended to the desires of the swarming crowd.

I only immediately paid attention to the tables because they were just beyond the entrance, I didn't want to bump into them, but the moment I cleared them, my eyes shot right up to the V.I.P booth, where the Queenz were seated, helping themselves to some food they'd ordered for the night. One bouncer stood at the entrance. However, I still couldn't make out their features for the distance, and dimness of the lights.

I didn't have any intention to eat anything else tonight but being that I'd paid thirty dollars to get in, and the aroma of the buffet taunted my nostrils. I decided to fill a paper plate with hot wings, potato wedges, and blue cheese dip. After receiving two Budweisers from the bar, I, surprisingly, managed to cop a seat by the stage, where two dancers were performing separate routines. I'd even brought a hundred dollars in single bills, to squander on some of the nude women while doing my best to look as normal as possible. That would be after I polished off these wings.

My mind drifted back on the sole reason I was here, I tended to my food while pretending to take interest in the atmosphere, though my eyes were locked in on the V.I.P booth. At that moment, I saw two of the Queenz exiting it, like they were headed for the restroom, which made me look around for the sign. Bingo! If this is where they were headed, then they would have to pass me, presenting me with a better chance to view their faces.

Seconds later, the two women were moving through the crowd, hugging and shaking hands with some of their admirers, almost about ten-yards of where I was sitting. The one in front was brown-skinned, about 5'6 to 5'7, and looked to be in her mid-twenties. The other one was a couple of feet taller, lighter in complexion, and maybe a couple of years older but was vaguely familiar to me.

Right then, they detoured, and approached the bar. They said something to one of the female bartenders, who came from behind the bar, and escorted them toward the restroom, while keeping my eyes on the taller one. I noticed her wince and grabbed her left side. That's when pieces of the puzzle fell into place. This was definitely the woman who was with Clarence Mikah when he was murdered last week, and she definitely fit the bill of a King's widow, though she wasn't legally attached to the late James Young, a.k.a King James.

Plus, although I wasn't all too familiar with other than live-in cousins, I would wager anything that Sheila Griffin was the one in the restroom with her right now or was one of the other two left in the V.I.P booth. Well, this bit of revelation put me in a dilemma because to hand Watson over to Detective McCoy, would be to throw a monkey wrench in an investigation that hadn't even begun yet. Surely, I couldn't do that.

As of now, I was still awaiting a reply from our analyst on the facial recognition report I requested on the two men responsible for Mikah's demise. Maybe, I'd hand *their* identities over to McCoy.

Moments later, the two Queenz emerged from the restroom, with the same bartender at their heels. I couldn't imagine what that was all about and didn't care to. As they moved through the crowd, headed in my direction, I kept my eyes on the shorter one, committing her face to my memory bank. For some reason, I was pretty determined that she was Sheila Griffin.

Instead of heading back to the V.I.P booth, they deviated, and headed for the DJ's booth, where Watson actually entered, leaving Griffin standing outside of it, where two men stood around like guards. Watson swapped a few words with the D.J., probably requesting a song, then exited. When they made it back to V.I.P, the other two Queenz got up to leave out.

While the two were descending the stairs, it seemed like the whole atmosphere in the general area I was in had changed, which prompted me to look to my right. Well, damn! Five men sporting Drop Squad chains entered the club, looking like they were ready to shoot up the place. Switching my gaze, I saw the other two Queenz moving through the crowd, hugging and shaking hands as their friends had, until they reached the five goons, who blocked their paths.

At this time, I couldn't see the men's faces, but by the look on the taller woman's face, shit seemed like it was about to hit the fan, as she traded words with one of them. Whatever she said to him was very brief because she spoke her piece, then basically plowed through them like a human bulldozer, with the shorter, light-skinned woman at her heels.

When the two Queenz approached the same bartender at the bar, I directed my attention to the goons, who went on about their business. Seconds later, the one swapping words with the Queen, whose posture was quite familiar, approached a light-skinned blonde giving someone a dance, and whispered something in her ear. Just like that, the dancer broke away from her customer, and followed the men to a table, in which she climbed up on and began entertaining them once they were seated.

I don't have to refer to my files to help me remember who the dancer is. I'm just surprised to see she's doing the same thing or hadn't upgraded to a more upscale environment. Minutes later, the two Queenz exited the restroom, headed back toward the V.I.P booth.

Consuming the last of my potato wedges, I wiped my hands on a paper towel, and handed off my trash to one of the catering service workers, pushing around a plastic trash bin. One beer left, I took a swig of it, then pulled a wad of one-dollar-bills and waited for the next pair of girls to come upon the stage, being that the current two were collecting their scattered bills before exiting.

Then, two more dancers, Peaches and Bubbles were introduced to the stage, but by a different male's voice. That's when I looked to see that the booth was occupied by another D.J., and the initial D.J. was headed for the V.I.P booth. Curious, I watched him interact with the Queenz, when one stood, and turned her back to him, so he could clasp a necklace around her neck. Now I knew who the Birth-day Girl was. This was the same one who had the brief encounter with the Drop Squad member.

As the man exited the V.I.P booth, headed back to the D.J.'s booth. I focused my attention on the dancer closest to me onstage, who must've been Bubbles considering the humongous ass cheeks protruding from her 5'10 frame, making her thong look invisible as she was leaning forward with both hands gripping the pole, waving them back and forth. Just like the other men and women who were now surrounding the stage, I was gladly tossing bills at her.

The dancers were in the middle of their second song, when the music came to an abrupt stop. Then, immediately, *Usher's Nice and Slow*, streamed through the speakers. At first, the stage dancers seemed confused, which only lasted a second. Then, they continued with their routines but much slower, and more seductively, staying synchronous with the tempo of the new playing song.

It wasn't until I heard the sound of women screaming, that I tore my attention away from the exposed assets of Bubbles. That's when I saw a stampede of women moving toward the V.I.P booth. For a moment, I thought the Queenz had found themselves in a fight or flight situation, until I saw the posted security guard, now inside the booth, going into a strip tease, and realized he must've been a dancer, hired to pose as a bouncer for the Birthday Girl.

All I could do was smile at the mob of women that stormed the V.I.P booth like they were ready to tear the poor man from limb to limb. I reverted my attention to Bubbles, who to my surprise moved closer while I wasn't paying her any attention. On all fours, with her goodies a few feet away from my face, she slowly gyrated her midsection while looking back at me, eyes drilling into mine.

A man in every sense of the word, I got out of my seat, and moved closer to the stage with the stack of bills clutched in my hand, and lust clouding my eyes. Usually, when I found myself yearning for another woman, my mind was interrupted by thoughts of Monique. That wasn't happening at this moment. Bubbles had my full attention and was definitely worth getting the rest of this money.

The second, and last slow jam played, then it was back to rap music. I watched the two dancers collect their earnings, before heading back to their dressing room. Looking up at the V.I.P booth, I saw that the male dancer was done with his routine, also. The mob of women that rushed the booth trailed behind him.

Once the booth was clear, The Queenz seemed to laugh and joke around for a few more minutes, before standing to leave. This was my cue. I still didn't have a definite plan, but I was gonna at least trail them to their destination. Sure, I could pull the addresses of Watson and Griffin up on our files, or obtain them from the DMV, but there was nothing like seeing an actual location first-hand.

Exiting the club, and making it to my car, I started the engine, and just sat, staring at the entrance of the club. It took almost ten minutes for The Queenz to exit. Once inside the truck, the driver immediately pulled off. I waited until they turned onto Brocket Street, before pulling out of my spot. Getting onto the expressway, the SUV stuck to the far-left lane, and I stuck to the far right, and as further back as I could without losing sight of them, although there weren't that many vehicles moving about.

We weren't on the expressway no longer than five minutes, when a black H-2 Hummer passed me, moving quite fast in the far-left lane, approaching the rear of the GMC Denali. What happened next was, indeed highly unexpected. The H-2 impacted the back of the GMC, which I'm quite sure scared the shit out of the women, because it almost made me lose the liquid, I was trying hard to hold inside my bladder.

The Hummer struck again, causing the other truck to swerve a bit. Suddenly, the GMC launched forward, gaining speed. The driver of the H-2 leaned in on its gas pedal, determined to do whatever it was he was determined to do. Of course, I slammed down on mine, in order to keep up with the potentially chaotic scene. The aggressor struck again, but the Denali didn't waver.

Watching this, had me thinking about last Saturday's incident. I toyed with the notion that Mikah's murderers may have spared Watson's life, but assaulted her as a message to stay away from the drug game, or some shit like that. Now, I'm more than convinced that it was some shit like that. Apparently, Watson and her girls didn't take heed to the warning and were now about to pay the Pied Piper.

Wait a minute! Now, I was thinking about Agent Town's report of how The Kingz were murdered. He said he'd seen four black H-2 Hummers surround their limousine, before occupants machine-gunned the truck down. Shit! Towns had witnessed the demise of The Kingz, and it looked like I was about to witness the—

"Oh, shit!" I exclaimed, when I saw bright flashes illuminate the interior of the Denali, before the rear window exploded.

A quarter of a second later, the interior lit up again. Suddenly, the Hummer veered to the left, crashed into the concrete median, then flipped onto its right side. Sparks flew as it slid along the asphalt, before coming to a halt. The Denali rolled on with its rear window missing, and I eventually rode by the H-2, trying to see as much as I could from my vantage point, though the darkness was not on my side. It was easy to see that the windshield had been shot out. It looked like there were two individuals inside, but I wasn't really sure.

I don't know who these guys thought they were dealing with, but they'd just found out the hard way that these women are no pushovers. However, I highly doubted they would survive, because I'm quite sure those point-blank, upper-body shots were fatally accurate.

As cautious as I could, I trailed The Queenz to a house in Norcross, Georgia, where they backed the SUV close to the house to conceal the damaged window and bumper. Knowing they would be extremely paranoid after this kind of ordeal, I remained parked a few houses down until a little after 3:00 a.m., figuring they were asleep by now, and not peering out of the window every thirty seconds.

Also figuring the rest of the neighborhood were in bed at this time, I got out of my car for the second time since leaving the club. The first time, I took a piss on the side of the house I was parked in front of. Now, I pulled my investigation kit from the trunk then made the short walk to the house I saw The Queenz go into.

As though I lived there, I dutifully marched up the driveway, darting my eyes from window to window, as I passed between a burgundy Cadillac, and a black Ford Mustang that could very well be the same Mustang I saw on the video of Mikah's murder, which was red in color at the time. Rounding the left side of the GMC Denali, I made it to the rear of it and peered into the spacious compartment, where an unkempt folded tarp was lying about.

I already knew the truck had a factory-installed alarm system, which was good, because it wasn't sensitive like the ones people buy. All I had to do was not open any of the doors, though I was being extremely cautious when I reached inside and pulled the tarp back. Revealing an AK-47 assault rifle. There's no doubt in my mind that this was the weapon used on the occupants of the Hummer.

I could take the gun in, and turn it over to our forensic unit, but that would be completely asinine. However, I was not going to let it disappear without recording its existence. Therefore, I placed my kit inside the truck, and opened it up, donning my gloves first. I knew it was a risk to use any kind of light, but I did anyway. I placed my pen light close to the gun to illuminate it, while I dusted it for prints.

Done with that, I took a picture of the gun, then of the rear of the SUV, making sure to capture the license plate. On my way back down the driveway, I took pictures of the Cadillac, Ford Mustang, and the Infiniti parked at the curb. Hell, it seemed like The Queenz will be a much easier case than The Kingz were. Who knows? I may end up taking them down in less than six months.

# Chapter 6

*Monday*

I was extremely happy to be back at the James P. Russell building today, because, ever since witnessing the ordeal with The Queenz on the expressway, this past Saturday, I couldn't wait to abuse my use of the FBI's criminal files, to see what I could dig up on Shonda Watson, ex-girlfriend of the late James Young, and her cousin, Sheila Griffin.

Well, according to the files, there was nothing to report on Griffin, but Watson was currently out on bail for two counts of simple assault. Just as I was about to delve into the facts of these infractions, a manila folder seemed to come out of nowhere, landing on top of the notes I had in front of me.

Looking up, I was greatly surprised to see our lead forensic scientist, Heather Vaughn standing over me, cloaked in her immaculately white laboratory coat with her dark hair pulled into a ponytail that barely graced her neck. Vaughn stood at 5'11, weighed 145 pounds, and had gray, cat-like eyes to die for. However, I was no fan of the uncanny look she was bestowing upon me at the moment, as though I requested her presence, when I knew damn well that she would rather send her subordinates out to do her dirty work.

"Well, good morning, Ms. Vaughn!" I beamed up at the thirty-eight-year-old woman. "I almost didn't recognize you. Did you do something with your hair?"

"Fuck you, Bishop!" she hissed in a low tone, suppressing a smile. "You know I don't make house calls."

"Which is why I feel quite special right now," I offered, now regarding the folder in front of me. "This would be the Clarence Mikah case, right?"

"No," she sassed. "It's the Erik Weisz case."

"Erik Weisz, huh?" I now conveyed a pensive expression. "Would this be the same Erik Weisz who died of gangrene and peritonitis, resulting from a ruptured appendix in Detroit, on the thirty-first of October, nineteen twenty-six? The same Erik Weisz who the world remembers as the famous magician, Harry Houdini?"

A smirk appeared on her face. "Wow! You know a little history. I have a few Scooby snacks back in my lab, if you feel the need to be rewarded."

"No," I replied. "But you do have some evidence in your lab that I'm highly interested in getting feedback on."

"Actually," she started. "That evidence hasn't reached my lab yet. Hell, it wasn't on my desk for more than ten minutes, when I set my heels in motion to personally drop in on you." She fixed me with narrow eyes. "I hope you're not rushing me, Bishop, which is something I highly caution against."

"No, ma'am!" I said, throwing my hands up in mock surrender.

I knew firsthand how Heather Vaughn would prolong her analysis report if she felt pressured, which is something I can't afford right now. "I was just inquiring to see if you've received it," I added, clearly lying. "Thanks for the confirmation. I'm sure you'll get back to me at your earliest convenience."

"You're full of shit!" Vaughn offered, slowly shaking her head from side to side.

"I do appreciate you, Vaughn."

"You'd better."

Then, with a look that had the potential to be passed off as flirtatious, she strutted off, with her head held high. Had it not been for the lab coat, I may have gotten a nice view of her buttocks as they bounced around in whatever kind of pants she had on. I was still looking, though. It's just too bad God didn't equip us with X-ray vision.

Putting my mind back on business, I opened the folder before me, and looked down at a stack of documents, whereas a photo of one of the two culprits in the Clarence Mikah case was clipped to the front page. Removing the photo and paperclip, I picked up the first stack that was stapled together, and scanned the criminal profile of Cecil Henderson, which only consisted of a few car thefts, and residential burglaries.

The other stack was of the same width but featured a photo of the other culprit. Removing the photo, I started reading, but didn't make it past the subject's name. Now, how is it that I'm familiar with the name, Jessie Bridges, but not with the face of the person it belongs to? After sitting there, jogging my memory for a good ten minutes, to no avail. I closed the folder and wrote, *Who is Jesse Bridges?* on the front of it. Just then, my cellular rang. I removed it from its case on my hip.

"Bishop," I answered, in my all-business tone.

"I'm quite sure you've heard about the double homicide that took place on the interstate this weekend," Detective McCoy's voice flowed through the device.

"I caught the news yesterday," I told her. "Are you working this one?"

"Unfortunately," she answered with a sigh. "A few more miles, and they would've been out of my jurisdiction. GBI was on the scene. Even District Attorney Paul Howard showed up, looking like he was on his way to a mid-night worship service."

"So, I guess the heat is on, huh?"

"The heat is always on," said McCoy. "But nobody pressures me into doing my job. I move at my own pace."

*Damn! Today must be National Feminist Day, or something.* "So, what do you have so far?" I inquired.

"Not too much," she told me. "A couple of theories, if you're interested."

"You know I can't resist a good bed-time story."

She cleared her throat. "Okay. These two guys were traveling, possibly stalking someone, along the expressway, in a black H-2 Hummer. However, the people they were stalking, were aware of their presence, and acted first, opening fire from their own vehicle, considering the breached windshield of the Hummer, and the impact angles of the gunshot wounds the occupants sustained. Subsequently, the truck crashes into the concrete medium, lands on its side, and slides to a halt."

"It's just too bad it didn't slide far enough, huh?"

"A couple of more miles, at least," she said, with a giggle.

"The media withheld the men's identities," I pointed out. "Any reason why?"

"That was at the D.A.'s behest," McCoy answered. "I don't question their motives. My job is enough weight on my back."

"But you do have their names, right?"

"That's just about all I have until autopsies and analysis reports come back."

"If you don't mind," I said, readying my ink pen. "What are they?"

"One second." I heard the brief sound of paper rustling, before she asserted, "Okay. Victim number one is a Cecil Henderson, and victim number two is a Jesse Bridges."

*Holy shit! There's no way she had this right.* The two guys I identified as Clarence Mikah's murderers, couldn't be the same ones I witnessed murdered by The Queenz. If so, then these men were either hitmen for someone, or a couple of renegades, with their own scores to settle.

"Are you there?" McCoy's voice interrupted my thoughts.

"Yeah, I'm here," I answered. "Are you sure this information is accurate? I mean, did you photo match their identities?"

"Of course, I did!" She took umbrage. "Surely, you don't think I just gave them names, do you?"

"That's not what I'm implying, Detective," I offered, hoping to ease some of the tension. "I was just looking at something pertaining to these guys, right before you called."

"Really?" she sounded surprised. "Do I need to get clearance, or will my FBI friend let me in on this top secret?"

"You're the only person I intend to share it with," I told her. "When will you have some free time?"

Being that I'm the only person in the world who doesn't own a portable DVD player, I borrowed one from Chad Hoffman, and managed to make it to the Turner Field stadium at 1:31 p.m. The black Dodge Challenger belonging to Lieutenant McCoy, sat alone in the semi-deserted lot. I parked beside the car, with the intent to join her, but before I could kill the engine, she was climbing from her car, clad in a pair of cream slacks, and a light-blue blouse. I had to move the DVD player off the seat, so she wouldn't sit on it upon climbing in beside me.

"Just out of curiosity," I spoke, once she was settled. "What made you pick this location? You plan on taking me to a game?"

"I had to file some paperwork with the Juvenile Detention courthouse," McCoy answered, nodding toward the building that sat across the street from the stadium. "So, what is this item of interest you have to show me?"

Since the DVD was already inside the player, I lifted the screen, powered it up, pressed play, and handed it to McCoy, who gently placed it on her lap, and surrendered her full attention to the visual playing out in front of her. Of course, I offered no narrative as I too viewed the footage that started off with the view of the front exterior camera of Jiffy Lube on Howell Mill Road.

I took it upon myself to edit the content, so the image slowed up, then stood still for ten seconds when the bright red pick-up came into view. Moving along, the image froze again when Bridges and Henderson re-entered onto the screen on foot, headed in the opposite direction, toward Howell Mill Road. After the ten-second pause, the picture enlarged to a close-up of the two.

At this time, I cut my eyes at McCoy, for a sign of recognition, but her facial expression never changed as she continued watching. The scene switched to the footage from the exterior camera of Kroger, where Clarence Mikah, and the woman I assume to be Shonda Watson, were already seated in Mikah's car. Momentarily, our subjects approached from the direction of Howell Mill Road.

"So," the Lieutenant finally spoke. "You went back and obtained the surveillance from Kroger?"

"Yes, I did."

"Where'd the other footage come from?"

"Jiffy Lube," I answered. "Which is on the opposite side of Howell Mill. Did you recognize the culprits?"

"Of course," she answered, disappointment ringing in her tone. "Considering what just happened to them. I'm almost concerned about these guys' agendas."

"Almost?"

"They were either hired hands," she offered. "Or troublemakers of the worst kind."

"I've concluded that myself," I told her. "So, this closes the case with them being suspects and opens a whole new investigation of them being victims, huh?"

Releasing a sigh, she said, "I'm afraid so, but I still need to find out the identity of the woman who was with Mikah when he was murdered."

"Why?" I asked, seeing no reason why she should pry any further into that particular case.

"I don't know," she answered with a shrug. "Maybe, she could give us some insight on them. I mean, she had to know them, in order for them to leave her behind to testify against them in court, though they did give her a good reason to keep her mouth shut."

"Yeah, they did."

"Anyway," the Lieutenant went on, stifling a yawn. "I gotta get back to the office. Could you make me a copy of this disc?"

"That *is* your copy."

On my way back to the James P. Russell building, I wondered why Agent Powell hadn't gotten back to me from the message I left on his phone earlier. Surely, he was busy with another case, but I figured I'd given him ample time to respond, which is why I was now getting off the elevator on the fourth floor, and marching in the direction of his cubicle, disregarding the stares I received from the other agents.

"Ah, Mr. Bishop!" Powell sprouted, as I approached. "I see you finally got my message. Have a seat." I took a seat beside him.

He asked, "So, what can I do for you?"

"What's the status of the abduction case?" I posed my own question.

"We'll be ready to begin round-up on the Johns next Tuesday," he informed. "I'll be briefing you all on Friday and Saturday."

"What about Phoenix?" I tried again. "What's the status of locating her, and their other location?"

"First of all," Powell said, leaning back in his chair. "We don't even know for sure if there *is* another location. As far as we know, those other children could have been sold off to people in other countries, or worse."

"And what could possibly be worse than that?"

'Dead, Bishop," He cleared his throat, before going on. "As far as locating this mystery woman, we keep hitting dead ends. We're still trying to connect the dots with the perimeter we've set up around the public phones she used. That region is still being can-vassed as we speak."

"What about the license plates of her vehicles?"

"We ran those," Powell informed. "Both vehicles are registered to Robert Delany."

"The sick fucker that ran the operation?" I asked of the host of who I still wanted to squeeze the life out of.

Powell nodded.

I shifted in my chair, reluctant to say what I came here to say. "I saw her," I finally let out.

"You saw who?"

"Phoenix," my answered spewed out, before he could fully get his question out. "This past Saturday at Six Flags."

Powell leaned forward in his chair, locking eyes with me. "Are you sure, Bishop? I mean, I can't see you encountering her, and not making a citizen's arrest, or whatever they call that bullshit."

"I know who I saw, Powell!" I forced out, taking offense to his assumption. "I spotted her in the crowd, watching me as my family and I were on our way out. Her hair was different, but I knew it was her."

"And you let her get away?"

I sighed, hoping I didn't have to reveal the reason why I couldn't apprehend Phoenix. "Someone bumped into me," I lied. "Which distracted me for a brief second. By the time I looked back up, she was gone, lost in the crowd."

A skeptical look appeared on his face, Powell leaned back in his chair once more, still eyeing me. "You know Hall got on my ass for submitting that pardon to Dr. Shoob in your favor, right?"

"I'm not fucking going crazy, Powell!" I hissed in a low tone, not liking what he was insinuating. "Thomas' death affected me just as it did everyone else here, but I'm not delusional."

"Nobody's insisting—"

"Were Delany's vehicles confiscated?" I cut him off, as my brain went into overdrive.

"As far as I know," he answered.

"The Range Rover and Aston Martin?"

"They're at the warehouse."

"Am I still invited to the round-up?" I purposefully changed the subject.

"Sure, Bishop."

There was an edge of uncertainty in Powell's response, as if he was hoping he wouldn't regret his decision, but I didn't dwell on it. Besides, I had more important things to do, which is why I got off the elevator on the sixth floor, marched dutifully to my cubicle, sat down, and placed a very important call to someone I would consider a very important person at this time.

"Vaughn," our lead forensic scientist answered the phone.

"Vaughn, it's Bishop," I announced, expecting her to hang up. "Are you busy at the moment?"

"Is that a rhetorical question?" she shot back.

"I really need your assistance."

"Doesn't everybody?" she continued, which is highly expected from the supervisor of forensics. "How may I offer my servitude to you this time, Mr. Bishop?"

"It's about the recent child abduction case I was on."

"Okay."

"Several vehicles were commandeered," I went on to explain. "And housed at the warehouse. However, there are two I'm particularly concerned with, both belonging to a Robert Delany."

"And what am I supposed to do with these two *particular* vehicles?" Vaughn inquired, after taking a breath.

"Dust them for prints."

"Now, that's an asinine request."

"How so?"

"Because," she explained. "If a commandeered vehicle has to undergo forensic analysis, that will take place *before* collecting dust at the warehouse, where any valuable prints are subject to become contaminated. However, even if I do decide to call and have these vehicles transported here for analysis, wouldn't the request have to come from Dan Powell, who's the lead investigator in that case?"

"I'm asking you to do this for me as a friend."

"Friends don't let friends drive drunk," Vaughn quoted. "But they damn sure don't mind getting a friend fired."

"Fired, Vaughn?" I questioned. "You're over-exaggerating. I've never seen a person lose their job for doing their job."

"What about Powell?"

"Fuck Powell!" I spat. "I'll submit a written request to you myself. If any issues shall arise, I'll have Hall back us."

"Don't make me have to kick your ass, Bishop."

"I got you, Vaughn."

There was a pregnant pause, before she said, "Fax me the request. I'll get to it as soon as I can."

"Thanks, Vaughn!"

"Yeah, whatever."

# Playa Ray

## Chapter 7

### *Tuesday*

"Pierce," Special Agent Andrew Pierce's voice came through the earpiece of my cellular.

"How're we looking?" I inquired.

"Still frosty," he replied. "The subject only came out for a smoke break, then disappeared back inside."

"Roger that. We're about ten minutes out."

During our mission brief that took place this past Friday and Saturday, which was conducted by Dan Powell, I was partnered with Agent Carlos Moreno, and was assigned seven of the thirty-six subjects to be rounded up in connection to the child abduction case. In addition to our two-man team, were two Fulton County deputies, who trailed behind us in one of their prisoner transport vans, and a camera woman for the Channel 5 news station, who was a ride-along, and would only record footage of us escorting the arrestees to the awaiting van.

So far, as of 12:58 p.m., we've only arrested one male, who was the owner of a small business association firm in Sandy Springs. Now, we were on our way to Marietta, Georgia, to apprehend a tax agent at a local tax firm.

When Moreno pulled the Crown Victoria into the plaza, I looked around for the Jeep Cherokee Pierce was driving but couldn't see it for how the sun rays reflected off the vehicles, causing a temporary distortion to the retinas.

"Park right in front of the establishment," I told Moreno, as I dialed Pierce's number.

"Talk to me!" Pierce answered.

"We're here," I relayed, finally spotting his borrowed Jeep. "You can go ahead and report to Powell."

"Yes, sir!"

When the Ford stopped in front of the United Tax Association building, the three of us didn't hesitate to dismount. The camera woman, who'd introduced herself as Erin Shepherd, leaned against the car, readying her camera. She and one of the deputies were to remain outside, while Agent Moreno, the other deputy, and I, who was in possession of the warrant and a photo of our subject, trooped through the tinted glass door.

The air-conditioned establishment was nothing more than a large room with four desks, file cabinets, and other miscellaneous items one may find in such a place. There were no customers, but all four desks were occupied by its staff members. Being that three of them were women, there was no need for me to refer to the photo.

"Mr. John Coston?" I said, approaching his desk.

"Um, that's me," the thirty-eight-year-old Causasian replied, apprehension in his eyes as he regarded the three of us.

"I'm Special Agent Bishop," I relayed. "From the Federal Bureau of Investigation, and we have a warrant for your arrest."

"A warrant for my arrest!" I haven't done anything!"

"This document begs to differ," I replied, finally shoving the warrant in his face. "Mr. Coston, you're under arrest for seven counts of child molestation." There were gasps from his co-workers. "Right now, you have two options. You can either stand, and let this deputy cuff you, or we can use force."

Trust me, I was silently praying for this sick bastard to choose the latter, so I could fuck him over for the seven times he'd been inside that building, and definitely for Rhonda Thomas, but he chose wisely. Getting to his feet, Coston retrieved his set of keys and cell phone off the desk.

"You won't be needing those," the deputy said, stepping forward, and confiscating the items.

Moreno and I stepped back and looked on as the deputy cuffed Coston while reading him his rights. I took this time to gander at the other employees, who were clearly in awe by the revelation of their co-worker being hauled off to jail for being sexually inappropriate with someone's children, which could've very well been their own.

Upon exiting the establishment, Moreno held the door open for the deputy to escort Coston out, and I brought up the rear finding it amusing how Coston spotted Shepherd's camera pointed at him, and quickly turned his head to the side, like his face hasn't already been captured, which would be plastered all over the six o' clock news tonight.

"You guys can go ahead and take them in," I told the deputies, as they assisted Coston onto their van. "As I understand, we'll be paired with two other deputies on tonight's mission. Thank you, gentlemen."

I didn't know about Moreno, but I didn't plan on lounging around the office until it was time for the next arrest, which would be around 8:00 tonight. Once I complete the mission report forms, I'm going home to have dinner with my family. Hell, I may even have enough time to put Monique in a few positions before heading out.

I was more than happy to doff my blazer, and loosen my tie as I approached my cubicle, where a manila envelope awaited me underneath my keypad disregarding my chair, I retrieved it, and immediately knew by the hand my name was written in, that it was from Heather Vaughn, which is why I literally ripped the envelope open, and couldn't help but smile at the color photograph of Shirley Plummer, who up until this moment, I've only known as *Phoenix*.

Keeping my eyes glued to the address on the document, I found myself taking long strides in the direction of Hall's office, knowing I was going out on a limb with what I was about to propose. As always, the director's door was closed, so I knocked, and waited impatiently. Not getting a reply, I was about to knock again, when the door slowly opened to Director Hall wearing a pair of her snug-fitted jeans, her hair in a ponytail, and an inquisitive look on her face.

"Do you have a minute?" I asked, testing the water.

"I opened the door." She pointed out, placing one hand upon her hip, with the other still poised on the doorknob.

"Right," I replied.

Seeing that she had no intention of offering me entrance, I got down to business. "I have an identification, and address on the woman we're looking for in that child abduction case."

"Okay." A shrug accompanied her response.

"As of now," I continued. "There isn't a valid warrant out for her arrest, due to the fact that no one knew her legal name. Now that we have that, plus an address, we can go ahead and bring her in before she skips town."

"Isn't Powell the lead investigator on that case?"

*Here we go with this shit again.* "Yes ma'am," I answered. "But I'm the one who rooted out this bit of information."

"So, you should be the one to bring her in, huh?"

Of course, I didn't answer.

"Bishop," the director went on. "You've been up close and personal with this woman, so she'll be able to spot you from here to Mars."

"I'm counting on that, Director."

Her eyebrows went up. "Really?"

"All I need is a warrant and your blessing."

"What about Powell?" she posed. "I mean, if you two are in a dick measuring contest with each other, I don't want any part in that. Now, if this woman is to be brought in, then I recommend you both do it. After all, he *is* the lead investigator, which makes it *his* case."

I didn't respond. I was too busy thinking of how much I dreaded being cooped up inside a vehicle with Dan Powell, especially alone.

"That's the only way I'll approve it," Hall urged, looking at her watch. "And I really don't have all day for you to make a decision."

Sighing inwardly, I replied, "I guess I have no choice."

Returning to my cubicle, minus the document on Phoenix that I should've made a copy of, I finally took a seat to begin filling out my mission report forms. While doing so, I began thinking about Theresa Joiner, a.k.a Queen Theresa, whose prints were recovered from the AK-47 that was used in the highway shooting that claimed the lives of Cecil Henderson, and Jesse Bridges. Seeing the way she interacted with the Drop Squad members that night, had me highly interested about this being, whose background I plan to look into at a later time.

Finishing up my reports, I made sure my cubicle was in order, before getting to my feet, with the documents in my hand. That's when a wave of dizziness swept over me at full force, causing me to stumble a couple of steps. I found myself squinting my eyes to parry the temporary darkness, though it did nothing for the migraine that rushed at me unabated.

"Are you okay, Bishop?"

That was the voice of Special Agent Knight, whose cubicle sat directly across from mine. I gave him an incoherent response, just as I realized the floor had uprooted, and was coming toward me. The last thing I remembered was the impact my body had taken, with my head sustaining a greater deal of the blow before darkness overtook me like a thief in the night.

# Playa Ray

## Chapter 8

"Hey, baby!"

I can never mistake Monique's voice for anybody else's. I mean, I could hear her clearly, but couldn't see her. Perhaps, she was the distorted figure standing to the left of me. Constantly blinking my eyes did nothing to dissolve the filmy curtains that altered my vision, so I used my right hand to assist.

Familiar with the smell of hospitals, I was able to discern where I was, before I was finally able to take stock of the one-bed recovery room I was laid in which resembled every other one I'd seen. Finally shifting my eyes over to Monique, I was a bit surprised to see how *appropriate* she was dressed in a pair of khaki pants, and a red Atlanta Falcons t-shirt. Plus, her hair wasn't the same as it was when I left the house this morning. She had taken her braided weave out and replaced it with the synthetic sew-ins that flowed past her shoulders. This marks the first time I'd ever seen her disassemble one hairdo and assume another on the same day.

"Are you okay, baby?" Monique, gingerly placed a hand on my chest.

"Water," I sputtered, though all I heard was a raspy gruff of a sound.

"You need some water?"

I slightly nodded my head up and down, which made it hurt, despite already feeling like somebody had me in a headlock. As Monique rounded the bed to fetch me some water from the portable table, I reached up and experimentally touched the bandage wrapped tightly around my noggin. Considering the coolness I was feeling, I could tell I was probably only wearing a gown underneath the extremely white sheets.

"Here you go, baby."

There was no need to reach out for the cup, being that my fiance already had it up to my face. Therefore, I parted my lips, and slowly took in the cool liquid that stung my throat as though I hadn't drunk anything for days.

"You want some more?" she asked, once I'd emptied the paper cup.

All I could do was shake my head.

"Well, I have to let the doctor know you're awake," she said, placing the cup on the table. "Be right back, baby."

As she made for the door, I began jogging my memory for an explanation as to why I was lying in a hospital, naked, with my head bandaged up. Doing this, caused the pain in my head to intensify, but the last thing I remembered was Agent Knight asking if I was okay, just before everything went dark. Of course, I remembered visiting with Director Amy Hall about obtaining a warrant to bring Phoenix in and filling out the mission report forms.

Momentarily, Monique re-entered the room behind a white-coat-clad black man, who looked to be in his late forties, and followed by Special Agent Dan Powell, who clearly had gone home and changed because he was wearing a different suit from the one I saw him in earlier. Now, the three of them surrounded my bed like a group of cultists on initiation day.

"Hello, Mr. Bishop!" The doctor spoke with a deep baritone. "I am Dr. Brown, and I've been tending to you since the day you were admitted. Are you experiencing any pain at the moment?"

"My head," I managed to get out, now feeling like I was in a time zone, considering what the doctor said about tending to me since the day I was admitted, as though I'd been here for more than just a day.

"On a scale from one to ten," he continued, scribbling something down on his clipboard. "How would you grade that pain?"

"A six, I guess."

"I'll have the nurse bring you something for that." He jotted this down. "Do you have any questions for me?"

"What's the deal with my head being bandaged?"

"You were received with a slight concussion," the doctor informed.

"From what I was told, you blacked out, and injured your head on the edge of your desk while falling. Lucky for you, your injury wasn't serious enough to require stitches—just stick sutures. However, we ran some tests to determine what may have caused you to faint, but only saw that your blood pressure was a little high, which wasn't at all detrimental, by the way."

"But, you do know what caused it, right?" Powell posed this to the doctor.

"Pretty much," he answered. "It's all mental, which is something we're highly familiar with. Mr. Bishop's episode was caused by a great deal of stress, which is the leading cause of death in the U.S. right now."

"The stress comes from working too hard," Monique finally chimed in. "He just won't take a break."

The doctor turned to me. "Is that so, Mr. Bishop?"

"I have a job to do, doctor," I blatantly pointed out. "I have to punch in and perform my duties like every other employed person in the world."

"And I respect that," he offered. "However, even the hardest working man in the world deserves a break."

"I'll remember that. How much longer do I have to be here?"

"I'm here to determine that right now," answered Dr. Brown, referring to his clipboard. "How's your vision?"

"I can see."

"How many fingers am I holding up?"

"Three."

"Okay." He jotted something down. "And what is your full name?"

"Brian Dorian Bishop."

After doodling something else, he said, "I don't see any reason to keep you for further evaluation. However, I'm gonna prescribe Tylenol Three for the pain. I recommend you take at least two weeks off work."

*"Two weeks!"* I exclaimed, causing the pain in my head to intensify. "Are you crazy! I can't afford—"

"It's already done, Bishop," Powell cut me off

I turned my menacing expression on him. "What!"

"The assistant director placed you on a four-week leave," he went on to explain. "And Hall signed off on it."

"Mr. Bishop," Dr. Brown interrupted. "Do you have any more questions or concerns, before I set out to sign for your release?"

I only waved a dismissive hand in response, to which he nodded, then exited the room.

I turned back to Powell. "How—"

"It's out of my hands, Bishop," he cut me off, throwing his hands up. "Hall brought it to my attention, letting me know that I had to put somebody in your place."

"I just talked to her today about bringing Phoenix in," I told him. "She agreed to let me do it, as long as you—"

"I brought Phoenix in yesterday," he interrupted me again.

Now, I was confused, and my visage must've shown it, because he and Monique exchanged parallel glances.

"Are you sure you're okay?" Powell asked me. "Maybe, it's best if you stayed another night or so."

"Cut the crap, Powell!" I hissed. "How in the hell could you have brought Phoenix in yesterday when I was just in Hall's office today, talking to her about it? What kind of games are you playing?"

They exchanged another glance.

"What is today?" Powell finally asked me.

"It's Tuesday," I said, matter-of-factly.

"No, baby," Monique offered, her worried expression still lingering. "It's Thursday. You've been here for three days and two nights, unresponsive."

As bad as I wanted to contend with her assertion, I couldn't. Hell, Monique's impromptu change of hairdo was enough to corroborate what they just revealed to me. I just couldn't believe that me bumping my head, had me dead to the world for three whole days. I also couldn't believe that I wasn't the one to slap the cuffs on Phoenix's wrists, and drag her ass, kicking and screaming, to the federal holding facility.

"So, I guess I'm off the child abduction case, huh?" I asked Powell, remembering there was another possible location, and six abducted children still missing.

"We're all off the case," he responded.

This brought on another wave of confusion. "How is this so?" I inquired.

"Upon reaching the residence you provided the address to," Powell started. "Pearson and I chose to watch the place, instead of ringing the doorbell, and shoving the warrant in Plummers' face. By doing so, we noticed suspicious activity. Nicely dressed people, driving nice cars, were in and out of the house like customers. Realizing what could possibly be taking place, I called back to the bureau, had Hall change the warrant to a no-knock, and summoned a tactical unit to the scene for an impromptu breach. However, upon entering the residence, where we were able to apprehend Plummer, we discovered something like a lair in the basement, where the remaining six children were found locked away in kennel-like cells."

"So, she was running her own independent operation," I stated, casting a glance at Monique, who was silently soaking all of this up.

"Pretty much," he replied. "Though she kept no records of any sort. Well, we didn't recover a record book this time." Stifling a yawn, then regarding his watch, he said, "I gotta get home. Believe it or not, but Hall ordered me to check in on you on my way home every day, until you recovered. However, let me be the first to welcome you back to the land of the living. Just do me one favor."

"What's that?"

"Try not to bump your head again," he joked, with a smirk. "I'll inform the boss of your condition."

\*\*\*

Still a hair stylist at a salon out in College Park, Georgia, Monique didn't have to be at work until 9:00 a.m. Being that she had to drop me off at the James P. Russell building to pick up my car, she had to get up, and leave out earlier than usual. The only good thing that came out of being hauled off in an ambulance, and leaving my car, was that it gave me a reason to return to the building, in spite of my leave, but I didn't give a shit about having a reason to wander inside.

Instead of the garage, I had Monique drop me off in front of the building, then marched inside as if it was a regular day at the office. I didn't punch in but moved about and congregated with other agents as I made my way up to the sixth floor. Hell, I even stopped in at our break room for coffee and a pastry and conversed some more. People inquired about the episode I had on Tuesday, but nobody seemed to know anything about me being on leave.

Upon leaving the break room with a fresh cup of coffee, I marched right up to Director Amy Hall's office, and rapped on the door.

"It's open!" I heard her voice assert, before turning the knob, and pushing it open to see my supervisor seated behind her desk, clearly in the middle of doing paperwork, considering the ink pen in her left hand that was poised over the document she was tending to before I interrupted. Yes, my boss is one of those *wrong-handed people*.

"No, Bishop!" Hall verbalized, the moment I closed the door back, and moved toward her desk. "The paperwork has been signed, sealed, and delivered. We'll see you in a month."

"I understand," I said, now standing before her. "But why a whole month? It's not like I'm fatally wounded, or anything like that."

"Maybe not physically," she offered, with furrowed eyebrows. "Anyway, Swint recommended it, and I concurred on the count of what you've already been through. It's not like you're being fired, Bishop. Enjoy the time off. Take the family to Egypt, or something."

"*Egypt?* Really?"

The director placed her ink pen down on the desk, then leaned back in her chair. "I know it's hard for a dedicated agent like yourself to do, but everybody deserves a break, which is why I signed my John Hancock in good faith, hoping you'll come back rejuvenated, with a fresh mind. Trust me, you won't miss anything."

She was right about everything, but you know how the human mind is. Once we feel we know what's best for us, no one can tell us anything otherwise. Well, in this particular case, I had no choice but to accept my fate. Therefore, upon leaving the director's office, I stopped by my cubicle, grabbed some files, then made for the parking garage, where the heat index was about one hundred and twelve degrees, though the interior of my BMW was around one hundred and forty.

While waiting for the air conditioner to do what it was installed to do, I stared into the rear-view mirror at the healing wound on the left side of my forehead. The sutures did a great job, though a visible scar will be left, which I'm not complaining about, considering the other blemishes on my body. I didn't sleep much last night and had no appetite this morning, which is why I didn't bother to eat anything. I was hungry now, though.

Most restaurants serve breakfast foods until 10:00 a.m., but I wasn't in the mood for any breakfast items. Therefore, being that it was only 9:42 a.m., I drove around until 10:17 a.m., and ended up at Burger King on Fulton Industrial, where I ordered from the drive-thru, but chose the parking lot to enjoy my meal.

Afterward, being that I had nowhere to be, I retrieved my accordion folder off the passenger seat, and fished out the report I had on The Queenz. Director Hall hit the nail on the head when she spoke about it being hard for me to take a break from my work, so the only break they gave, was a break from the office, because I was definitely going to continue doing what I do best.

Theresa Joiner. Twenty-eight years old. Native of Dallas, Texas. Medically discharged from the Army in October of last year. Single. No children. No criminal history. Currently resides in Riverdale, Georgia. Besides the mentioning of her enlistment, there was nothing in Joiner's file to indicate that she was the ruthless killer, whose prints were found on the assault rifle used in the highway shooting. It was her birthday, so maybe she was under the influence of more than just the alcohol I watched her consume that night. Or, maybe her militant instincts kicked into survival mode, once realizing that her life, as well as the lives of her friends, was in danger. Whatever the case may be, I'm well convinced that if put into another situation as such, altered mind frame or not, she's gonna do everything in her power to make sure she comes out on top.

"Bishop," I answered my business cellular.

"How're you feeling?" Homicide Detective McCoy's voice sounded through the earpiece.

"A lot better," I replied, closing the folder on my lap. "Thanks for asking."

"You know I have to make sure my FBI friend is okay," she purported. "So, what did the doctors determine?"

"It was a stroke."

*"You had a stroke!"* the detective exclaimed.

"Yeah." I looked out at the traffic on Fulton Industrial. "Right now, I have paralysis in my left leg, and my member doesn't work anymore."

*"Your member?"*

I said nothing. Perhaps, I was too busy smiling.

"You know what?" McCoy stated slowly. "You really need Jesus. Why would you joke about something like that? Having a stroke should never be taken lightly."

"I know," I replied, seriously. "Thank God I didn't have one!"

"You didn't?"

"They say I blacked out from stress," I told her. "Anyway, what's going on with my APD friend? Anything new?"

"Of course," she replied. "While you were lying in the hospital, pretending to have a stroke, I made contact with one of my C.I.'s, and found out that your subjects had some kind of Fourth of July shindig at Grant Park."

"The Queenz?" I asked, wishing I was there, taking pictures, instead of at Gloria's barbecue this past Monday, the day before I had my incident.

"Yes, The Queenz."

"Is your C.I. close to them?"

"Close enough."

"Could you set an appointment for me to interview them?"

"Now, Bishop," she replied, sounding like a high school principal, addressing a student. "There's a reason why they're called *confidential informants*. If I introduce you—"

"I get the point," I cut her off, not disappointed that she chose
to not reveal the identity of her source, which is forbidden.

"If I hear anything vital about the group," she continued. "I'll
make sure to bring it to your attention."

"I'd appreciate it," I told her. "How's the highway shooting going?"

"I'm not done telling you about your girls."

"Okay. I'm listening."

"These women are not crumb pushers," McCoy let on. "According to my source, they supply local dealers, and have personal
bodyguards. Am I telling you things you already know?"

"Not really," I replied, now curious, "What made you question
your informant about The Queenz?"

"I didn't." there was a hint of attitude in her tone. "I contacted
my informant on another matter. During the course of our conversation, he mentioned being in attendance. Don't worry, Mr. Bishop,
I have no interest in these women, unless they show up on my radar.
Like you said, I'm Homicide, not Narcotics."

Wait a minute! There was something about McCoy's statement
that didn't sit well with me. Not to mention the tone she used to
deliver it. She knows something and is withholding it from me. I
mean, I do the same to her, but this is different. If she somehow
linked The Queenz to the murders of Jesse Bridges and Cecil Henderson, and has launched her very own investigation, this could become a huge problem. Plus, it'll put a strain on our professional re-
lationship. Now, I feel like I have to find out who her informant is,
consider how close they are to The Queenz, and liquidate this individual if I feel they're anything more than a moderate threat.

After concluding my call with the homicide detective, I found
it hard to re-focus on what I was doing beforehand. Therefore, I
pulled out of the parking lot, and continued my joyriding along busy
Fulton Industrial. It wasn't long before I realized I was coming up
on the warehouse building that was once owned by the late Kingz.

As I neared it, I expected to see it flourishing, with tractor trailers roaring in and out, not to look the same as I last saw it, almost two years ago, with the same four tractor trailers backed into the loading dock, no traffic, and—Damn!

I'm not much of a dog lover, but I didn't think the guard dog lying motionless, several yards away from the building, deserved to die the way it did, because I'm certain it wasn't just sleeping out in the sun, on the hot asphalt like that. There was no sign of the other one.

I suppose I was moving on instinct, but, for some reason, I found myself pulling up to the gate of the warehouse. Clearly, no one had been here since the demise of its owners, which had me inquisitive as to what they may have left inside. Drugs? Guns? A safe? A few body parts?

I looked over at the security booth, but figured it wouldn't do me any good, being that the power was out. However, there was still the lock and chain I'd have to wrestle with, which wouldn't be much of a problem. Putting my gear into park, I went to the trunk, and rummaged around in my investigation kit for the required implements.

As though I was doing nothing wrong, I disengaged the security lock with precision, pushed the gate wide enough for my car to fit through, then drove toward the building, making sure to ride close enough for a better look at the expired canine. For some reason, the scene had an uncanny way of putting me in the mind of Bernadine Yarborough's discovery, with the multitude of insects feasting away on its partially mauled carcass. I found the other one under one of the trailers, in the same condition, before circling back around front, and parking at the entrance of the building.

Donning a pair of latex gloves, I exited my car with a flashlight, and my lock-impregnating tools. Again, applying what I learned in the academy, I breached the two locks on the steel door in less than five minutes, but when I pushed the door open, I was hit by a fetid odor that almost caused me to swoon. I retched once, but quickly recovered, being that I'm, unfortunately, immune to such stink.

Yeah, I mentally joked that there may have been body parts left behind, but that thought was no longer amusing. There was actually some kind of human remains lying about somewhere inside this large warehouse, which put me in the mind of the child abductors' building in Sandy Springs except this carpentry had actually been done in wood.

The steel door slammed behind me, but I wasn't left in the dark. Though not as bright as one may expect, the ceiling lights were actually illuminating the place, like someone was keeping up payments on the electricity. I wasn't worried about encountering anyone, though my Glock was in my side holster, but that horrid smell!

I came upon an office to the right of me, but the wooden structure to my left is what had my full attention, whereas the first door I came upon had some kind of ancient-looking lock clamped to a chain. Plus, it seemed like that stench was coming from beyond it. To me, it doesn't matter how old a lock looks, or actually is, I can breach it.

However, for some reason, I chose to bypass the room, and pushed the double doors open to the next one. Well, damn! Just as Chambers described, the room had rows of foldable chairs, facing four thrones that sat parallel, at the head of the room. This is where The Kingz took on the role of magistrates, handed down death sentences, and executed motherfuckers on the spot. They also did a good job of cleaning up behind themselves because the floor was spotless.

I saw no need to enter this particular room but couldn't help myself when I reached the third one, which was outfitted into a shooting range, with five booths for individual target practicing, though there were no targets hanging about, just a large amount of sandbags piled along the far wall. There were also over a dozen handguns sprawled out on a table, along with cartridges, and various calibers of ammunition.

Leaving there, I crossed over to the office, where the door was ajar, and the light was on. Pushing the door open, I entered and just looked around. There was a black oak table, surrounded by four, black leather chairs, with only a telephone sitting in the center of it. Of course, I picked up the receiver, to see if the phone bill was also being maintained. Nothing.

Replacing the receiver, I moved over to some wooden, boxed artifact that had a large Mona Lisa painting, and four two-way radios, docked in a charger, on top of it. I mean, these fuckers actually walked around here with walkie talkies, like they were running a drug empire.

I was ready to get out of there, but I knew I couldn't leave without, first, locating the source of the horrid smell. I didn't bring my camera, so all I could do was get an eyeful, then get the hell out of there.

Back at the door with the uncanny security lock, I didn't waste any time. It took a lot longer than the one at the front gate, but I did manage to breach it. Dropping both, chain and lock, to the floor, I pulled the wooden door open, and caught another wave of the nauseating stench, plus a face full of angry and disturbed insects. Once I was sure I was remotely safe from bugs flying into my eyes, I opened them back up, and wasn't a bit surprised at what I was seeing.

There was a steel, cage-like cell, a tin tub with a battery charger beside it, a wooden chair made for restraining people, and some kind of contraption that actually had a decomposed body strapped to it, in something of a praying position.

I frowned at the rats that scattered upon my approach. I was so familiar with the black Reeboks on the feet of the carcass, I felt I didn't have to view the features to identify him. Despite the gag in his mouth, and the loss of facial tissue, I was one hundred percent sure who it was, and why he was here, awaiting trial, which never took place, due to the sudden tragic that befell The Kingz.

# Chapter 9

*Two Weeks Later*

I thought Fort Sumter, in South Carolina, would be a whole lot bigger than what I was looking at right now. As I pulled my BMW behind the third vehicle from the two-man security check booth, I saw a fighter jet landing on their air strip, at about five hundred yards out. Plus, there seemed to be an exercise drill going on, whereas I could see cadets in full Army fatigues, backpacks, and assault rifles, running an obstacle course. My windows were down, so I could hear a cadence being called in a distance, along with periodic reports from a sniper rifle of some sort.

Hearing the shots, caused me to think about the shooting range I discovered at the warehouse on Fulton Industrial, two weeks ago. Perhaps, The Kingz, along with their Kingsmen, had a little gun-control training of their own, taking place inside the building. Steven Chambers died a horrific death, but I felt no pity for the rat bitch, which is why I locked the place back up, and left his ass exactly how I found him. However, I did place a call to animal control about the two deceased Rottweilers. Once they were picked up, I replaced the lock and chain on the front gate and got as far away from that place as possible.

"State your business!" the female military guard said, once I pulled up to the booth.

"Special Agent Bishop," I replied, handing her my credentials. "I'm here to see Drill Sergeant Moore."

"Right." She checked something off on her roster, handed my credentials back, then pointed beyond the security gate. "Do you see that soldier standing beside that Jeep?"

I looked, saw the military-clad man standing beside the Jeep Wrangler with no doors, and nodded.

"Just follow him," she told me. "He'll escort you straight to the D.S.'s office."

"Thanks!"

She signaled to the man in the security booth, then radioed to the awaiting man at the Jeep. As the security bar slowly raised, I saw the man respond to his radio, then climb into his truck. My car wasn't even halfway past the gate, when my escort took off down the gravel road, leaving behind a thick cloud of exhaust fumes that wafted through my open windows.

My tour of the base lasted no more than two minutes, but I made sure to take in all I could, which was enough to make me wonder if I made the right decision by joining the force, and not enlisting in the Army.

The Jeep parked in a reserved spot, and I found one in the visitor's sections. By the time I climbed from the car, the soldier was already standing at the entrance of the one-story building, with his hand poised on the doorknob. In my gray, two-piece suit, sunglasses on my face, badge dangling from the thin rope around my neck, and notepad in hand, I crossed the lot over to the man, who was courteous enough to hold the door for me.

"Thank you!" I gratified.

"You're welcome, sir!" he replied, moving ahead of me. "Right this way, sir."

The walls of the corridor we traveled along, were decorated with many photos of much older, military-clad women and men. Just beyond the first office we passed, was a water cooler, in which I was highly tempted to grab one of the complimentary, cone-shaped, paper cups, and help myself to some of the liquid that I'm sure was highly refreshing, considering the hot temperature outside.

We passed two more offices, before turning left, passing more photographs of decorated soldiers that led to an office dead center at the end of the hallway. The bold, black letters across the obscured glass of the door, pretty much let it be known that the office belonged to none other than Drill Sergeant Bernard Moore.

The escorting soldier rapped on the metallic door, and, without waiting for a response, stuck his head inside, announcing my arrival. I didn't hear the response, but he pushed the door open, then stepped aside.

"Come on in, Special Agent!" said Moore, who was standing behind his desk, both hands behind his back.

When I entered, the soldier pulled the door shut, and I wondered if he would actually stand outside the office until I was ready to leave. Drill Sergeant Bernard Moore was dark-skinned and stood at about 6'2. If I had to guess, I would say he was about forty-seven years of age. His salt and peppered crew cut was neatly trimmed, and he was clean shaven.

"How was the drive?" he asked as I approached, extending his hand.

"I made it in one piece," I replied, shaking his massive hand. "Thanks for seeing me!"

"No problem." he gestured to a chair in front of his desk. "Please, have a seat." Once we were both seated, he asked, "So, which one of my cadets is the FBI interested in?"

"*Former* cadet," I rectified, casting a glance at an array of trophies lining a shelf behind him.

Moore's eyebrows went up, questionably.

"Do you remember Theresa Joiner?" I plunged in.

A hint of recognition sparked in his eyes. Moore slowly leaned back in his chair, and interlocked his fingers, with his elbows resting on the armrest, "Yeah," he said. "I remember her."

"What do you remember about her?" I asked, producing an ink pen, and opening my notepad up.

"Well," the drill sergeant replied, looking toward the ceiling, as if in deep thought. "She was really dedicated. She had no problem speaking her mind, which is what made her standout. In fact, Joiner won the most purple ribbons in her platoon, got the highest points in sharp-shooting, and mastered in weapons specialist."

"But she was discharged," I pointed out, still jotting in my notepad.

"Medically discharged," he made sure to rectify. "You'll have to speak with our medical personnel about—"

"I'm not interested in a prognosis," I told him. "Just a condition. Whatever you jotted down in your file if you don't mind."

Moore took a deep breath, before entertaining me further. "She was having complications during certain drill exercises," he explained. "As I said, she was really dedicated, so she wouldn't dare give in to complaining. I only learned of her complication, because I drilled her harder than I did the others, which is something I do to every prospective soldier who gets off that bus, and think they know my job better than I do. Anyway, during certain exercises, or afterward, I'd catch her wincing from pain, and reaching at her back. Knowing she was gonna play the tough role with me, I didn't waste my time inquiring about it. Instead, I put in a referral to have X-rays ran on her."

Upon his pause, I looked up from my notepad, expectantly. Now, he leaned forward, resting his elbows on the desk. "It was discovered that Joiner suffered from some kind of congenital spinal defect."

"Spin a bifida?" I offered.

"Um, yeah," he stammered, a surprised look on her face. "That's exactly what they said it is. I'm not in the medical field, so I can't tell you much about it."

"That's okay," I said, jotting this down. "However, I'd like to know more about Joiner's character. What was she really like?"

\*\*\*

On my drive back to Georgia, I thought about everything Drill Sergeant Bernard Moore told me about Theresa Joiner. After putting everything in its proper perspective, I had a mental picture of a mean, and haggard woman, holding an AK-47, in my mind. Hell, in the Army, ordinary men and women are trained to kill. That, mixed with the drill sergeant's delineation of Joiner's character, brought me to the conclusion that she may be the most dangerous one out of the four Queenz. Granted, the Kingz were a dangerous bunch, especially James Young, but it's my theory that Joiner's *dangerous* supersedes that of her late male counterparts, altogether.

Monique's car was in the driveway when I returned home. Pulling in beside it, I shut the engine off, and just sat there, thinking about my fiance's demand to go ahead and *jump the broom* in January of next year. She had been doing a lot of shopping, and pretty much planned the whole wedding. However, I agree. Why prolong, right? My cell phone rang, interrupting my thoughts.

"Hello?" I answered.

"Is this a bad time?" Chief John Moody's voice came through the earpiece.

"Not at all," I replied, looking out at the house, to see if anyone was peering out of a window. "What can I help you with?"

"A profile," he answered. "Are you still on leave?"

"Who do you need a profile done on?" I blatantly disregarded his question.

"Some guy who goes by the name of *LKS*."

"Would that be his initials?"

"Maybe," he answered. "Or it could be some kind of acronym."

"Please, tell me that you have a picture of this person of interest, Moody."

"I'm afraid not," the Chief of Decatur police admitted. "I've had a couple of my C.I.'s mention his name, saying that he's a huge supplier, though it seems that no one has ever met the guy."

"Are you sure he's a guy?" I asked, already preparing myself to turn this wild goose chase down. "LKS could be a female, or some drug syndicate. I'll need a little more than three letters to do a profile, Moody."

"Yeah, I know," he concurred. "I was just hoping you'd heard of the person, thing, or whatever the fuck."

"Well, I haven't," I told him. "When I do, you'll be the first to know. Until then, see what else you can find out. Something substantial, Moody."

"I'm on it."

# Playa Ray

# Chapter 10

## Monday

## *August 1, 2005*

"Welcome back, Bishop!" Special Agent Knight spoke, once I made it to my cubicle, and began extracting files from my briefcase.

It seems like it took forever for this day to arrive. I've been anticipating this day for a whole month. Hell, I didn't even sleep last night, thinking about how I was going to drop my spiel about The Queenz to Director Hall. During these past two weeks, I was able to follow The Queenz and their guards around, and catch several pictures of them as they, apparently, made drops to some of their workers. I'd even ascertained the names and places of residence of their four-man security team.

Hopefully, my being able to connect The Queenz to Cecil Henderson's and Jesse Bridges' deaths, is enough to persuade the director.

"Thanks, Knight!" I replied, nodding at the agent seated across from me. "I've never seen you come in so early. What gives?"

"I'm investigating a loan shark," he said, as I sat, powering up my computer. "He owns a legit insurance business but lends drugs to local drug dealers."

"Are you working this investigation alone?"

"Actually," Knight began." I'm working alongside GBI, ATF, and the DEA on this one."

"Intelligence operations?"

"That's me!" He gave a smile. "Hall's gonna be gone for two weeks, so—"

"Two weeks!" I exclaimed, cutting him off, not liking the fact that I'd have to postpone my pitch.

"She and her husband had been saving up for a cruise," Knight explained.

"I know," I admitted. "So, when did her two weeks start?"

"Today." He slowly shook his head. "That means we'll have to deal with that dickhead Swint for two whole weeks."

"Yeah," I grunted, just as my desk phone rang. "Bishop," I answered.

"Welcome back!" a familiar, masculine voice came through the earpiece.

Shit! Speak of the devil!" Thank you, sir!" I offered, though I wanted to say something more offensive.

"Hall insisted that I make sure you pay a visit to Dr. Shoob upon your return," the assistant director informed. "But I don't deem it necessary. However, I do have to honor her second request, which is to team you up with Agent Knight on the investigation he's currently working on. I'm quite sure he'll put you up to speed. If you need anything, you know where to find me."

Leaving it at that, the son of a bitch hung up. It's not like I had anything to say to him. Hell, I'm just glad we'd gotten that conversation out of the way, and he'd chosen to do it by phone, rather than summon me down to his office, just to rub it in my face that he's the head honcho for the next two weeks, while Hall is out.

Well, there's no reason to dwell on it. I've been handed my new assignment, so it was time I climbed back into my saddle and did what I do best. Returning the receiver to its cradle, I looked over at Knight, who'd resumed whatever paperwork he was working on before I arrived.

"It looks like we'll be working together," I told him.

Knight looked up from his work. "Bullshit!"

"It's what the doctor ordered," I remarked making a face. "So, what do we have so far?"

Saying nothing, the agent passed a manila folder across the partition to me. I opened it, to see a 5.5 x 8.5 photo of a very large man, who looked to be in his late thirties or early-forties. The next document contained two addresses, and the third was a scratch piece of paper with several notes jotted down by Knight. After reading the notes, I looked up at my new partner, who was regarding me expectantly.

"I guess I'm following our lead," I told him, "What's on the agenda?"

"I was gonna do a little bird watching," Knight replied. "Are you up for it?"

"Sure," I said.

As it went, Special Agent Knight and I left the building a little after ten o' clock, taking one of the government-issued SUVs with dark tinted windows. The weather was fine, so we had the windows partly rolled down, and the V-103 radio station playing at a decent volume, as we made our way to East Point, Georgia.

"So, what's your take on the Flenory case?" Knight finally asked, as he pulled the GMC Denali off on the East Point exit.

"I really can't say I have a take on it," I told him. "To be honest, I really don't know much about the case, other than what I was told."

"But Agent Count said you'll be a part of the interagency Task Force, headed by DEA Agent Bell."

I was now regarding the Caucasian agent through the lenses of my sunglasses. "Bob Bell requested my assistance."

"What!" Knight expressed, gazing over at me with admiration. "Just out of the blue? I mean, you two have never met?"

"Never," I answered, looking out at the road we were now travelling on. "Maybe, he inquired into the Bureau about—"

I stopped mid-sentence, when Knight pulled the truck into the parking lot of the Worldwide Insurance Agency building, which is the same building I followed The Queenz to on last Tuesday.

Shit! This was why one of those addresses on Knight's documents looked familiar. I had no clue why the women had visited the place, but I'm quite sure I'm about to find out today.

"What's here?" I inquired, looking out at the six-story building, wondering if we were going to enter it.

"This is Calhouns' most lucrative business," Knight explained, as he searched for a spot to park. "As I'm told, this is where he spends most of his business hours. It's possible that he meets his street clients here."

"If that's a possibility," I started. "Then there's a possibility that his product is shipped here and is stored somewhere inside the building.

An amused expression appeared on Knight's face as he backed the SUV into a spot closest to the main road. "Well, damn!" he expressed. "I didn't even think of that."

"Is this a legit functioning business?" I was looking at the large number of vehicles already parked, and the few people meandering to and from the building, all casually dressed.

"As far as I'm told, it is."

"What about his criminal history?"

Knight shook his head. "He doesn't have any."

"Perhaps, we're dealing with a person of great intellect," I offered, powering up my camera. "First, we have to determine which of these wandering people are insurance agents, and which ones are drug dealers."

"Hell, some of the insurance agents could be playing both fields," offered Knight

"Perhaps." I lifted my trusty Nikkon, adjusted the lens, and snapped shots of the handful of people who'd just so happened to be in the parking lot at this time. "Does GBI have a man inside?"

"I was told they're working on that."

"Working on it," I muttered, snapping a picture of a sky-blue, four-door Chevy Caprice on chrome wheels, that entered the lot.

Letting the camera hang from its strap around my neck to let my arms rest, I kept my eyes on the older-model car as its driver searched for somewhere to park. At this time, we had the tinted windows rolled up, and the engine still running, for the sake of the A.C., but we could still hear its customized sound system, though the music was low.

Once the Caprice finally docked, I raised my camera again, ready to add someone's picture to the FBI's data bank, if it wasn't already there. Just then, the driver's door opened, and a black male in his mid-twenties, dismounted, clad in a gray two-piece suit and red tie. His cornrows were neatly braided, and I caught a glimpse of the gold watch on his right arm, as he checked the time on it.

*Click! Click!*

I panned my camera to keep the 5'10 man in sight as he sauntered toward the entrance of the building, with nothing visible in his hands. Upon entering, he stopped at the front desk that was occupied by a blonde, white woman.

"Person of interest?" Knight inquired.

Pulling my camera away from my face, I looked over at him. "Friendly bet?"

"It all depends," he replied. "Whatcha got?"

"I think this guy's a dealer."

Knight casted a glance over at the building, then back at me, before asking, "And you base your opinion on the vehicle he arrived in? You don't think insurance agents ride around in tricked out hoopties?"

"Are you saying he's an insurance agent?" I questioned eyebrows arched.

"He could be both."

I held my right fist out. "So, is it a bet?"

"You don't think he's both?"

"Nope."

Knight now glanced in the direction of the Chevy Caprice. "So, how would we confirm—"

"We'll get the confirmation," I cut him off, hand still lingering.

"What's the wager?" he wanted to know.

"Lunch," I answered, plainly. "Loser has to buy lunch."

"Today?"

"My arm is getting tired, Knight."

"Fuck it!" he prompted, bumping his fist into mine. "You're on!"

"My man!" I gave a smile, then raised my camera to take shots of a few stragglers.

After fifteen minutes of *bird watching*, I had to reload my camera, swapping the cartridge out for a fresh one from my investigation kit on the back seat, where I also retrieved my small tape recorder, making sure it was fully functional, before dropping it into the inner pocket of my blazer. Another eight minutes crept by, when our target emerged from the building, carrying a large, brown paper bag that was rolled down at the top, but displayed a bulging shape I was all too familiar with.

"Here's our guy," Knight announced.

"Indeed," I responded, taking a couple more shots of the man, as he made for his car.

"So, what's the plan?" Knight wanted to know.

"We follow his ass."

"Then?"

"Then, we get confirmation."

Knight waited until the Caprice pushed out onto the main road, before pulling out of the spot we were in. Though traffic was a little heavy, it wasn't hard to keep the bright-colored vehicle in sight, before Knight was able to secure a good three-car link behind it.

"Make sure you stay on us!" I said, seeing the older car coming to a stop behind another car at a traffic light.

"Do what!" Knight let out.

I didn't respond, before he could bring the truck to a complete stop, I was lunging from it, taking long strides in the direction of the Chevy, with my camera dangling from my neck, and my tape recorder in my left hand. The windows weren't tinted, so I was able to tell that the doors weren't locked, before reaching it. Using my free hand, I yanked the rear-passenger side door open, and slid into the back seat.

"What the fuck!" the man exclaimed, looking back, apprehension in his eyes.

"Shut up!" I voiced, pulling my Glock from its holster. "Cut that bullshit off and keep both hands on the steering wheel!"

When he killed the music, I pressed play on my recorder.

"Where's your driver's license?" I inquired, as the car in front of us moved forward.

"In the glove compartment," he answered, a skeptical expression on his face, "Why would you—"

"Hand me your license!" I demanded. "And drive like you got some sense!"

"How can I hand you my license?" he questioned. "You told me to keep my hands on the wheel."

"You picked a fine time to become a comedian, don't you think?"

Perhaps, the seriousness of my tone prompted him to wise up, because he reached over to open the glove compartment. Of course, I was peering over the front-passenger seat, to make sure he wasn't about to attempt something he'd probably seen in some action movie. The nickel-plated .45 caliber handgun was prominently on display, as it seemed to take up a great deal of the small space, but his hand moved beyond it, taking hold of the plastic identification card. Using the same hand, he closed the compartment back, then passed it back to me.

"Henry Lofton," I pronounced, reading from the card. "College Park, Georgia. Is that where you move your product?"

Lofton didn't respond. Perhaps, he was surprised at my acknowledgment of the paper bag on the floorboard beside him, and its contents.

"Here you go, sir," I said, handing his license back. "Pass me that paper bag you got there.

"I think you're making a big mistake."

"Oh, and how's that?"

"By robbing me."

I smiled, clearly seeing how he easily concluded this scene as a robbery. "It's not what you think, my friend," I assured him. "Just do as you're told, and I promise you'll suffer no loss."

"That shit don't even sound right."

"Just hand me the fucking bag!" I was becoming agitated. Plus, I was sure Knight was concerned about my well-being right now. "Like I said," I resumed. "This is not what you think it is. It's not a robbery, it's an investigation. I'm FBI, and my partner is in the black SUV, about three cars behind us."

I paused to let that sink in, and allow him time to regard his rear-view mirror for confirmation. My shield was clipped to my belt, so when he chanced a glance back at me. I made sure it was visible, along with my gun. I'd placed the recorder on the seat beside me.

"There's a strong possibility that you could end up in an eight-by-nine cell today," I went on. "There's an even stronger possibility that you could reach your destination unscathed or as I said, with no loss suffered. It's your decision."

Henry Lofton seemed to cogitate this for a moment, before reaching for the large paper bag, and handing it to me. Placing my weapon in my lap, I turned the bag over, dumping its content onto the other seat, which was, undoubtedly, a kilo of cocaine, wrapped in red cellophane. After taking a couple of pictures of it, and a good side view of Lofton, I returned the drug to the bag, folded the top back down, and left it on the seat.

"What can you tell me about Vincent Calhoun?" I inquired, retrieving my recorder. "Don't forget—the ball is in your hands."

"Would I have to testify against him in court?"

"That won't be necessary," I replied. "What I'm doing now is gathering intelligence, which goes into my anonymous file."

"Well, I don't know much about the dude," Lofton let on. "Other than he's a loan shark."

"How'd you come in contact with him?"

He shrugged. "The same way everybody else does. He's responsible for the success of a lot of drug dealers in Atlanta. I just so happened to know one. My dude connected Vincent, Vincent set up a meeting."

"And, that meeting was today?"

"No," answered Lofton. "That meeting was almost a month ago, which was pretty much an interview. Said he had to run a background check, before deciding to do any kind of business with me."

"What kind of information did he require of you?" I wanted to know.

"The basic stuff," he answered, with another shrug. "Full name, social security number, two addresses, and other things."

"Where's his office located?"

"On the sixth floor."

"Any bodyguards?"

"Four," he answered. "They sit right outside the elevator and search you the second you step off."

"Then, escort you to Vincent's office, right?"

"Right."

"What about the blonde at the front desk?" I asked, glancing out the rear window, seeing that Knight was now two cars behind us. "Doesn't she keep records of these appointments?"

"In some kind of logbook," Lofton replied." That's where she checked my name off on both visits."

"You've been very helpful, Mr. Lofton," I said, returning my gun to its holster, before dropping the paper bag onto the front-passenger seat. "If you could just pull over, I'd be on my way, and you'll never hear from me again."

"I'm not counting on it," he sneered, pulling his car to the curb.

All I could do was smile at his state of skepticism, as I pressed stop on my recorder, then dismounted, making for the GMC Denali that was just coming to a halt behind the Chevy.

"What the hell just happened!" Knight demanded to know once I slid in beside him.

"You lost the bet, my friend," I told him, tossing the recorder into his lap. "I have a taste for some fish, so swing by the next Captain Ds you come across."

"This guy actually admitted to being a drug dealer?" he asked, disregarding the recorder, as he drove on.

"It's all on tape."

"So, what was in the bag?"

"A kilo of cocaine."

Knight glanced over at me. "Did you see it?"

"I took pictures of it," I replied, removing the strap from around my neck, and placing the camera on the rear seat with my kit. "Captain Ds got this new—"

"What if he mentions this to Calhoun?" Knight cut me off. "That could tip him off that he's under investigation."

"It could," I said. "But this guy isn't stupid enough to bring this encounter to Calhoun's attention."

"And, what makes you so sure of that?"

I started, "Because then he'll have to come up with the world's greatest excuse as to how he was stopped by the FBI, questioned, and not arrested for possession of cocaine. From what I've learned about Calhoun so far, he doesn't seem like the type you can piss on and tell him it's raining. If Lofton mentions this encounter, he'll be dead within twenty-four hours.

"So, Calhoun will automatically gather that this guy had given up some kind of information on him and his operations," Knight summarized. "Yeah, I can see how that scene would play out."

"Listen to the tape," I said, pulling my vibrating cellular from its clip. "Bishop," I announced through the device.

"I have that information you asked about," Homicide Detective Kowanda McCoy's voice reached my ears.

"Which information?"

"The ballistics on the highway shooting case," she reminded. "Should I fax them over?"

"I'm not at the office right now," I told her. "Would it be too much to ask for a verbal account?"

"Not at all," the detective replied. "According to our expert, both victims sustained fatal shots from one A.K. forty-seven assault rifles, though the weapon has yet to be recovered."

I was already aware of all of this. The document would be a plus, but what I really needed were the projectiles extracted from the bodies of the two victims, which would only be possible if the FBI had justifiable reasons to wrest jurisdiction from the hands of the locals. Well, we don't have justifiable reasons, but if I can persuade Director Amy Hall to grant me permission to investigate The Queenz, I think I'd be able to pull a rabbit out of the hat.

## Chapter 11

*Two Weeks Later*

"This is my first day back, Bishop," Director Hall groaned, upon bidding me to enter her office, where she was seated behind her desk, hands poised on the keypad of her computer. "I was hoping to have this day to myself, without having to hold anybody's hand, or break up a quarrel between you kids. Now, how may I help you ruin my day?"

"That's not my intention, Director," I purported, taking a seat across from her, still clutching the documents I came in with." I just need you to hear me out, view a few documents, and give me an answer. Then, I'll be out of your hair, and you won't hear from me for the rest of the week. I promise."

Exhaling a sharp breath, Hall tapped keys on her pad, leaned back in her chair, and said, "I'm listening."

This was my moment, so I took full advantage, and told her everything I knew about the four-woman group known as The Queenz.

While explaining my discoveries, I handed my documents over to the director, for her own confirming evaluation, in which she seemed highly interested.

"You mean to tell me you watched these women murder two men?" Hall inquired, once I was done. "Did you even report this to anyone? I mean, clearly, you didn't report it to *me*."

"I was in the middle of conducting my surveillance on them," I offered as a pretext.

"Yeah, an *illegal* surveillance," she made sure to point out, sitting my documents down on the desk. "You let these women get away with murder?"

"They may have gotten away for now," I contended. "But if you grant me permission to launch a full-scale investigation on them, I'll make damn sure they're held responsible for the act, amongst whatever other charges I bring against them."

Hall leaned back in her seat, as she steepled her fingers under her chin, with those ocean-blue eyes boring holes through me. "If I'm not mistaken," she began. "Director Hopkins gave you his blessings to investigate a similar, male group, and you botched the investigation."

"You are *highly* mistaken," I begged to differ, shifting in my seat. "The investigation wasn't botched. The Kingz ended up being murdered on the same night I was set to arrest them. The file still exists if you need further confirmation."

She seemed to consider this for a moment, then asked, "So, are these women really the widows of The Kingz?"

"Neither of The Kingz were married." I sat up in my seat now. "However, both groups were intimately familiar with one another, which leads me to believe that these women learned what they know about the drug game from their counterparts and are hell-bent on making a name for themselves."

"From what I've gathered," Hall stated. "They haven't kicked up enough dust to wind up on the Bureau's radar, except for the murders, in which we do not have concrete evidence at the moment." She raised her hand to silence my protest. "I know what you conveyed to me," Hall commenced. "But the President, nor the DOJ, wouldn't even bat an eye at your proposal, unless you were in possession of the actual weapon that was used. Do you think it's possible for you to obtain it?"

"I doubt it," I answered, seeing my investigative work going down the drain. "These women are smart. They've probably gotten rid of it by now."

Now, leaning forward, and resting her elbows on the desk, the director said, "I understand what you're trying to accomplish, Mr. Bishop, but out of concern for your well-being, I'm ordering you to cease with this unauthorized investigation. As of now, your current assignment is to assist Agent Knight with —"

"What if I get my hands on the murder weapon?" I cut her off, in my attempt to salvage my investigation. "Would that be enough to get your approval?"

Hall let out an exasperated sigh. "Bishop, let the GBI and local authorities deal with the low-level crimes. You're the FBI for Christ's sake! Now, can I count on you to perform your duties as such, or do you need a little more time off?"

"I'm good, Director," I said, standing, and retrieving my documents off the desk. "My apologies for wasting your time."

"I'm only looking out for your best interest, Mr. Bishop," she replied also getting to her feet.

"Sure," was all I had to offer, before spinning on my heels, and heading for the door.

"Oh! I almost forgot," Director Hall asserted, stopping me in my tracks.

I turned to face her but said nothing.

"DEA Agent Bell excluded you from his interagency Task Force roster," she apprised.

"Okay." As if to say, *"So what?"*

"Wouldn't you like to know why?"

"He's probably looking out for my best interest," I sneered, sarcasm lacing my voice, then made my exit.

Clearly, Miss Goody Two Shoes didn't know that I was not keen on taking *no* for an answer. If she thinks I'm just gonna cease with my investigation, and let my hard work go down the drain, then she had another thing coming. I mean, there's more than one way to skin a cat, right?

Special Agent Robert Knight was ready for our outing when I returned to my cubicle. Therefore, only having to grab my investigation tool kit, we took the elevator down to the garage, and climbed into a dark green, '97 Buick Skylark, then made for East Point with me at the wheel, since it was my turn to drive.

August was putatively the hottest month of the year, and it was definitely rearing its ugly head, smack dab in the middle of its reign. I had the windows sealed tight, sun visor down, and the air condition howling like an electric leaf blower, that was the only sound inside the car, being that I was pretty much in my thoughts, periodically entertaining my partner's questions or whatnots.

"Something's bothering you," Knight now asserted, pulling me from my thoughts.

I glanced over at him. "Huh?"

"You're quieter than usual today," he tried a different approach. "What's on your mind?"

"I was just thinking about this illegal investigation I've been conducting," I said, after taking a deep breath.

"Illegal?" There was a hint of surprise in his voice.

"Pretty much," I answered, pulling into the parking lot of the Worldwide Insurance building. "I'm looking into a body of female drug dealers, who calls themselves *The Queenz*."

"The Queenz," Knight repeated, pensively. "I don't think I've ever heard of them. Are they supposed to be a spinoff from that male organization you were investigating two years ago, The Kingz?"

I shot him a questionable look.

"I overheard other agents talking about it," he went on to explain. "Nothing bad, of course. In fact, I've heard nothing but high praises for you on how you handled that investigation. I think the tragic outcome of it is what makes it one of the most talked about inside the Bureau."

I backed the Skylark into our regular stakeout spot and regarded Agent Knight. Yeah, I'm quite sure other agents have spoken amongst each other about the misfire of The Kingz investigation, but he's making it seem like it's perpetual. Knight hadn't been with us for a year, so he definitely wasn't here at the time. Are my fellow agents still chattering about something that happened almost three years ago? Praising me, perhaps?

"It's definitely my belief that these women are trying to mimic The Kingz," I finally responded. "But they haven't even scratched the surface of the drug game.

"Do you think they have the potential to build an empire?" asked Knight.

"Of course, these women are new to the game, but not to the knowledge of it. With the right connections, they could become a force to be reckoned with."

"Or, with the right male figure behind them," offered Knight. "I mean, I'm quite sure there's some kind of male influence in the background."

"There isn't." Now, I was looking out at the building, wondering what The Queenz may have borrowed from Vincent Calhoun.

"Well, you'd know better than anyone," said Knight. "When do you plan on presenting it to Hall?"

"I already have."

"Yeah? When?"

"This morning."

"Shit! That's great!" he expressed, playfully punching me in the shoulder. "I just hope I'm a candidate for your preferred agents list. It would be a pleasure to—"

"She turned me down," I cut in, raining on his parade.

Naw, Knight was regarding me with a surprised look. "She what! Why the hell would she do that?"

"I have no idea." I shrugged. "But I'm not giving up, though, for some reason, I just have a hard time taking no for an answer."

"So, I've heard." He smiled. "Well, if you need a sidekick, or whatever, I'm in."

"I'll remember that, Knight."

"Subject B," Knight informed, nodding toward the building.

I looked in that direction, and I'd be damned if subject B, a.k.a Brenda Lane, wasn't leaving the building, headed in the direction of her silver Mercedes-Benz hard-top convertible, clad in a tan skirt suit with her blonde hair pulled into a bun, and her large pocketbook hanging from her shoulder.

There was no reason to take pictures of the secretary, I pretty much had enough of her from multiple angles. For the past week or so, Agent Knight and I had been running surveillance on the thirty-one-year-old Caucasian woman, gathering whatever substantial intel we could dig up on her, after considering her an asset to this investigation.

"It's a little too early for lunch, isn't it?" Knight asked, checking his watch, prompting me to do likewise.

It was 10:03 a.m.

"Pretty much," I replied, watching Lane climb behind the wheel of her vehicle. "Maybe, she's running an errand for the boss."

"Then, why wait?" Knight became animated. "We can apply the pressure right now. This could be the only break she gets today."

I didn't have to cogitate this for long. We did choose this day to accost the secretary on her break, in the lot of some non-descript restaurant she favors, in an attempt to squeeze information about Calhoun's operation out of her, and to use her as our own personal mole. Of course, we weren't authorized by the lead investigator to do this. We knew it had a ninety percent chance of backfiring but I was pretty much calling the shots on this one. Sure, it would be the end of my career if I botched this case but I could never forget that I built my career by improvising and pulling off such feats. However, all in all, I had a good feeling about this one.

Before the Mercedes could push out into the main road, I pulled the Buick out of its spot, driving toward the exit. Every day during her break hour, Brenda Lane would make a right turn onto Birch Parkway, today, she was headed in the opposite direction. As I caught up, hanging a good three-cars behind her, I wasn't the least bit worried about her spotting us. Although women from what I've learned are the least likely to be concerned about who's driving behind them.

"Let me hear it," Knight said, after we'd been trailing the woman for a good ten minutes. "I know you've come up with a contingency plan by now."

"Not really," I responded, turning the A.C. down a notch. "Considering this unpredictable change, we'll definitely have to improvise. Since I think she's running an errand, maybe we should approach her afterward. I mean, I'm assisting you, so it's your call."

"Fuck that!" He waved a dismissive hand. "We're both assisting the Georgia Bureau of idiots. If you feel that's the best time to approach, then that's when we'll approach."

While he was in the middle of his *I had a dream* speech, my cell phone vibrated on my hip. Of course, seeing Detective McCoy's information on the screen, pushed me to answer immediately.

"Bishop," I said through the mouthpiece.

"There's an event taking place on the tenth of next month," she explained over the chatter, and the perpetual ringing of telephones in her background.

"The battle of the D.J.s?" I asked, a bit surprised that she would be interested in anything secular.

"So, you already know about this."

"I just find it strange that you're interested in such a shindig."

"I'm not particularly interested in it," McCoy declared. "I just stumbled upon some valuable information that I thought my FBI friend would be interested in."

"What information?"

"About The Queenz being in attendance."

"Say what!" I sputtered, now thinking about her confidential informant, who could just as well be one of The Queenz for all I know.

"The Queenz are attending the event," the homicide detective rephrased. "There's a rumor that they'll either be hosting or judging the event."

"Information from your C.I., huh?"

"My *reliable* C.I.," she corrected. "Anyway, I figured you'd like to know that."

I didn't detect a hint of attitude in her voice, but she did hang up before I could respond, which was the first time in our history of phone conversations. Now, I was more than certain the lieutenant was looking into The Queenz, and had linked them to the highway shooting, perhaps from something her informant overheard. I already know what I need to do, though it seemed like time is against me at the moment.

We ended up following Brenda Lane to inland Seafood, which is a small packaging warehouse located on some back street. Still not worried about her spotting us, I pulled into the lot right behind Calhoun's secretary, and attempted to back into a spot several yards across from her.

Before I could fully complete the task, Lane exited her car, tossed the purse strap over her shoulder, and strutted toward the small office building, resembling a call girl on her way to milk some old man, who probably couldn't even spell *erection*. Seconds after rapping on a windowless door, it was opened to her, but we were unable to tell by whom.

"She'll probably be in there a while," Knight said, unbuckling his seat belt and looking around. "I gotta piss like a racehorse!"

He got out and moved toward the rear of the car. Curious, I looked back to see where he'd planned to relieve himself, and saw the agent stomping in the direction of a small, wooded area that boasted a gamut of barren trees providing little to no shelter from the eyes of anyone driving by.

Redirecting my attention toward the building, I almost thought my eyes were playing tricks on me, when I saw Lane exiting, moving fast to her car with her heels clawing the asphalt. There was no time to think about Knight, who probably hadn't got his zipper down yet. Therefore, I quickly unlatched my seatbelt, grabbed the manila envelope from between the seats, and lunged from the Buick with purpose.

The secretary was at her car now. Upon pulling the driver's door open, she stopped, and regarded me, now resembling a deer caught in headlights. I must've resembled a thug, clad in khaki shorts and tank top underneath my unbuttoned button-down shirt with my *Highway Patrols* glued to my face.

"FBI, ma'am," I announced, approaching and flashing the badge on my hip, withholding my name. "You can go ahead and sit down."

Apprehension now registered on her face, she shot a glance back at the warehouse, then did a quick survey of the area, before settling behind the wheel of the coupe, and placing her bag on the seat beside her. I pulled my recorder from my pants pocket and stood between her and the door.

"Mrs. Lane," I spoke, after activating the recorder. "I understand that you work for Vincent Calhoun who happens to be a loan shark for drug dealers?"

"I'm a secretary for the Worldwide Insurance agency," Brenda Lane huffed. "I don't know anything about any drug dealings, or any other false accusations you may have against my boss."

"I figured you'd play hard ball," I said, handing her the manila envelope. "This is for you."

There was a look of uncertainty on her face as she extracted the 6x9 photo. Then, the apprehension was back, once she realized it was a picture of her and Calhoun, cuddling beside her car in the parking lot of their workplace. Giving her a moment to let that set in, I looked up to see Agent Knight approaching, amusement was written all over his face. I turned back to Lanes.

"According to our files," I resumed. "You're married to a Mr. Ronald Lane, am I correct?"

She looked up at Knight, who'd just joined us, then back at me, but said nothing.

"Clearly, that Biggie-Smalls-looking motherfucker isn't Mr. Lane," I pressed on. "I have other pictures of you and this cheese-burger-eating son of a bitch and I am highly tempted to mail copies to your husband, so he'll see what kind of trash you're opening your legs up to. Hell, with this kind of evidence, I'm quite sure Ronald wouldn't have a hard time getting a judge to side with him in divorce court."

I know I came off a bit crude, but that's how the game's got to be played during investigations, whether dealing directly with a criminal or not. Everybody has something to lose. Even so, everybody had something they can't stand to lose. Once you point such things out to a person, and apply the right amount of pressure, nine times out of ten, you'll get the results you desire.

The secretary looked up at me with tears forming in her eyes. "Why would you do this to me?" she asked, hurt registered in her voice.

"Why would you do this to yourself?" I countered, leaving no room for sympathy. "Now, you have a very important decision to make. Which one of these men are more important to you?"

\*\*\*

It was well after 9 p.m., when I made it to Riverdale, Georgia. A wave of relief swept over me as I entered Lawrence Street, and saw the black GMC Denali parked in the driveway of the home belonging to Theresa Joiner and Ebony Davis. Passing the house, I darted my eyes from window to window, looking for any sign of movement. The only thing I saw was the constant flicker of light coming from the television set in the living room. I chose the fourth house beyond theirs, to turn my car around in, then drove one house up, and parked, killing the engine.

Someone was apparently up at the residence, so, knowing I had to wait, but not for how long, I reclined my seat a little, and let my mind wander. I was thinking about Monique, and how acquiescent she was tonight, by not wanting to have sex, prior to me leaving the house, like she'd always been hell-bent on doing. A part of me wanted to believe that I could be overreacting. You know, reading too much into it. Maybe, she was just tired, or tired of putting up a resistance when it comes to my duties as an investigator. However, the other part of me wanted to stick to my guns on this one. There had definitely been a shift in my fiance's demeanor that shouldn't be ignored, and probably needed to be looked into. Hell, honestly, I wouldn't be surprised if it came out that my woman was stepping out on me.

Anyway, at 12:12 a.m., and with my mind back on business, I finally emerged from my car, eased the door shut, then marched in the direction of the house, furtively scanning houses on both sides of the street for signs of enthusiastic *Neighborhood Watch* members. Everything was quiet, except for the occasional rustle of tree leaves ruffled by the cool, late-night breeze.

Reaching the house, I diligently searched the windows, and noticed that the living room was dark, indicating that the television was turned off. Without altering my steps, I approached the rear of the SUV with some gizmo I'd acquired from Hoffman. It resembled a very small hand drill, but he said it would efficiently copy the mold of any security lock within three to four minutes, with two to three minutes for the mold to cool down and harden. Shit, that's damn near ten minutes of me standing in these people's driveway, in the middle of the night, looking like a damn fool.

Oh well, as my good friend instructed, I nudged the pointed end of the device into the lock of the rear door and squeezed the trigger. The whirring noise was barely audible, and the vibration wasn't much to wink at but I'm not a man of great physical steadiness, which made it a bit aggravating trying to keep my hand steady, for the sake of the mold. Plus, as dumb as it sounded, I had to do all this while trying not to look out of place.

After five minutes, the whirring stopped, but the vibration continued. Figuring this to be the cool-down phase, I waited with a little more patience than before, being that this was all about to come to an end, momentarily. Of course, I took another casual glance around, though I really couldn't tell if I was being watched. I'm quite sure if I were being watched, the local authorities would already be here by now, arresting me for trespassing, which would be the least of my worries, compared to what Director Hall would do to me.

The trigger on the device pushed out and locked, bringing me from my abstract musing. Seeing that it had completely shut off, I carefully pulled back, extracting the newly made mold from the keyhole. Now, all I had to do was get the flimsy mold turned into a sturdy alloy key, which would entail a trip to the local locksmith, but that would definitely be a journey saved for tomorrow, or what-not.

# Playa Ray

# Chapter 12

## *Saturday*

"It doesn't get any more *out-of-place* than this," Agent Knight commented, as the delivery truck sporting the *Inland Seafood* logo pulled into the lot of the Worldwide Insurance agency building.

We've been parked across the street in the parking lot of the Ace Hardware store since 7:43 a.m. Only because it was our assignment, although we felt as if we'd documented everything there was to document about Vincent Calhoun, and the associates we'd encountered him with. However, since the day we'd followed Calhoun's secretary to the seafood packing warehouse, not once had we seen any of its delivery trucks at this particular establishment until now.

Lifting the camera off my lap, I snapped shots of the truck as it roared toward the building, parking directly in front of it. A good seven minutes eased by, before the driver dismounted, carrying a clipboard but that was right after Calhoun, and his four henchmen exited the place. They all met up at the rear of the vehicle, where the driver lifted the rear door for them to inspect the cargo, before handing the clipboard over to Calhoun for his signature.

"There's definitely something fishy about this," Knight voiced, looking over at me. "And I don't mean that literally."

"Noted," I replied, still photo documenting. "I think ol' Miss Lane left this part out."

"Indeed."

Now, the truck driver produced two hand trucks from the rear and began loading them with boxes. Once the first one was loaded, one of the goons hauled it toward the entrance, accompanied by another, who held the door for him, then they disappeared inside. It went the same with the other two goons, when the second-hand truck was loaded. In all, they made nine trips. With no handshakes, hugs, or goodbye kisses, Calhoun and his men re-entered the building, leaving the deliveryman to secure the cargo area of his truck.

I looked over at Knight. "Follow that truck!"

"We already know where he's going," my partner protested. "Besides, I highly doubt there's anything left inside it."

"I agree with you one hundred percent," I told him. "However, those are not my concerns right now. I'm curious about something else."

"Hell, that's good enough for me," Knight said, starting the engine of the gray Ford Crown Victoria. "Would I get to play with the siren, and pretty, flashy lights?"

"I'll let you know when."

"Yippee!"

When the delivery truck entered onto the main road, Knight put the car in motion, and followed, taking my instruction to stick close to it. According to my watch, it was 11:23 a.m., so there should be enough time to implement the other impromptu plan I'd recently devised, in which I'd spring on Knight once I was done harassing this delivery guy.

"Light 'em up!" I told Knight, when the truck turned onto Preacher Road, which is the same road Inland Seafoods is located, though the building was a little over half a mile away.

Knight sounded the siren and turned on the red and blue flashers located in the grill of the Ford. The driver immediately beared down on his brakes, pulling to the side of the street but I had to shoot an *are-you-serious* look over at Knight, who was clearly having a field day with the siren.

"Guess I got a little carried away," he offered, apologetically, bringing the car to a halt behind the truck. "So, what's the plan?"

"Just follow my lead," I told him, dismounting.

Clad in dark-blue slacks, and a light-blue Polo shirt. I crossed between the car and truck, feeling a bit relieved to be taking a small break from the A.C. The stench of raw fish assaulted my nostrils, but it wasn't as pungent as the odor of stale cigarettes and sweat that wafted from the open window of the cab.

"Why'd you pull me over, officer?" the thick-mustached Caucasian man questioned, after staring at my badge that dangled from the Nike sport rope around my neck.

"Step out of the vehicle, sir!" I ordered, after snatching the door open. Knight was standing beside me.

"As you wish, officer," he replied, unbuckling his seatbelt, and climbing down from the cab.

"My partner and I want to take a look at your cargo area," I said to the man who stood a few inches shorter than myself. "Will you have a problem with that?"

"N-no, sir," he stuttered. "I mean, there's nothing back there, which is why I'm returning to the shop for a shipment."

This fucker could be smarter than he looks because he meticulously made sure not to say for *another* shipment.

"We would still like to inspect that area, sir," I said, then told Knight to accompany him.

I waited until they were directly behind the truck, before making my move. The object of my interest was lying on the passenger seat, but I dreaded climbing inside, lest the stench finds itself embedded in the fabric of my clothing. Therefore, I reached across the driver's seat, and took hold of the metal clipboard that contained a small stack of delivery receipt forms.

Being that the truck had just left Vincent Calhoun's place, I expected to see his receipt with his signature on top but that wasn't the case. Not only did the form not contain Calhoun's signature, there were no indications as to any kind of product being delivered to anybody, at any location. More out of instinct, than curiosity, I scanned the next two forms beneath the first one, and came up with the same results, which doesn't necessarily prove my theory that the truck driver *knowingly* dropped drugs off to Calhoun, but what person in their right mind would endeavor to confute?

Hearing the cargo door sliding shut, I tossed the clipboard back onto the passenger seat, and pretended to search through the trash on the floorboard until Knight and the driver were back in my presence. I turned to them.

"The cargo hold is empty," Knight announced.

I regarded the driver. "We apologize for the inconvenience, sir. Ever since one of our fellow officers busted a delivery truck carrying illegal immigrants, the chief has been on our asses about some human smuggling ring supposedly operating somewhere in Georgia."

"I understand," he offered with a nod. "We all have jobs to do."

As the driver climbed back into his truck, Knight and I returned to the Ford. He made a U-turn and proceeded in the direction whence we'd come. I sat quietly, waiting for Knight to question my motive for stopping the truck, but it occurred to me that he was waiting for me to offer my own explanation. Oh, what the hell!

"I was curious about Calhoun's shipment receipt," I finally offered, after minutes of riding in silence.

"Oh?" Knight shot a glance over at me. "What did it reveal?"

"Nothing."

He shot an inquisitive glance in my direction.

"The form was blank," I went on to explain, "No order, no address, no signature."

*"No signature!"* he expressed. "But we saw Calhoun—"

*"Pretend* to sign an order form," I intervened.

There was a pregnant pause, before the agent said, "That smart son of a bitch! It was all a show just in case he was being watched."

"Exactly."

"Well, he for damn sure fooled the hell out of me."

"Keep driving!" I told Knight. As we neared the Worldwide Insurance agency building, I noticed the secretary's car was missing from its lot. "Maybe, we can drop in on our dear friend, while she's having lunch."

"Do you think the truck driver will report the stop?"

"I doubt it," I responded. "If he does, he'll be sure to let it be known that it had something to do with human trafficking."

"To keep down panic," Knight summarized. "If the dealers panic, it interferes with shipments, as well as the money he makes on the side."

"Right."

"Well, let's just hope he's smart enough to think like that."

About eight minutes later, Knight pulled the Ford into the lot of Bernie's, the non-descript restaurant Brenda Lane likes to visit on her break hours. Sure enough, her Benz was docked in its usual spot, and Knight made sure to park beside it. I insisted we leave our badges in the car, before dismounting.

As expected, the windowless building was a small bar and grill like establishment, which contained a bar that served food and drinks, a stereo system played some soft rock music, and tables and chairs lined along the far wall. The place wasn't packed, but the handful in attendance were pretty much dressed casually, that had me wondering if this was a low-key place for the well-to-do to hang out and be themselves during their breaks.

It wasn't hard to spot Lane, seated at a table, alone, clad in a purple, sleeveless dress, matching pumps, with her blonde hair pulled into a bun. Not giving it any thought, I marched right over to the table, and dropped right into the seat beside the secretary, who was picking over her Fruit salad. She scowled at me, but we both shot disapproving looks over at Knight, who scooped up the chair across from her, and straddled it backwards.

"Are FBI agents always this rude?" Brenda Lane asked, sarcasm heavily lacing her tone.

"Only when we find out we've been lied to," answered Knight.

"Why didn't you tell us about the shipment of drugs delivered to your boyfriend, through Inland Seafoods?" I took the reins.

"You didn't ask," she said, nonchalantly, before plucking a slice of avocado from her salad, and forking it into her mouth.

"So, this is all a joke to you, huh?" Knight pushed, sticking his hand into her bowl, taking hold of a slice of watermelon, and pointing it at the woman. "It's funny until you're sharing a cell with your hippopotamus of a boyfriend."

"You mean to tell me that prisons now have co-ed living quarters?" Lane sneered. "Which planet is this on?"

"Where does Calhoun store his drugs inside the building?" I intervened, shooting my partner a look for him to back off.

"I don't know anything about that," she said, now regarding me with a softer expression. "He doesn't tell me what comes off those trucks, or where he stores the stuff. As far as I know, it's seafood, that is what's advertised on the packages."

"But you know better," I reminded, considering what she told us on our initial encounter. "Is there a basement floor?"

"No."

"A secret alcove, or something like that?"

She hesitated.

"We had a deal, Lane," I reminded.

"*Somebody* didn't hold up their end," Lane accused, shooting daggers across the table at Knight. "I was told that if I cooperated, I wouldn't see you two again."

"We were just curious about the shipment," I said, apologetically.

"I just told you what I know," the blonde fussed.

"What about the hidden alcove?" I was not gonna let her off the hook with this one.

Brenda Lane drew a deep breath, before asserting, "I don't know about any secret rooms but Vincent has a secret door behind a large mirror in his office, that leads to a flight of stairs, that takes you all the way down to a door that leads out into an alley beside the building."

"Which side?"

"Your right, if you're facing the building."

"Thanks!" I told her, getting to my feet." I apologize for the inconvenience. Hopefully, after today, you won't be bothered by us again."

Knight and I moved away from Lane's table, but not before Knight, disrespectfully, dropped the sliced watermelon back into her bowl. Honestly, I wasn't even mad at him for doing this. Maybe, it'll teach her some manners, and she'll show a little more respect on our next visit. Yeah, I know what I told her, but there always seems to be a *next* visit.

As it went, we returned to the James P. Russell building a little before 5:00 p.m. to compare notes and file our findings away. Then, it was off to do the family thing, although I had an engagement tonight. By now, I'd gotten over my suspicion of Monique letting some other man have his way with her behind my back, because ever since that night the thought entered my mind that she had been her same sex-craving self, never failing to satisfy, and refusing to take *no* for an answer. In fact, she initiated our sexual romp tonight, a couple of hours before I had to leave.

It was 7:38 p.m. when I turned Monique's Lexus truck, onto Lawrence Street in Riverdale, Georgia. Immediately, I spotted the other black GMC Denali belonging to The Queenz' bodyguards, parked across the street from Joiner's and Davis' home, and occupied by the four of them. As I passed the house, where Sheila Griffin's Cadillac was parked at the curb, I kept my head and eyes forward, though I could just feel the heat coming off the four pairs of eyeballs behind the dark windows.

It wasn't dark out yet, but it didn't bother me. I did my same routine, made a U-turn, and parked in front of the same house I parked in front of on my last visit. Considering the scene, I figured The Queenz would pile into their own SUV, and the guards would tail them to the club, where the Battle of the D.J.s was taking place. Of course, I'd be somewhere in the midst. I just hoped they didn't have a parking spot reserved for them in front of the building, that would compel me to revert to plan B.

The moment I thought of this, a white, stretch Cadillac Escalade entering the street caught my attention. I pretended to be searching the glove compartment for something when it slowly rode past me. At this moment, I didn't need a rocket scientist to tell me who'd ordered the truck. Hell, I'm just glad they did, because it would make tonight's mission much easier.

Minutes later, the limousine eased back by me from the opposite direction and parked behind Griffin's car. The driver blew the horn, as I retrieved my camera off the passenger seat, to snap shots of The Queenz, when they exited the house. However, the only movement that ensued was one of the guards stepping from the Denali and approaching the driver's side of the Escalade. After a short exchange, the guy returned to the SUV.

Just as I was about to pan my camera toward the house, the driver's door of the limousine popped open, causing me to halt. The casually dressed man that dismounted, was the last person I expected to see right now, or anywhere near The Queenz. Philip

Lakes, from what I gathered from running intelligence on him owns P.L.'s Limousine service, but will double as a chauffeur, if needed.

Of course, I snapped shots of Lakes as he rounded the large truck, and took position on the right side of it, presumably to await the four women, who were probably all piled up in one bathroom, fighting over one mirror, doing last-minute preparations, which reminded me of Monique, and how it would take her an hour to do last-minute preparations, I smiled.

Just then, the women finally emerged from the house, all wearing skirts, and the same diamond-encrusted tiaras they'd worn on Theresa Joiner's birthday. I snapped away as they trooped toward the limousine.

Wait a minute! Ebony Davis paused to have a few words with Lakes, who was holding the rear door open for them, as if they were old friends, or something. Quite interesting if I may say. No, maybe she was just flirting with the guy, thinking he was just some underpaid chauffeur, who probably didn't get much attention.

My favorite part of the scene was when the limousine pulled off, and the Denali occupied by the guards was right behind it, leaving me to cogitate this new change of plan. Seeing that there was no reason to be discreet, I started the Lexus, and pulled up to the house, parking behind Griffin's car.

I didn't even care to look around to see if I was being watched, as I stepped out with my camera dangling from my neck, and a keyring in my hand that contained three partially similar keys. The locksmith provided me with the three, ensuring me that one of them would be the right fit.

Approaching the driver's door of the GMC Denali, I blindly selected one of the keys, stuck it in the lock, and tried to turn it. No luck. I inserted the second key and was in business. Climbing into the driver's seat, I closed the door like I was the rightful owner of the vehicle.

After taking a moment to relish the faint aroma of various perfumes and cosmetic items, I climbed between the front seats to the rear seats, which took some time, being that my over-grown ass was too big to even be thinking about doing such a thing. It didn't matter, because now I was one step closer to completing my mission for tonight. All I had to do was take pictures of the AK-47, then take it with me, to present to Director Hall. After the ballistics is done, and the director gives me her permission to pursue The Queenz, I'd find a way to obtain the projectiles extracted from the bodies of Cecil Henderson and Jesse Bridges.

Now, with my knees planted into the cushion of the rear seats, I wasted no time pulling the cloth tarp back and wasn't too surprised to see that the AK-47 wasn't there. In fact, it had been replaced with an Uzi.

Feeling defeated, I covered the sub-machine gun back up, and planted my bottom onto the seat. At this moment, I was trying to figure out another way to win Amy Hall over, while my mind was telling me to search the truck. That's when it dawned on me that there could possibly be something else left behind, like an overlooked shell casing from the assault rifle, being that it was actually fired from *inside* the SUV.

I didn't have any gloves, so I was skeptical about sticking my hand under the rear seat, but I did it for the sake of this investigation. After blindly, and gingerly, moving my bare hand over the carpeted surface underneath, to no avail, I did the same with the two seats up front, finding nothing but a lipstick capsule, or whatever women refer to it as.

The only spot to check now was the glove compartment. I was not about to climb back between the seats, so I just placed my upper body between them, which enabled me to reach it. Pulling the door open, I saw there were only a couple of folded documents. Figuring one to be the SUV's title, I was inquisitive about the other, which looked like some kind of receipt.

Unfolding the piece of paper, I saw that it was a receipt from a body shop in Henry County. It boasted of repairing a rear window, and rear bumper of a 2003 GMC Denali, on the twenty-sixth of June, which was the day after the highway shooting. I don't know why, but I found myself smiling at this revelation. It may not be as effective as the murder weapon would've been, but I deem it would be effective nonetheless.

# Chapter 13

*Monday*

"What's here?" Knight asked, pulling the Crown Victoria onto the property of Riggs' body paint shop in Henry County.

The place didn't have much of a parking lot, being that no concrete had been laid over the uneven earth, vehicles that were present, were obliquely parked. Considering the sparsely scattered parts of various shapes and sizes, I was hoping like hell that Knight didn't run over anything capable of piercing the tires.

Once he found a spot between a Dodge pick-up, and an older model Mercedes-Benz, we dismounted, and moved toward the entrance of the dilapidated, steel frame structure of a building. To the left of us, and a few feet away from the establishment, a Caucasian male seemed to be doing repairs to the engine of a Jeep Wrangler, while another guy, presumably the owner of the vehicle, stood around, chatting on his cellular.

The mechanic, leaning into the hood of the Jeep, stood about 5'11, clad in a pair of dingy, dark-blue cotton fabric pants, and a tank top that may have been white once upon a time. A walking canvas, he was overlaid with tattoos that went all the way up to the peak of his shaved head. As we were passing, he stopped what he was doing, stood erect, and sternly regarded us through black-framed eyeglasses.

"May I help you guys with something?" he inquired, looking us up and down, clearly able to see our guns and badges that were attached to our hips.

"Sure," I replied, stopping in my tracks. "We're looking for the owner, Danny Riggs."

He held his skinny arms out and palms up. "You're looking at him. What am I accused of now?"

"Nothing," I told him. "We just need to question you about some work you did on a vehicle of interest. Any idea how long it's gonna take you with this one?"

"I'm pretty much already done," Riggs replied. "Once I make sure the fan belt is secure, I'll join you boys inside."

I nodded my consent, then Knight and I entered the small establishment that was much cleaner than expected. Objects on the counter were neatly arranged, as well as the magazines on the low table of the waiting area. Knight busied himself with one as we both sat to wait on the shop's owner, who didn't have us waiting for long.

A man of his word, Danny Riggs walked through the door a few minutes after we were seated. Instead of approaching, he went behind the counter to cash in, and to log in his recent work, which took another two to three minutes. Finally putting his ink pen down, he fixed us with a gaze through his bifocals.

"I don't suppose I could interest you boys in a couple of beers, huh?" he asked.

"Nope," I answered, standing, and crossing over to the counter, pulling the receipt from my pocket. "You serviced a two thousand and three GMC Denali, on the twenty-sixth day of June. Do you remember that?"

"Two women," Riggs answered, reflectively, now leaning forward on the counter. "Shit these women had some of the fattest asses I've ever seen walk through that door, I tell ya'!"

"The truck, sir," I pushed him to stay focused, placing the receipt in front of him. "I'm only interested in the work you did on it."

"It's right here on the receipt," he said, after surveying the piece of paper, and sliding it back toward me. "I replaced the rear window and corrected the rear bumper."

"Did you question them about the damage?"

"Of course, not." There was a look of contempt on his face. "I'm never concerned with the cause unless it'll help me locate and fix the problem. However, one of 'em did mention something about a jealous boyfriend."

"And you believed her?"

"Hey!" He threw his hands up in mock surrender. "As long as I'm being paid for my labor, I'll believe whatever people want me to believe. Besides, with a woman as fine as the owner of the truck,

I can understand why a man would undergo such a violent frenzy, I think I may have—"

"Is this your true signature?" I cut him off, holding the receipt up.

"It is," he answered. "I guess what they did is top secret, huh?"

"Not really," I responded, stuffing the receipt back into my pocket. "The owner of the truck is the plaintiff in an insurance fraud case. However, thanks for your time!"

Knight and I left the establishment, to resume our daily surveillance on Vincent Calhoun. Well, that's what I wrote in the missions book, but being that we felt we'd obtained enough intelligence on the loan shark, Knight and I decided to mosey around for the duration of the investigation.

A married man, Agent Robert Knight had a *side piece* he wanted to harass on her job, so we ended up riding out to the hotel she does housekeeping at, located in Clayton County. When he went inside, I chose to stay in the car. In fact, I decided to call and check on the Decatur Chief of police, John Moody.

"Talk!" The older man answered, sounding grumpy.

"Have you gathered anything else on the ghost?" I asked.

"What damn ghost, Bishop?"

"LKS."

"Oh!" Moody let out, chuckling. "You wouldn't believe I was just thinking about that son of a bitch."

"So, LKS is a male?" I inquired, figuring he'd come upon more information on the subject he'd been searching out.

"That's the impression I've been getting," he said, with a sign. "I can't get a link on where the fucker resides, but from what I understand, he's one of the biggest drug suppliers in Georgia, if not *the* biggest."

"Even though no one has ever seen him?" I asked, meaning to sound sarcastic.

"Right," the Chief replied. "Honestly, I believe it's some kind of syndicate, and my C.I.s are sending up smoke screens."

"Well, you and I both know that informants can't be one hundred percent trusted," I reminded, watching a white couple emerge from the entrance of the hotel. "If they'll volunteer information to us for free, they'll definitely misinform us for the right price."

John Moody laughed at this. "I've never looked at it like that, Bishop," he admitted. "The fuckers will tell us anything to keep themselves out of the clink."

"Exactly!" I stared at my watch. "So, what made you pursue LKS?"

"I was doing a routine check-in with some of my C.I.s," he went on to explain. "While doing so, two of 'em mentioned this guy, or whatever the fuck it is, and it sparked my interest. Right now, I don't have a positive ID, but I was informed of a night club employee, who's a possible customer, or worker of LKS. According to the source, he receives drops at the club, but the schedule is undetermined at the moment."

"But you do have eyes on this guy, right?" I asked, seeing Knight exiting the hotel.

"I wish I did," the older man grunted. "With this fake-ass budget cut, I can barely pay myself to do the piece-of-shit job I signed up to do."

"I'll tell you what," I said, speaking faster now. "Text that information to me. I won't make any promises, but if I can find the time, I'll swing by the club and see if I can shed some light on this thing for you."

"Thanks, Bishop!"

"No problem, Moody," I replied. "I'll talk to you later."

Knight and I usually didn't retire to the James P. Russell building, until a little before 5:00 p.m., but I made sure we made it back a little before 4:00 today, being that I had one more task to complete, prior to quitting time. Knight had already committed himself to logging in our daily movement. So, once we exited the elevator, he settled in at his cubicle, while I only stopped for a moment to grab a folder from my file cabinet and resumed toward Director Amy Hall's office.

To my surprise, the door that's normally closed, was standing wide open, and I found Hall standing behind her desk, stuffing documents into her briefcase, preparing to leave for the day, which was a bit too early for her schedule. Usually, as with the former director, I'd linger in the threshold until acknowledged, but not this time. I marched right on in, and took a seat across from her, like I'd been rightfully summoned, placing the folder in my lap. Oh! You better believe the director stopped what she was doing, to regard me with a disapproving look.

"To what do I owe this extremely rude intrusion?" she asked, narrowing her eyes at me.

"Are you leaving this early?"

"Don't answer my question with a question, Bishop!" Hall chided. "What is it that you want?"

"Five minutes of your time," I said, immediately becoming serious.

Closing, and snapping the latches on her briefcase, the director thrust her hands upon her hips, before asking, "Does this have something to do with those women you were trying to get my permission to harass?"

"If that's the term you prefer to use," I conceded, letting her have her moment. "Yes, this is pertaining to them."

"I've already given you my answer," she pointed out. "What makes you think—"

"Just five minutes." I actually held up five fingers for emphasis.

After a moment of staring me down, she drew a deep breath, then threw her arms over her chest. "You got three," she told me.

"That's good enough," I responded, thankful for the opportunity. Standing, I handed the folder to Hall, who accepted it with a quizzical expression.

"I hope you don't expect me to read this," she said, glancing at her watch.

"It's not much," I assured. "Just a document, and a few notes I jotted down."

Another moment of eyeing me passed, before she finally opened the folder to view the contents, which were the receipt from the body shop that did the repairs to the SUV belonging to The Queenz and notes I'd written down to corroborate, and further illustrate prior evidence I presented to her.

While she busied herself with these things, I found myself looking at her red, newly polished fingernails. I only knew they were
newly polished, because of the faint scent of nail application that
still hung in the air. Considering this, and how early it was, I was
under the impression that this married woman was on her way to
commit adultery, which made me smile. I'm not judging her. She's
human and she has needs. Maybe, her husband isn't hitting those
spots he used to hit. Or maybe he's never hit those spots, and she's
only with him because he's the nicest guy she's ever met. Hey! It
happens.

"I'm assuming Ebony Davis is one of The Queenz?" Hall finally spoke.

"Yes, she is."

"You didn't mention it."

"Sure, I did," I begged to differ. "I mentioned all of their
names."

"Oh!" the director let out, after looking back over my notes. "I
see where you're going with this, Bishop. However, despite what
you've witnessed, and documented, the DOJ will only brush it off
as hearsay. Hell, you don't even have the murder weapon."

"I presented you with photos of it," I made sure to point out.
"Also, if granted permission to proceed, I'd be able to obtain the
projectiles extracted from the bodies of Henderson and Bridges,
which were fired from this weapon."

"And, how sure are you of this?"

"About ninety-eight percent."

"That's quite a bold number, Mr. Bishop!" she asserted, handing the folder back to me. "However, I'm not moved by inflation,
so I hope you're not exaggerating this, in order to get my approval."

"I'm quite sure you've read the file I built on The Kingz," I said,
thankful she'd given me the opportunity to play this card. "The former director, even the Department of Justice, said I did an outstanding job with that investigation, which I initiated, and built from the
ground up."

"Just like this one, huh?" There was a sly smirk on her face.

"Of course."

Casting another glance at her watch, Amy Hall took hold of her briefcase, then scooped her keys and cellular off the desk. Regarding me through narrow slits, she said, "I'm gonna stick my neck out for you on this one, but I'll be orchestrating the investigation."

"Meaning?" I inquired, not liking how this was going.

"Meaning, I'll choose what agents work the case," she replied. "I'll also decide on who'll be running point."

# Playa Ray

## Chapter 14

*Tuesday*

*September 20, 2005*

"How does the defendant Mrs. Shirley Plummer wish to plead to the outstanding number of charges brought against her?" asked Judge Larry Dean, a Caucasian male in his early sixties, seated on his bench, bedecked in his immaculate black robe.

Today's proceeding was a bond hearing for the bunch we arrested in the child abduction case, not including the Johns. Considering the number of defendants, and defense attorneys, it was arranged for the defendants to sit in the jury box, and the attorneys to gather awkwardly around the defense table, with the family members of the accused, taking up three of the benches, leaving us participated agents squeezed in on the last two.

Being that this was a high-profile case, there were news personnel from three different news stations set up around the room, sending live feed out to their stations, who sent it out to the rest of the world via satellite. Well, I assumed that's how it works.

"Your Honor," Attorney Peter Hines who'd already spoken for three other defendants, got to his feet. "Mrs. Plummer also joins the group's plea of nolo contendere, as well as the group's joint motion for a bond in which we pray the court will grant in good faith."

"The court accepts the defendant's plea," Judge Dean asserted, as the attorney took his seat. "However, the court, hereby, denies motion for bond. Defendants will remain in custody until a trial date is set." He banged his gavel. "Court is adjourned."

I couldn't help but glance over at Phoenix, who was staring at me, just like she'd been doing from the moment she was escorted into the courtroom in her red jail-issued jumpsuit. Even when I was on the witness stand, giving my account of the investigation, I felt the heat from her eyeballs burning into the right side of my face. It's not like it's uncommon for an arresting official to get stares from an arrestee, but Shirley Plummer's stares didn't pair with the ones I was used to getting. In fact, they were almost unreadable. Just as she was being escorted from the courtroom, Phoenix cast one last glance at me, and winked.

Of course, I thought about this on my ride back to the James P. Russell building. Despite the range of charges, and the kind of time she was facing, Shirley Plummer seemed to not have a care in the world. Like she possessed some kind of secret, or magic power that would make this all go away for her. There was definitely some kind of secret behind those eyes and for some strange reason, I felt like it involved me.

It was shortly after 2:00 p.m., when I finally reached my cubicle, and collapsed into my chair, exhausted from hours of being cooped up in that courtroom. Knight had come down with the Flu, which is why his area was empty.

I yawned and stretched for the umpteenth time today. While in the midst of doing so, my desk phone became active, its soft ringtone blending in with those of the others. As my very own custom, I waited for the conclusion of the second ring, before snatching the receiver from its cradle.

"Bishop," I announced, opening my logbook on my desk.

"I tried calling your cellular," Homicide Detective Kowanda McCoy's voice came through the earpiece. "Are you busy?"

"I was just about to jot something down in my logbook," I told her. "Other than that, I have nothing else going on."

"We need to talk," she plunged in. "Can you meet me somewhere when you're off the clock?"

As a habit, I looked at my watch. "Yeah, I suppose so. What's the location?"

"I'll make it convenient for you," said McCoy. "We'll meet up at Club Magic City."

"The strip club?" I asked, figuring she had to be joking, considering her devotion to her religion. "I'm quite sure there's a Catholic church, or even a mosque, somewhere in that same area."

"It's not like we're going inside the place, Bishop," the detective let on. "But, if you feel like you won't be able to control yourself, I'll select another location."

"I see you got jokes, Lieutenant," I replied, just as Agent Dan Powell approached, and stood over me. "I'll call you when I'm en-route."

"That'll work," McCoy replied.

I hung up the phone and looked up at Powell, who was giving me an uncomfortable look.

"Hall wants to see both of us," he informed, then turned, and headed toward the director's office, leaving no room for me to pose questions he may, or may not have had answers to.

Of course, I was a bit addled about this. I'm not doubting Pow-ell's word, but if the director wanted to see both of us, why would she notify him, and not me? This made me look down at my phone, as if it was gonna ring at any moment, though I only waited a few seconds, before forcing myself to my feet, and trailing behind Pow-ell, who was already halfway to our destination.

I made it to the door, just in time to hear Hall bid us entrance. Being that Powell was the first to enter, I was left to close the door behind us, before taking a seat beside him, across the desk from Director Amy Hall, who seemed to be having one of her informal days. She was dressed in a pair of jeans, and a gray sweater with *UCLA* stenciled on the front of it. Plus, her dark hair was pulled into one of those loose ponytails.

"Thanks for coming, guys," Hall said, leaning back in her chair, elbows propped on the armrest. Then she bared her blue eyes down on me. "Mr. Bishop, I already told you I was gonna stick my neck out for you on this investigation. I also told you that I'd be orches-trating it, choosing my own agents, and who I'll use as a point, did I not?"

"You did," I said, with a slight nod, though I was leery of her introductory.

"Are there any issues about how I plan to proceed with this in-vestigation?" she inquired. "Speak now, or forever hold your piece."

"No issues on my part," I lied.

She turned to my co-worker. "That goes for you too, sir."

"Hey!" Powell lifted his hands in surrender. "You're the boss."

"That's music to my ears!" Leaning forward, Hall collected a piece of paper from atop her desk and handed it to me. "These are the initial agents I've chosen for this assignment."

Looking at the paper in my hand, I saw that there were seven names, including mine, which was the second one on the list, right up under Dan Powell's. Surely, the erroneous positioning of our names wasn't an indication of something that's not meant to be, right?

"Agent Powell?" our supervisor resumed, garnering my full attention. "I hope you still got your rodeo boots, because I'm assigning you as point."

"Again?" I blurted, thinking of how she gave this fucker the same position in the child abduction case.

Director Hall fixed me with a stern look. "I beg your pardon!"

"Nothing, Mrs. Hall," I deferred, handing the list over to Powell, her golden retriever.

"I thought it was nothing," she hissed. "From here on out, you'll be required to put Powell up to speed on your discoveries of this group of women who calls themselves The Queenz. Relinquish the file to him to take home and familiarize himself with it. Powell, once you brief the other agents, you have my blessings to proceed. Just make sure I'm notified of all movement in reference to this assignment."

"Yes, ma'am," Powell agreed, like a true bootlicker.

"Now, get out of my office!" Hall spat, turning her attention to her monitor, pretty much indicating that this meeting was adjourned.

Of course, I was the first to stand. Maintaining my cool facade, I strutted right out of the office with Powell close on my heels. He had to know I was heated about the director's decision. Hell, the director knew I was heated about her decision. For some reason, I could not help but feel like these two had already rehearsed the scene, before calling me on stage for a fucking cameo appearance.

"I know how you're feeling right now, Bishop," Agent Powell spoke from behind me." Trust me, I wasn't expecting her to make me the lead investigator over an investigation you'd put your time and energy into building. Yes, I could've declined, but I don't think Queen Sheeba would've taken *no* for an answer. Hell, you know how she is."

"Yeah," was all I cared to offer through clenched teeth.

By the time, we'd made it to my cubicle, where I chose to remain standing, while logging today's movement into my logbook. Finishing with that, I was about to gather my things, and get out of there, when I realized Powell was still standing around, like he was waiting for something.

"What's up?" I inquired.

"I was gonna look through that file tonight," he professed obviously choosing his words carefully, considering the state I could possibly be in.

"It's at my home," I lied. "I'll make sure to drop it off to you first thing tomorrow morning."

Oh! You better believe the cocksucker shot me a skeptical look, before quietly moving toward the elevators. I'm a firm believer that great minds do think alike. Especially FBI agents. Therefore, I'm willing to bet anything he's under the impression that he won't receive the full file I have on The Queenz. I mean, of course he won't receive the full file, fuck Director Hall!

The clock on my dashboard read 2:45 p.m., by the time I pulled my BMW into the lot of Atlanta's most prestigious strip club. It wasn't packed at this time of the day, so McCoy's silver Range Rover wasn't hard to spot, as it was parked further away from the building. Docking my car next to the expensive piece of machinery, I killed the engine, dismounted, and climbed in beside the homicide detective, who was clad in khaki pants, and a black turtle-neck sweater that bore down on her C-cup breasts, making them stand out like a couple of warheads. As her jet-black hair was parted at the center of her head, cascaded to her shoulders, she was as flawless as ever without the help of any man-made cosmetics.

"Thanks for coming," Lieutenant McCoy said, as she turned the volume down on her stereo playing gospel tunes. "I won't hold you up for too long."

"I'm in no rush," I told her, reclining my seat a little. "What'cha got?"

"A homicide took place on the eleventh of this month," she explained. "In Riverdale, Georgia."

"Riverdale, Georgia?" I was now looking at her. "Did you transfer?"

This brought a smirk on her face. "I see you brought jokes."

"I try to keep a few in my pocket," I replied. "Are you referring to the deadly carjacking that left one man dead?"

"Yes, I am."

"And, what sparked your interest in this particular case?" I inquired, now looking out at two men approaching the entrance of the club.

"I knew the victim," McCoy told me. "Being that I have a few colleagues in Riverdale, not only will I be following the case, but I'll be assisting with it."

"Off the record, right?"

"Of course, Bishop." She narrowed her eyes. "This is personal for me."

"And I assume you'll be needing my help?" I asked, stifling a yawn.

"You know I'm gonna need your help," admitted the homicide detective. "I need you to keep your ears to the streets."

"Okay. What will I be listening for?"

"The victim's name was Spencer Kelly," she went on to explain. "He was known to most as Spenz, or D.J. Spenz, being that he was a D.J. at a nightclub. The vehicle taken from him was a blue, eighty-four Chevy Caprice, with chrome wheels."

"Is that all?"

"Yeah, the basics."

"Got it." I grabbed the door handle, preparing to depart, then looked back at her. "How close were you to the vic?" I asked.

"Close enough for me to get involved."

"One of your C.I.s, huh?" I pressed "This wouldn't be the one you were so secretive about, would it? The one you claimed to be close to The Queenz?"

In response, she directed her attention out her side window.

"Don't I get some kind of prize for getting it right?" I was not letting this go. "At least tell me more about this guy."

McCoy took a deep breath, before turning to me and saying, "He was dating one of them."

Holy shit! This can't be true, because I'm quite sure I have the names of every man I've encountered these women with, and Spencer Kelly does not ring a bell. Surely, this guy has been pulling the detective's leg, just to feed her information. I'm all too familiar with the type.

"Which one?" I challenged, more than anxious to hear the nonsense.

"Joiner," she seemed to draw from her memory bank. "Theresa Joiner, I think."

Wait! Time out! Out of the four of these women, Joiner is the *only* one I haven't seen hanging onto any man's arm. Hell, I'm still under the impression that she's a lesbian, and has been secretly rocking Ebony Davis' boat, with whom she shares a house with. However, if what Detective McCoy says is true, it means I need to tighten up on my investigation. Now that other agents will be working the case, I'll learn a lot more, though I'll be playing my cards close to my chest, keeping certain information out of circulation until I feel the right time to reveal them. Until then, I'll be working on a way to supplant Agent Powell and claim the lead investigator's position that rightfully belongs to me.

Playa Ray

# Chapter 15

"Do I need to go back over anything?" asked Special Agent Dan Powell, who stood at the front of the war room on the fourth floor.

Me and the other five agents chosen to work under Powell, were seated, and taking notes, while the lead investigator went over *my* notes as though *he* was responsible for the discoveries. Tacked to the board were photos of all The Queenz, and a number of associates I'd connected them to. Plus, there were sticky notes containing information, including phone numbers and addresses.

"Yes, Agent Pierce?" Powell acknowledged the guy's hand that went up in the air in response to his question.

"Just one thing," the young agent replied. "My subject is Sheila Griffin, who, from what I gathered, is the cousin of and also resides with Shonda Watson. Being that Agent Bishop's subject is Watson. How do we pursue them if, and when they split up?"

"You're already making me regret you were chosen for this assignment, Pierce," Powell voiced, garnering snickers from some of the others. "You'll both be in separate vehicles. Stay on your subject, and Mr. Bishop will stay on his. As I said, gentlemen, until other agents are available to me, you'll all be flying solo, and your missions may change sporadically without notice. Now, if there aren't any more time-consuming questions, I'd like you all to return to your cubicles, and familiarize yourselves with these files, because you'll be on post first thing tomorrow morning.

As we gathered our files to leave, I cast a glance over at Agent Andrew Pierce, who had to be disconcerted after being mocked by the lead investigator. I looked up to see Powell exiting the room, then scooped my folder off the table in front of me and crossed over to Pierce who was just getting to his feet.

"Are you good?" I inquired, falling in-step with him as he made for the exit.

"Yeah, sure," he answered, giving me a mere glance.

"It's clear to see that you two aren't the best of friends," I pried, thinking of why Powell would never be considered my BFF.

"I don't know what his problem is," Pierce admitted. "I barely said two words to the guy since I've been here."

"Don't let him get to you," I advised. "Sometimes, you gotta—"

"Bishop!"

We had just crossed the threshold of the war room when my name was called by that all too familiar voice. Stopping in my tracks, I turned to see Agent Powell standing just beyond the entrance, twirling an unlit cigarette in his hand. "I'll catch up to you later," I told Pierce. He nodded, then moved on behind the others. Turning to Powell, I asked, "What's up?"

"You're already familiar with this case," he told me. "If you want, you can go on out in the field. I'll log you in for twelve."

"I'll go out tomorrow," I told him. "Right now, I need to research something."

"Pertaining to the case?"

"Of course," I replied, then made for the elevators.

Getting back to the sixth floor, I stepped off the elevator just as Agent Knight was about to get on, carrying a manila folder.

"Where are you off to?" I inquired, standing in the threshold to keep the elevator doors from closing.

"We're supposed to swap intel with the GBI, remember?"

"Shit!" I mumbled. I can't believe I let that slip my mind. Knight and I always reported our findings on Vincent Calhoun, to the lead GBI every other week in exchange for whatever they were willing to let us in on.

"Don't worry," Knight insisted. "I'll tell them you were assigned to another case. I mean, I know how important that case is to you.

"Thanks, Knight!"

"Don't mention it," he said with a wink, then pressed the button for the ground floor.

Moving along, I got to my cubicle, and immediately powered up my computer. For some reason, while Powell was going over what intel I gave him on The Queenz, I periodically found myself thinking about Decatur Chief of Police John Moody, and this *LKS* character he was looking into. That's when it finally dawned on me that the local authorities' data base wasn't as advanced as ours, just as ours isn't as advanced as the CIAs.

I'm quite sure Moody has logged *LKS* into his search engine on a witch hunt for someone whose name may bear the initials, which would pretty much be foolish, because only a fool would use his actual initials while conducting any kind of illegal transactions. Therefore, I typed in the three letters, in reference to nick names and entities in Georgia.

After a few seconds of loading, over a dozen legitimate businesses appeared on the screen. These definitely didn't spark my interest, so I took a moment to rub my naked arms, then scrolled down, until I came upon Latin Kingz, which is a gang that was founded in 1940, on the southside of Chicago, by a group of disgruntled Puerto Ricans to protect themselves, and African-Americans, from the ongoing racial acts committed toward them by white and Italian extremist.

*Blah! Blah! Blah!*

Moving along, I found myself frowning at criminal profiles of male and female members of the aforementioned organization which at this present time, is on the FBI Gang Task Force's terrorist list. These profiles included photos of the affiliates, and every part of their bodies that boasted tattoos of the *LK* in various forms and fashion, indicating that they were true to what they vowed their loyalty to. However, none of this shit had a thing to do with what I was looking for.

Just as I was about to skip to the next column, the bold letters that spelled *WANTED* caught my attention. Tweaking the rotor on my mouse, I brought the screen up, until I was staring into the eyes of a man who looked like he'd never had a good day. Tattoos decorated his shaved head and face, but I was focused on the one on the right side of his temple, which was an *L* and a *K*, topped with a slanted crown.

According to the electronic report, Jason Garcia, a.k.a Loko, after being arrested for multiple homicides in Puerto Rico, his homeland, in 2004, was placed on house arrest, but ended up fleeing to the states, where he was now wanted in connection to a multiple homicide in Texas. A Georgia address showed that he had a sister, who resided in Savannah. I'm quite sure that residence was being watched by the National Guard right now.

The next organization that rolled onto the screen was the North Side Lokos, which had me wondering about one of its leaders I'd had under investigation years ago. In fact, I think I'll pay a little visit to Ruben Rodriguez, a.k.a Oso, which means *bear* in Spanish. If anybody knew who LKS was, it would be Oso, who seemed to have connections to every major drug dealer, no matter what region they lived in. If he didn't know them, he knew of them.

The moment I began tampering with my mouse, a figure appeared to the left of me. The first thing that caught my attention was the white, shell-toe Adidas, that were definitely in fashion with the bell-bottomed jeans, black and white Adidas sweater, and the white hat that was clearly a knock off of the Kangol. Don't get me wrong, the ensemble wasn't out of place, just the person wearing them.

"Are you auditioning to be a back-up dancer for Run DMC?" I asked the director, who seemed greatly comfortable in her new look.

"For who?" she asked, clearly unfamiliar with the famous rap group of the eighties.

"Never mind," I gave in. "It's like a UFO sighting to see you out of your office. What gives?"

"Just stretching my legs," Hall replied. "Also, to let you know that someone has requested your presence."

"Do I have to dress like that?" I asked, looking her up and down.

"That's strike two!" she warned, and I knew better than to defy her whenever her facial expression took on the form it was taking on at that very moment.

"Would this be the assistant director?" I became serious. "Surely, it's not Dr. Shoob."

A smile slowly spread across the director's lips. "It's your little girlfriend Shirley Plummer."

Director Amy Hall had never been known as someone with a keen sense of humor, and only a fool would think otherwise, but what does Shirley Plummer, a.k.a Phoenix, want with me?

I've done my part in that investigation. The only thing left to do is testify against her and her co-defendants once the case goes before a trial judge.

"Did she contact you?" I finally inquired.

"Her lawyer did." Hall shifted her weight to her other foot. "Maybe, she's trying to get a lesser sentence by making a confession but would only make the confession to you. Are you going to see her?"

"Nope," I replied, shutting off my computer. "Right now, I'm working a whole new case, and the lead investigator has me extremely busy."

"Alright." Hall shrugged. "I'll relay this to Peter Hines."

Only regarding Hall for a second, as she retreated to her office, I gathered my briefcase, keys and cellular, then made for the elevator, dialing Detective McCoy's number, while waiting for the elevator to arrive, and the lines to connect. I thought about Phoenix, and the way she kept watching me in the courtroom that day. The woman definitely had a trick up her sleeves and as I suspected, it involved me.

"McCoy," the homicide detective announced through the device.

"What are you up to right now?" I inquired, stepping onto the elevator, pressing the button for the fourth floor.

"Well," she said with a sigh. "I'm on my way to interview a possible witness to a homicide."

"Who's the vic?"

"A Mario Ballard," she answered. "He was murdered on the eleventh in an abandoned house off Bankhead Highway."

*"On the eleventh?"* I was stepping off the elevator now. "Isn't that the same day Kelly was murdered?"

"I know where you're going, Bishop," McCoy stated. "There's no clear connection to these cases."

"Do you mind if I tag along for the interview?" I asked. For some strange reason, I felt compelled to take this ride. Plus, this gave me a chance to meet up with her, which was my sole reason for placing the call.

"I don't mind at all," she told me.

When the homicide detective gave me the location, I concluded the call, then approached Agent Powell's cubicle, only to inform him that I was going out in the field. Once he vowed to log me in for a twelve-hour shift, there was nothing else to talk about. I journeyed off to the garage, where I dove into one of our black unmarked Crown Victoria's and hauled ass up out of there.

For it to be the end of September, the sun was beaming, and it was a bit warm out, which is why I rolled the windows down, upon exiting off the Bankhead Highway exit. Keeping the emergency lights still flashing, I twiddled with the siren all the way up the notorious westside Atlanta Road until I reached Grove Street. The moment I turned onto the street, I spotted the familiar black Dodge Challenger, parked off to the side, with the engine still running.

Pulling to the rear of the governmental vehicle, I killed the engine, and waited for Lieutenant McCoy to get out. After a moment, she only flashed her brake lights. Taking it as my cue, I stepped out, and circled the rear of the Dodge. I didn't see any need to don my FBI windbreaker, but my gun and badge were prominently displayed on my utility belt. I was clad in a blue Polo shirt tucked inside my tan chinos.

"I hope I didn't delay you," I said, climbing in beside McCoy, who was wearing one of her turtleneck sweaters that left a man no choice but to wonder how it would feel to titty-fuck her fine ass.

*God, forgive me!*

"Not at all," she replied, drilling those pretty, brown eyes into mine through my Highway Patrols. "She's not in yet. When she arrives, I have someone who'll notify me."

"Does *she* have a name?"

"Olivia Whitley."

*"Whitley!"* I exclaimed, highly familiar with the name.

"Do you know her?" McCoy wanted to know.

"I can't say I do," I told her. "But I know that last name."

"Well," she started, now looking out of her window. "From what I know so far, she's a drug addict, and was with Ballard at the time he was murdered."

"What if she's able to identify the murderers?" I asked. "I don't suppose you're a sketch artist or have a photo book in your trunk that she could look through."

"If I feel she's competent to give an accurate description," the lieutenant said. "I'll have her come down to the station, next week, to look through a photo-lineup, and have a sketch drawn up." She reverted her attention back to me. "Now, what's *your* reason for being here?"

"I actually called you for a whole different reason."

McCoy raised her eyebrows in anticipation but said nothing.

"I need your help to obtain the projectiles extracted from the bodies of Cecil Henderson, and Jesse Bridges," I plunged right in.

"I don't see how you'll need *my* help," she said. "You're FBI. As long as you have the proper documents, you're welcome to every piece of evidence inside that place."

It was my turn to remain silent.

"And why wasn't I informed of this change?"

Before I could come up with something plausible, the loud roar of a diesel-powered engine caught our attention, as an oil tanker crawled to a halt beside the Dodge. Momentarily, the passenger's door came open, and some frail-looking woman, dressed in dingy blue jeans, a pink sweater, and a wool skull cap pulled over her head cautiously climbed down from the rig. After waving to the driver like a love struck teenager, she slammed the door, and watched the truck move up the street, before crossing over toward a house that was clearly abandoned, considering the boarded up windows. The particles of yellow crime scene tape left hanging on different parts of the place is what got my full attention.

"I guess one murder doesn't stop a show, huh?" I commented, now watching the woman climb the steps to the porch and enter.

"Of course not," McCoy replied, slowly shaking her head. "I hear addicts still use it as a place to sleep and get high."

"So, was that her?" I asked. "Do you have a picture of the woman?"

"Yes, I have a computer-generated photo of her," she answered, "But I couldn't see her face. Like I said, I have a—"

McCoy stopped short, when the front door of the house came open again, and a man in his mid-fifties with an overgrown beard stepped onto the porch, clad in extremely soiled pants that I couldn't tell the color of, a brown corduroy overcoat, and a green ballcap with a missing team's logo. He looked right in our direction and nodded before retreating back inside.

McCoy killed the engine, then looked over at me. "That was her. Are you ready?"

"You didn't tell me she had a beard," I responded, reaching for my door handle.

"You and your jokes," the lieutenant said, giggling.

We exited and crossed the street together, both visually surveying our surroundings out of instinct. I didn't have a bad vibe about this, but as we neared the house that looked like one of the last places that I'd rather be. I rested my right hand on my sidearm just as McCoy did. She was the first to climb the steps, and push the wooden, knob-less door open with one of her gloved hands. The smell of burnt cocaine immediately reached my nostrils, which upon entering was followed by body odor, feces, urine and other things my nose wasn't able to identify.

I thought the homicide detective was going to announce her authority, as it is customary. Instead, she just proceeded through the living room, stepping over discarded food wrappings, cans, bottles, syringes, and drug paraphernalia. Plus, there were four men and a woman present. Two men and the woman were huddled on a naked mattress in one corner, sharing a glass pipe, which they used to smoke their crack cocaine.

One man seemed like he was already on cloud nine; he was standing by the boarded windows with his arms tightly wrapped around himself like he was about to freeze to death. His eyes were the size of saucers, and they darted back and forth at nothing in particular making him look like something out of a horror film.

They stopped what they were doing to glare at us. Even the guy who'd stepped onto the porch and gave McCoy the signal. He was sitting Indian style on another mattress, against another wall with some alcoholic beverage in his hand, concealed in a brown paper bag. He tilted his head, indicating that the woman we were looking for was in one of the other rooms.

Still following the homicide detective, we circumvented two more stained mattresses, before exiting the living room. There was no need to enter the kitchen, that was also a mess. A bedroom came next, I only glanced inside, as McCoy had done being that the door was open. Passing the bathroom, she shot a disgusted look over her shoulder at me. It was enough for me to save myself the image, though the stench was inescapable.

The door to the next bedroom was closed, even though it had no knobs or visible fasteners. Keeping her right hand rested on her weapon, McCoy knocked twice, then pushed the door open with her other hand. Accustomed to the procedures in tactical breaches, she crossed the threshold, and sidestepped to her right, as I brought up the rear, positioning myself to the left side of the door.

The room wasn't as trashy as the others, but there wasn't a huge difference. Despite the littered floor, there was also another stained mattress and the woman we saw get out of the truck was sitting on it with her arms wrapped around her bent knees, rocking back and forth, bumping her back against the wall. She was looking at us almost like she wasn't seeing us.

"Ms. Olivia Whitley?" Detective McCoy spoke.

The woman stopped rocking and blinked her eyes several times like she was trying to blink her high away.

"I'm Homicide Detective McCoy," she went on. "Can you tell me about Mario Ballard's murder? He was your boyfriend, right?"

"They took my Mario from me," Olivia stated calmly, drilling her large eyes into McCoy. "He wouldn't tell them where he hid the kilo and they killed him."

"Did Mario sell drugs?" the detective inquired, I knew she was fishing.

"They said he stole it from somebody," the small woman answered now rocking back and forth again. "All I could do was watch. I was too scared to move. They killed him right over there."

We looked in the direction of where she nodded. There was no mistaking the dark, dried-up substance that stained the wall, and a large section of the carpet, reminding me that the forensic guys are not responsible for cleaning up such messes, after documenting them.

"How many guys were there?" McCoy inquired, brandishing her small notepad and pen.

"Two of 'em."

"Do you remember what they looked like?" the detective went on. "Have you ever seen them before?"

"I'd never seen them a day in my life," Whitley admitted, coughing twice into the sleeve of her sweater. "One was chubby, and the other was skinny. The chubby one was light-skin with a lot of tattoos. The only tattoo I remember is the one on his right arm, a dog with an arm in its mouth. The arm had blood dripping from it."

McCoy jotted this down. "What about the other man?" she asked. "Did he have any outstanding marks?"

The woman shrugged. "Not that I know of. He had on a long-sleeved shirt."

"If you were shown a photo line-up," McCoy said. "Do you think you could pick these guys out with certainty?"

"Sure, I can."

"Can we do this next week at my office?"

Olivia Whitley stopped rocking, and just stared at the detective.

"I'll pick you up myself," my friend tried to reason, knowing she couldn't force the woman downtown without a warrant. "Plus, I'll buy you lunch. You can choose the restaurant."

After another moment of staring at the female authority figure in front of her, Olivia shrugged again. "Okay, it's the least I can do for Mario."

I was so glad to get out of that house that I found myself greedily inhaling the fresh, wintry air, until my nostrils started burning, though it seemed like the stench was embedded in my senses, and definitely in my clothes. Reaching McCoy's car, she unlocked the doors by remote, and I took the initiative to pull the driver's door open for her.

"I guess this was a blank trip for you, huh?" asked the detective, who was now standing with her face just inches from mine.

"Yeah, I guess so," I said, though it was the total opposite. "What else do you have planned for today?"

"Not much," she answered. "Right now, I'm about to return to the station. You should be on your way to the evidence warehouse. Henry Wilcox is working today. So, you don't have to worry about going through the hassle of waiting too long or dealing with someone's nasty attitude."

"That's good to hear," I replied, gesturing for her to get into her car, she complied. "Keep me abreast of the Ballard case."

"You know I will," McCoy promised, starting the ignition. "Just make sure you let me know how the highway shooting investigation goes."

"Of course."

Returning to the Ford, I started the engine, then pulled out my cellular, and dialed a phone number I'm all too familiar with. At this moment, I was kind of hating that I lied to Detective McCoy about the FBI now having jurisdiction over the highway shooting case, although she had one of her underlings working it. The only way she'd find out I lied was if she decided to question the investigator about it. Well, I guess I'll have to diffuse that bomb when I get to it.

"Information Center," the familiar voice came through the earpiece of my phone. "Hoffman speaking."

"Chad, I need your help," I spoke fast, ready to pile a load of work on top of my friend.

"Lay it on me," he said.

"Have you been on break yet?"

"No."

"Listen," I went on. "First, I need you to pull up files on two people. A Miles Whitley who's affiliated with a group known as Drop Squad, and a Mario Ballard who's recently deceased. On Whitley, I need the names of every female family member on file with that last name."

"Okay," Hoffman replied. "What do you need on Ballard?"

"Everything," I told him. "Print those out for me. Also, I need you to doctor some paperwork for me."

"What kind of paperwork?"

Watching the rear of Detective McCoy's car as it pulled off, I explained the highway shooting to my friend, including the names, and what I was trying to obtain. Of course, it was up to him to draw up the document, fabricate a case number, and forge the appropriate names on it, which, if discovered, could get us both thrown in jail on all kinds of impersonating and fraud charges.

"Am I to secure these things until you return?" Hoffman asked, after taking everything in.

"Negative!" I replied. "I'm on my way to the evidence building right now. I need you to meet me there in about twenty. Is that enough time?"

"Of course, it is."

"Great!" I said. "See you in a bit."

Making a U-turn on Grove Street, I was heading for the evidence warehouse, thinking about Olivia Whitley's description of the two men that murdered her lover. Of course, it was highly impossible for me to conjure up rightful images of the men, due to the lack of information, but I was, indeed, anxious to find out what pair of idiots were dumb enough to kill Ballard in front of someone who had all the reasons in the world to identify and testify against them in court. Plus, I was eager to find out what drug dealer allowed a drug addict close enough to steal a kilo of cocaine from them. I swear, these modern-day street punks have a lot to learn.

It took approximately forty-two minutes to reach my destination. Before I could even turn into the parking lot, I spotted that bright-ass orange Astro van belonging to Chad Hoffman, sitting amongst the other vehicles and couldn't help but shake my head. One of these days, I'd have to have a long talk with my friend about adopting a whole new paint job. Hell, I'd even pay for it myself.

Making sure to park as far away from the van as possible, I got out and dawned my windbreaker before crossing over to it and climbing in beside Hoffman who was wearing a gray suit and pink necktie.

"This should be everything," he said, handing me a manilla folder. "Also, I hacked into Homicide's database, and ascertained the correct storage numbers for the items you're seeking. You did say you were after the projectiles, right?"

"Yeah, I did." At this time, I was looking down at the open folder in my lap, where the doctored document sat atop the other information that I asked Hoffman to print out for me. "But wouldn't it be less suspicious if I took possession of every piece of evidence connected to the case?"

"That's the point," Hoffman said, smiling. "The projectiles are all they have right now. No weapons, or spent shell casings."

"So, we should be good, huh?" I asked, now regarding him.

"Are you nervous?" he asked. "I mean, if you have no confidence in it, I'd be glad to go inside."

"But your name isn't on the document," I pointed out.

"That's why I'll be running an errand for Special Agent Brian Bishop," Hoffman pushed, clearly anxious to participate in whatever I had going on. "It's not like they're gonna call the Bureau for verification."

"Yeah, you're right," I said, glancing out at the building, then back at my friend. "Did you bring your credentials?"

"I sleep with them."

"That's entirely too much information, my friend." Extracting the information on Mario Ballard, and Miles Whitley, from the folder, I handed the folder over to Hoffman. "A Henry Wilcox should be on post. Tell him that Detective McCoy sends her regards."

"Got it," Hoffman said, before dismounting.

As I watched the big guy march toward the building with sheer confidence, I was hoping like hell everything worked out, because being hauled off to jail was not on my agenda for today. I waited until he entered the place, before directing my attention to the documents in my hand.

I already knew whose photo I was looking at, before seeing the name Miles Whitley. I wasn't interested in his bio, so, leaving the paperclip intact, I flipped the page back and found myself looking at a photo of a female name Brenda Whitley. According to the mini bio she was the aunt of Miles Whitley.

The next woman was a Carol Whitley-Stokes. Then came Caroline Whitley, Geneva Whitely, Janet Whitely, Kimberly Whitely-Bettis, Louise Whitley, Mary Whitley, and Monica Whitley. I started losing hope when I got to Octavia Whitley-McCray. Well, that was until I flipped over the final page, and saw a much better image than that of the strung-out drug addict McCoy and I encountered less than an hour ago.

Like the others, I wasn't at all interested in her bio. Once I saw that she was Miles Whitley's sibling, this packet was no longer valuable to me. However, now that I knew of this kinship, it made the capture of Ballard's murderers a bit more interesting, considering Miles Whitley's position in his organization, though it depends on whether or not she cried on her brother's shoulder about it.

The next stack of papers was pertaining to Mario Ballard, whose picture I found myself staring at to see if I could place him anywhere but there was no recognition. Therefore, I casually perused the file that contained the subject's criminal history, and personal information like date of birth, place of birth, contact information, emergency contact information, and names of immediate family members.

Like most drug addicts, Ballard had a history of petty thefts and burglaries. In the midst of scanning his prior bad acts, an Atlanta Police squad car, containing two police officers, caught my attention as it entered the lot, and cruised in the direction of the entrance. I watched the two male officers' get out. Upon one ringing the call button, the steel door buzzed open. That's when I half expected to see Hoffman plowing into them, in an attempt to flee. Just the image of his big ass trying to outrun someone was enough to make me laugh to myself.

However, once the officers disappeared inside, I reverted my attention to the documents, skipping past Ballards' criminal history that was as interesting as watching a goldfish swim around in a coffee mug. None of the addresses stood out, so I scanned the names of his immediate family members until I came across the name Shonda Watson, listed as his girlfriend.

Surely, there was about at least 1.4 million Shonda Watson's in the U.S. alone, right? This was definitely not the same Shonda Watson I'd been investigating. Hell, the address listed for this woman was located in Decatur, Georgia not Norcross, which is where Shonda Watson a.k.a Queen Shonda resided. Along with this address was a phone number. Considering I wasn't familiar with Watson's I made a mental note to check this one out when I got the chance.

I looked up from the papers, just in time to see Chad Hoffman emerge from the building carrying a cardboard box that was about twelve inches in width and six inches in height with the manila folder sitting on top of it. Though we were not yet out of the woods, this was an accomplishment, nonetheless.

"Piece of cake!" Hoffman said, as he slid behind the wheel, and handed the box over to me.

"Was Wilcox there?" I asked, placing the papers back inside the folder with the doctored document, before placing it on the dashboard, freeing my hands so I could explore the contents inside the unsealed box.

"Of course," he answered my question. "I relayed the message, and he lit up like a Christmas tree. Said he and McCoy attend the same church."

"Yeah, I'm quite sure," I mumbled, pulling the flaps up on the box.

Inside, were two Ziploc bags each containing three spent projectiles, and a label with the name of which victim they were extracted from, which were Cecil Henderson, and Jessie Bridges. For a closer examination, I picked the bags up, and studied the projectiles that had their own unique marks that came from impacting the windshield of the H-2 Hummer and the skeletal of the two men.

Right now, I was hoping these, and the photos I took of the murder weapon were enough to have The Queenz convicted in this case. Plus, I was hoping like hell Detective McCoy didn't go snooping around and find out I lied to her. If so, there was no telling how things would play out. I just knew it wouldn't be pleasant.

# Playa Ray

# Chapter 16

## *Saturday*

For it to be the last week of September, it still felt like the middle of August with the exception of the cool breeze that seemed to creep up out of nowhere and leave a few chill bumps from time to time. However, I still didn't roll my windows down as I left the barber shop, and made for the expressway, hoping I'd make it back to the house in time. Monique and I were taking the children to catch a movie around one o' clock, then to some restaurant Monique heard about from one of her clients.

Being that I left my business cellular charging in the car, I checked it for any missed calls, and saw there was one from John Moody the Decatur Chief of Police. Being that I was assisting him with one of his investigations. I was more than obliged to call him back. Hopefully, he'd tell me something that would make me abort this drive to Norcross, Georgia.

"You just take your precious time getting back to your friends, huh?" the older man grumbled through the device, upon answering.

This made me smile. "I miss you, too," I said. "Tell me something good."

"I do have something to tell you, but it's not good."

"I'm listening."

John Moody cleared his throat before going on, "I finally caught up with my C.I. You know, the one I told you was close to one of LKS' customers?"

"I remember."

"Well," the chief resumed. "He just informed me that the guy is dead. Not LKS, but the customer."

"What was his name?" I asked, thinking of Mario Ballard for some reason.

"Spencer Kelly," Moody answered. "He was a D.J. at that club I asked you to check out for me."

*Damn!* I had planned to stake that club out tonight, to see if I could spy LKS or whoever was running for him, her, or it. I was shaking my head at this moment. It's crazy how Moody's informant was giving up information on McCoy's informant and McCoy's informant who was supposedly dating Theresa Joiner was giving her information on The Queenz. Now, all of a sudden, he'd been murdered.

Wait! Joiner's birthday party was at Club Strokers. Now, I remembered the D.J. entering the VIP booth where The Queenz were celebrating and presenting Joiner with a necklace, that he clasped around her neck himself. It was definitely Spencer Kelly a.k.a D.J. Spenz, but that was the only time I saw them together.

"That was the only lead I had on LKS," Moody went on. "I want this guy, or whatever the hell it is, but I think I'm gonna have to sit this one out."

"O' ye of little faith?" I quoted from the Holy Bible. "You used to tell me not to be a quitter. Now look at your old ass. Thou hypocrite!"

This made him laugh. "You know what?" he said. "I deserve that one. I really do.

"Just be patient," I told him, as I took the Norcross exit. "As long as LKS has any kind of human traits, mistakes will be made, and handcuffs will be applied."

"Amen to that!" the chief let out, chuckling.

It was 11:23 a.m., when I turned my BMW onto Mitchell Road which is where I hadn't been in over two years. The house I was looking for was on my right, and the yard was full of men and women of Spanish descent, they were smoking, drinking, talking and dancing. Some guy was cooking on a makeshift grill and tricked-out vehicles lined the street, but I was only concerned with one, the dark blue '89 Cadillac de Ville on gold Daytons parked in the driveway.

Spotting an opening right across the street from the house, I parked, and didn't bother with shutting off the engine, knowing I wouldn't be here long. Dismounting, I circled around, and leaned against the fender, scanning the partying crowd. Seeing all the red bandanas, pretty much let me know that this was a North Side Lokos' thing, considering this was the home of Oso, one of its fearless leaders.

Speaking of the fucker, he must've spotted me at the same time I spotted him. Seated in a chair on the porch, he was slowly getting to his feet as realization seemed to kick in. I'd had these same mirror-tinted sunglasses for more than five years, so I'm quite sure they were what gave me away.

Keeping a stoical look on his face, the 5'8, 235 pounds leader descended the steps and maneuvered through the crowd, almost unnoticed. Despite how cool Oso looked as he made his way toward me, I must warn you that he was one mean, and ruthless son of a bitch. He hated cops with a passion. In fact, his gang had a history of being suspected of numerous murders involving law enforcement officials, which is how I ended up investigating him years ago though we could never link anything back to him.

Now, wearing a pair of blue jeans, red and black Air Force Ones, and a tank top, Oso made sure to look both ways before crossing the street. Perhaps, he was looking to see if there were any unfamiliar vehicles lingering which would indicate I was not alone.

"What the fuck are you doing here, pig?" he spat, as he approached, maintaining his cool facade.

"I came to partake in the festivities," I answered, gesturing to the goings-on across the street. "Is it Cinco De Mayo already?"

"Fuck you, puto!" Oso leaned against the car beside me, and crossed his arms over his chest, as I had mine. "It's my primo's birthday, and we're trying to celebrate it in peace. Why are you at my house?"

"Tell me what you know about LKS," I plunged right in.

He shot me a questionable glance.

"Think about your answer, Oso!" I warned. "You're still a drug and arms dealer. I can't even imagine what our Task Force would find on your property. Plus, Immigration would have a field day with your company, because I'm quite sure sixty percent of them are illegal aliens."

"I don't know any LKS," the gang leader reported.

"So, you're really gonna play this game with me, huh?" I said, now regarding him. "Maybe, I should have my boys in Texas knock on Irene's door. Shake her up a little."

"Don't you dare threaten my mother!" Oso hissed, while trying to penetrate my sunglasses with his eyes. "I'll have your whole family chopped up and fed to my pet alligators!"

"You're plugged in with too many drug dealers," I acknowledged, disregarding his threat, though I knew he was capable of making it happen. "Hell, you know El Chapo, but you're telling me you've never heard of LKS?"

"Don't you have snitches?" he shot back. "Maybe, you should be talking to *them*. That's not my department."

By now, I had directed my attention back across the street, where everyone seemed to have stopped what they were doing and were now watching us. While scanning faces for signs of familiarity, I almost thought my eyes were playing tricks on me, when I spotted a face that was very familiar to me. I'd only seen it once, staring back at me from the screen of my computer's monitor. This was strange, because, if I was not mistaking, his affiliation was Latin Kingsz not North Side Lokos.

"I'm assuming Jason Garcia is your cousin?" I spoke, still watching Garcia, a.k.a Loko. "Is it *his* birthday?"

Oso just looked at me.

"Are you serious right now?" I was now facing the NSL leader. "Not only do you sell drugs and guns, but you also harbor fugitives? This dude is wanted by every law enforcement agency on this planet, and you have him right here at your house. I wouldn't be surprised if the CIA was watching him from a satellite right now."

"I think you need to leave."

"I think you need to tell me who LKS is," I countered. "All it takes is one call, and I'll have agents crawling from sewers, and jumping out of airplanes like an extraction team in Iraq."

"¡Chupa mi verga!" Oso spat, before starting in the direction of his house.

"Lo tienes bien chiquito," I said to his back. "Besides, you're not my type."

I didn't know what was going through Ruben Rodriguez's mind, but I knew he was really upset, and if he wanted me murdered right here on the spot all he had to do was give the word and *September 24, 2005* would be the last date on my tombstone.

Therefore, maintaining my cool posture, I moved around to the driver's side of my car, and climbed behind the wheel, just as my business cell phone started vibrating in the cupholder. I cast a glance across the street to see Loko following Oso inside the house, before retrieving my phone, and regarding the screen to see Detective McCoy's name.

"I'm listening," I said, upon answering.

"You're not gonna believe this," she said, sounding sad.

"Lay it on me."

"Olivia was murdered yesterday."

"*Olivia Whitley?*" I asked, knowing damn well who she was referring to.

"Olivia Whitley," McCoy sassed, obviously upset about it. "She was murdered in that same house. Same bedroom Ballard was murdered in."

"Was she also shot?"

"Twice," answered the detective. "Upper body. According to my report, she was the only person inside the house at the time."

# Playa Ray

# Chapter 17

## *Monday*

I don't know where the headache came from but my head was throbbing like hell, when I peeled myself out of bed at 6:45 a.m., after my alarm clock disturbed me from a provocative dream I was having about Shirley Plummer a.k.a Phoenix. This was strange because I'd never dreamed about Phoenix. Not even after that night in her hotel room, with Rhonda Thomas which was quite common.

In spite of the headache, I was wondering if I should take the dream as a sign? I was pondering her request to see me, while en route to the James P. Russel building. I mean, what could she possibly want with me? If she was looking to be reprieved, then she was barking up the wrong tree, because I had no power to spare her of whatever execution was owed to her for her crimes.

I didn't notice my headache was gone until I found my usual parking spot in the garage and shut the engine off. By that time, I was done wracking my brains about Shirley Plummer's motives, and more focused on The Queenz investigation. Retrieving my briefcase and investigation kit, I got out and made for the elevators.

For as long as lead forensic scientist Heather Vaughn had been with us, I'd never seen her out of her laboratory coat, so it was pretty much like a UFO sighting to see the 5'11, 145 pounds woman, now waiting on the elevator, wearing dark, snug-fitted jeans, and a black, fleece-laced, waist-length leather coat with an American Eagle on the back. Apparently, she saw my reflection off the metal frame of the elevator, because she turned to face me with one hand on her hip, and the other gripping the handle of her lunch pail.

"Look at what the cat dragged in," Vaughn joked, although her facial expression showed no sign of humor.

"That's exactly how I feel," I replied, approaching. "Like I was dragged in by a cat. Good morning to you!"

"Same to you," she said, now eyeing me with those gray eyes. "You look like a detective from one of those eighties movies."

---

"I can live with that comparison," I said, just as the elevator arrived. When we entered the shaft, I pressed the buttons for the first and sixth floors.

"So, how are you and Powell getting along?" the forensic scientist posed.

The question caught me off guard, which is why I only looked at her. This time, there was a smirk on her face, though I knew better than to think she was being facetious. Before I could inquire on it, the doors opened on the first floor. Vaughn punched me lightly on the shoulder, before exiting with that same smirk, leaving me more confused.

Making a mental note to harass her about it at a later time, I made sure to punch my timecard in, before heading for my cubicle. I dropped my things off and grabbed my thermos. The place was buzzing with only a handful of agents. So, there were plenty of doughnuts and coffee left in the break room. After filling my thermos, and wrapping a bear claw inside a paper towel, I returned to my station.

Agent Knight had just gotten in, and was pulling documents from his briefcase, while still standing.

"Morning!" I spoke, setting my thermos down, before taking a seat, and starting up my computer.

"Morning!" Knight responded, regarding me with a smile. "How's the investigation going?"

"It's coming along quite well," I answered, then bit into my pastry.

"It shouldn't take long though, right?" he asked. "I mean, being that you've already been gathering intelligence on these women."

I shrugged. "Maybe, but these girls aren't exactly Fed status yet. Hopefully, we'll be able to take them down within a year."

"I wish I was working on the case with you," the agent said. "I just don't think I could tolerate working under the supervision of Powell. How's that working out, anyway?"

"It's not all that bad," I offered, now thinking about Heather Vaughn's question, realizing that Powell may have put these two up to inquiring on my feelings toward him, for whatever reason. "Are you going out in the field today?" I asked, taking the spotlight off myself.

"Unfortunately, no," he answered, now holding his coffee mug in his hand. "I'll be doing miscellaneous paperwork that should hold me over till lunchtime. What about you? Are you going out?"

"When I finish with my bear claw," I told him, taking another bite.

"Well, I'm about to grab myself some of this coffee before it's all gone," Knight said, then took off in the direction of the break room.

Once he was gone, I took a sip from my thermos, typed my password into the computer, then pulled up Shonda Watson's profile. Remembering she was once employed at the Dekalb County Jail, I searched her employment record, where she listed herself as single, and made no reference to having a boyfriend. Scrolling further, I came upon the address she used, and it was not in Norcross, Georgia but Decatur, Georgia. Without having to turn to the documents given to me by Chad Hoffman, I could already tell it was the same exact address Mario Ballard had given of his girlfriend as an emergency contact. Even the telephone number matched.

This is where my mind went into overdrive. Clearly, from what I'd just discovered, Shonda Watson and Mario Ballard were once an item, however long ago that may have been. According to Olivia Whitley, Ballard's murderers asked him about a kilo of cocaine that he'd stolen from someone, before killing him. Now, suppose Watson or The Queenz is that *someone* Ballard had ripped off. This would mean, either way it goes, Watson is responsible for the death of Mario Ballard, and she was familiar with his murderers.

Shutting off my computer, I stuffed my thermos inside my briefcase, then stood. Collecting it, and my investigation kit, I turned, and took no more than two steps, when my desk phone began ringing, causing me to stop in my tracks. Being that I considered all my calls important, I spun back around, sat my investigation kit down on the floor, and snatched the receiver from its cradle.

"Bishop," I announced, thinking it was Hoffman.

"How are you, Mr. Bishop?" a vaguely familiar male's voice came through the earpiece.

"I'm good," I answered, trying to place the voice. "Who am I speaking with?"

"Pardon my manners," he said. "I'm Attorney Peter Hines. One of my clients, a Ms. Shirley Plummer asked me to contact you."

"What does she want?" I asked, just as Knight returned to his cubicle.

"For you to visit her," answered the attorney. "Please, don't ask me what for, because I'm just as in the dark about this as you are. I'm just doing what I was paid to do."

"Yeah, I'm quite sure you are," I said, being sarcastic. "Tell your client I said she can go to hell."

I slammed the receiver down, then looked over at Agent Knight who was now seated, regarding me with a puzzled look.

"Sometimes, you have to tell people how you feel," I offered, retrieving my investigation case off the floor. "I'll catch you later."

I had to stop by the front desk to collect the keys to the blue Honda Accord I signed out from Motor Pool yesterday. Then, I was on my way to Norcross, Georgia. At that time, it was hard to keep my mind on my current assignment, especially after receiving that call from Plummer's attorney. I didn't believe he was going to give her my message. I also didn't believe that would be the last time I heard from him, considering how adamant his client was. However, I am curious about Plummer's motive, which had me wondering if I should give in, and pay her a visit, although I was starting to feel that I'd be damned if I do, and damned if I don't.

It was a little after 9:00 a.m., when I pulled the borrowed car onto Palmer Street, and cruised past the house shared by Shonda Watson and her cousin, Sheila Griffin. Both of their cars were parked in the driveway and the GMC Denali was sitting at the curb. It wasn't hard to spy the beige Chrysler 300 that was occupied by Agent Andrew Pierce and parked a few houses down.

We nodded our acknowledgments, as I drove by, but to keep from compromising either of our positions, I chose to park further down where I would have to use my binoculars, and the detachable lens of my camera to identify anyone other than The Queenz, or their bodyguards.

I had already freed my thermos from my briefcase while en route. After parking, I downed the remainder of the coffee, before extracting my camera and binoculars from my kit, making sure I had enough film, before snapping the lens into place. Figuring there would be no action today, I decided to place a call to Detective McCoy to inquire on Olivia Whitley's case, but ended up getting her voicemail.

Without leaving a message, I ended the call, and set the cell phone in the cupholder. Just last week, Director Hall approved two more agents for this investigation, who'd be doing night duty. Though I'm not yet committed to the idea, I was thinking of asking Powell to place me on temporary night duty. At least from 12:00 p.m., to 12:00 a.m., being that most criminal activities took place somewhere along this time period.

After another hour and twenty-seven minutes of inaction, I felt the coffee running through me, and knew it was time for another restroom break which was one of the things I hated about solo steak outs, because one was forced to choose between the investigation and their health. I just didn't see how racecar drivers could drive around in circles, for several hours, and not have to stop to drain their bladders.

Anyway, I knew I couldn't just sit there, and risk damaging my sac, so I had to place a call to Pierce, and let him know that I was about to head out to the nearest establishment with a public restroom, and to advise me if my subject made a move. I grabbed my cellular, but before I could stroll through my contacts for Pierce's number, the device vibrated. I found myself smiling at the name on the screen.

"Talk to me!" I answered it.

"I'm sorry I missed your call," Detective McCoy explained. "I was on the phone with a friend of mine from missing persons. He was telling me about an abduction that took place over the weekend."

"A *child* abduction?" I asked, thinking about Shirley Plummer.

"Adult," she answered. "According to witnesses, the guy was sitting on the passenger side of a car, accompanied by another, when a dark colored van supposedly came out of nowhere. Masked gunmen jumped out, and smashed the windows in on the car, before ordering the passenger, who was a resident of the community to step out, subsequently forcing him into the cargo area of the van and hauling him away, leaving the driver behind."

"Does your friend suspect foul play on the driver's end?" I inquired.

"The driver fled the scene immediately after the incident."

"A non-resident, I presume?"

"Exactly!" the detective let out. "This case is definitely reminiscent of Clarence Mikah's case."

"How so?" I asked, not seeing any similarities between the two.

"The car that fled the scene was a black Ford Mustang," she went on to explain. "Driven by an unidentified female. Do you not see the connection? Unidentified female? Ford Mustang? I think this woman is using herself as bait to lure her targets in."

"I hope you didn't sell this theory to your friend."

"Why not?"

"Because, it doesn't add up."

"What doesn't add up, Bishop?"

"In Mikah's incident," I began. "The woman was beaten by Bridges and Henderson. If these three are working together, why would they assault the bait?

"I think it was staged," McCoy persisted. "I think they made it *look* like they were assaulting her to throw authorities off *her* trail, and not be able to link her to them."

"But she didn't wait for the authorities," I was proud to point out.

"She also didn't wait for the authorities in this recent case," McCoy must've been even prouder to point out. "Two Ford Mustangs, Bishop. Both with female drivers, fleeing separate crime scenes. I mean unless Ford Mustangs have become popular getaway cars."

"Wait!" I said, as realization kicked in. "Didn't you say the abductors smashed the windows in on the Mustang?"

"I was only telling you what Gatson relayed to me," said the detective.

While she was in mid-sentence, I grabbed my binoculars off the passenger seat with my free hand and put them up to my face. Upon adjusting the sight, I focused on Watson's Ford Mustang in the driveway. The windows were all there, but I think I had a way to find out if this exact car was the one seen fleeing the scene of this recent abduction.

"Have you made any progress in Whitley's case?" I purposely changed the subject, preparing to end the call.

"Not yet," she answered. "Her funeral is this coming Saturday, and it seems that nobody's seen, nor heard a thing. Mayor Franklin signed an order to have that house torn down?"

"Well, let me know if you hear anything," I said, as my bladder sent warning pulses through my body.

"I will," she promised, before hanging up.

I was finally able to access my contact list in my phone, but I was not searching for Pierce's number. This was one of those times I chose to go out on a limb with one of my own theories. Finding the number I was looking for, I pressed the call button, and waited.

"Rigg's Body and Paint Shop," the familiar voice answered. "Danny Riggs speaking."

"Mr. Riggs," I spoke. "I'm Special Agent Bishop, and I need to question you about a Ford Mustang you serviced yesterday. Do you remember it?"

"It was just yesterday," the mechanic remarked. "Of course, I remember."

"Do you remember the owner's name?" I asked, already feeling like I'd proven my point.

"Shonda Watson."

"What about the color of the car?"

"It was black."

"One more question, Mr. Riggs," I said, ready to put the icing on the cake. "What kind of repairs did you make to the car?"

"I don't repair windows," he said. "But the windows on both of her doors were broken out. I ordered a pair from a guy I know and put the windows in myself. That was all the work I'd done to it."

*Bingo!* This was full confirmation that Shonda Watson was on the scene of yet another major crime, which also left a great number of questions floating around in my head. I already know Detective McCoy's *friend* would keep her informed on the progress of the case, so I'd eventually attain information about the man Watson was with before he was snatched from her car at gunpoint. The more I thought about this, the more McCoy's theory about Watson being used as bait to lure targets in, started to take shape in the back of my mind.

# Chapter 18

*Friday*

*September 30, 2005*

It didn't take any method of persuasion to get Agent Powell to alter my shift. All I had to do was ask and give a half-ass excuse why I was making such a request. To my surprise, he granted it right on the spot, without having to confer with Director Hall. Now, my temporary shift starts at 12:00 p.m., and ends at 12:00 a.m.

At this moment, with 1:12 p.m. showing on the digital dashboard of the gray Audi released to me from Motor Pool, I was once again parked on Palmer Street, stationed three houses away from the home of Shonda Watson and Sheila Griffin. Their cars were parked in the driveway, but they were not in. According to Agent Pierce, who was currently tailing them, Ebony Davis and Theresa Joiner had picked them up in their company's truck and they were being escorted by their security team in the other GMC truck while conducting their routine drug run.

It wasn't until a little after three, that I spotted The Queenz' convoy enter onto the street. I already planned to pretend like I was fidgeting with my cell phone when they drove by, but the first SUV stopped in front of the house. Momentarily, Griffin and Watson exited. Watson stopped to check the mailbox, and Griffin continued toward the front door. The convoy didn't move on, until both women had gone inside.

That's when I was able to implement my front, appearing to be searching for something on my phone. Once the two trucks rode by, I followed their movement through the rear-view mirror. I didn't know what kind of car Agent Pierce was riding in today, but I was almost certain it was the black Cadillac that entered from the other end of Palmer Street, now passing the two Denali's and coming up on my car. As it passed, I looked over at the driver, it was definitely Pierce. He drove a little further past the house, taking up position on the other side of it.

Another thing about solo mission steak-outs, they are boring. Things didn't become interesting until another four hours or so, when two cars pulled up, and parked across the street from the home of Watson and Griffin, one a gray, four-door '84 Chevy Caprice, and the other a white, '85 Buick Regal.

For as long as I'd been watching these women, I had yet to see anyone other than Ebony Davis and Theresa Joiner visit the place, and neither one of them owned either of these cars, which had me wondering if these were the men who were responsible for the abduction Detective McCoy informed me about. Yeah, I suppose McCoy's theory grew on me. Especially the part about the Ford Mustang fleeing the scene with a female at the wheel.

However, I am not one hundred percent committed to this theory, because, like I told the homicide detective before, it didn't add up. If Watson was luring these men in for whatever reason, then why in the hell would she use her own car that could easily be traced back to her? No matter how many times she had the car painted, all it takes is for someone to memorize her tag number, and it would definitely be the end of her career.

I had my camera powered up and ready, just as the occupants of the two cars got out. Immediately, I recognized the two men as Anthony Moody, and Shelton Payne, two of The Queenz' guards. Their presence only meant that Watson and Griffin were about to step out, but where to? Better yet why were the men driving their personal cars, and not paired up in the GMC truck? Could Griffin and Watson be going in separate directions? Surely, they were not conducting an act of unprofessionalism by dating their employees, are they?

I figured the men would cross the street, but they remained by their cars, talking, apparently waiting for the women to exit the house. I snapped a few shots of them, for documentary purposes. At approximately 7:38 p.m. Shonda Watson emerged from the house, wearing a dark-colored evening dress, and matching heels. When she locked the door back, I realized Griffin wasn't joining her, with her purse dangling from her shoulder, Watson approached her Ford Mustang that was now painted yellow with a black racing stripe running from the hood to the trunk of it.

*Click! Click!*

Both guards climbed back into their cars, but when the Mustang started for the main road, only the Buick Regal followed, which was driven by Anthony Moody. This was my cue, but I had to move with caution, being that the other guard was still stationed, and was probably smart enough to peg me as a government official the moment I rode past him.

Once both vehicles made a right turn on the main road, I started the Audi, and pulled out, moving as casually as I could. As I passed the Caprice, I regarded Payne from the corners of my eyes, and saw he had his head down, toying with his cellular. Passing the black Cadillac further up the street, I received a nod from Agent Pierce, who'd be relieved in the next thirty minutes or so.

Making it to Branch Avenue, I didn't immediately spot Watson and Moody for the bend in the road. However, once I rounded the bend, I spotted them at about one hundred yards out, entering onto the expressway. Thankfully for the light traffic, I accelerated a bit, and was able to maintain a good fifty-yard distance behind my targets, while still trying to figure out what Queen Shonda was up to, since she was dressed like she was on her way to meet somebody of interest. If this turned out to be one of those incidents like Mikah's, or that recent abduction case she was involved in, I'd have no choice but to report her to Director Hall and begin the process of taking her and her accomplices down on their next mission.

I didn't know what to think, when I saw them exiting off in Smyrna, Georgia, which is the city I reside in. Again, it still made no sense, why Watson would use her own car in these ordeals, which had me wondering if someone spotted her car on Grove Street, on the day Mario Ballard was murdered. What about the day Olivia Whitley was murdered? Hell, I'm still waiting to find out what happened to Trent Williams, who was abducted from the East Lake Meadows community in Decatur, Georgia. I'm quite sure he's dead by now.

Momentarily, I saw Watson and Moody enter the parking lot of The Enchanting restaurant, where there were no more than ten vehicles present, which wasn't enough cover for me to sit in the car for a long period of time without looking suspicious. Therefore, I opted for the gas station across the street from the establishment, parking by the public phone beside the giant ice cooler that was just beyond the entrance of the store. By the time I got out and approached the phone like I was about to place a call, I caught a glimpse of Shonda Watson's tall, and voluptuous figure, entering the restaurant, leaving Moody sitting in his car that was parked alongside hers.

Figuring she'd be inside the restaurant for a while, I entered the store, where there were only three customers moving about the aisles, and one at the check-out counter that was manned by an older white woman, who looked to be in her late sixties. Just as I approached the counter, the purchasing customer received his change, and headed for the door.

"How can I help ya'?" the woman inquired her voice thick with a Southern accent.

"I'm looking to gain access to your restroom," I told her.

"Sure, darling."

The woman turned around and retrieved a key that had a Buick hubcap attached to it, like we were back in the nineteen fifties, or something. My baffled look must've been quite amusing to her, because she smiled from ear to ear, resembling a carved pumpkin, with the way her teeth were intermittently missing.

Anyhow, leaving the woman to her personal pleasures, I exited the store, and found the restroom on the far side of the building. The lighting was extremely poor, which had me wondering how many people had been mugged in this exact spot. The big-ass hubcap clanged against everything, including me, as I managed to unlock the steel door to the lavatory, and pushed it open. At that moment, I thanked God that I didn't' have a weak stomach, because such a person would instantly become ill at the sight, and smell of this dump.

174

I mean, I didn't expect the place to be squeaky clean, but I also didn't expect it to look like it had never been sanitized since the day it was built, with a puddle of urine consuming a large portion of the floor, and feces smeared all over the walls. Some Pablo Picasso-inspired individuals even got creative with the shit, drawing pictures, and writing obscene quotes. I didn't have to cross the threshold to see the flies and cockroaches feasting on the excessive amount of excreta and used toilet paper cluttering the toilet bowl.

It didn't take but a second for me to make a moral decision. I pulled the door shut, then looked around to make sure I wasn't being watched, before moving toward the rear of the store, where I relieved myself of the liquid stored in my kidneys. When I returned to the store, there were customers lined up at the counter. I know they were only innocent bystanders and had nothing to do with this psychological war I had going on with the cashier, but I didn't care at the moment.

Approaching, I slammed the hubcap down on the counter with so much force, it caused the cashier and customers to flinch out of fear. A satisfied smile appeared on my face, as I turned, and marched out of the door, wondering if I should report this place to a health inspector.

Making it outside, I looked across the street at the restaurant as I moved toward the public phone but saw no movement. After pretending to drop coins into the device, and dialing a phone number, I leaned my back against it, with the receiver to my ear, and pretty much set up shop right there. It was a little cool out, but I was able to maintain in my black leather coat and skull cap.

Still maintaining my view, I found myself just staring at Moody's car, until I saw something being tossed from the driver's window of a dark-colored Lincoln Navigator that was parked closer to the entrance before the window rolled back up. Come to think about it, this SUV was already there when we arrived. Considering the make and model of the vehicle, I toyed with the notion that it was from some limousine company providing service for a couple that was currently dining inside the restaurant. On the other hand, I was thinking of how Watson arrived under escort, which brought me back to whoever she was in there dining with. I mean, surely, she didn't drive all the way out here to dine alone, right?

When Watson exited the restaurant at 8:49 p.m. I was still struggling with the decision to either continue following her or wait here until I spotted a sole individual exit the place and climb into the awaiting Lincoln. Then, trail the person to their destination, with the intent to get an identification on them. However, sticking to the initial mission, I strolled over to the borrowed Audi, and waited until Watson and Moody were a good distance, before pulling out onto the main road.

Just as I did, I saw a man exit the restaurant, casually dressed in a dark suit, and move in the direction of the Navigator. Though it was dark, the lamps in the parking lot produced sufficient lighting, whereas I was able to get a decent look at him, in spite of the distance. Within the seven-second window I had, I thought I recognized familiarity in his features, even though I could only see the right side of his face. Right then, I made a promise that if Shonda Watson ever met up with this guy again, I'd make it my business to identify him by any means necessary.

As it went, I trailed Watson and Moody back to Norcross, where I waited until Moody and Shelton Payne were long gone, before attaining the same spot I was parked in, prior to leaving. Pierce's relief, which was a female agent, was occupying a green Ford Explorer that was parked where he was parked earlier.

The rest of the night was neutral, as I figured it'd be, neither Watson or Griffin ventured out, and no one visited their residence. So, when 11:50 p.m. showed up on the digital dashboard of the borrowed Audi, I was more than happy to be on my way back to the James P. Russell building, which took about thirty-two minutes. It took another thirty-eight minutes to log my movement into the logbook and document my findings. Then, I was back inside my BMW, headed home.

As I traveled along the highway, I found myself thinking about the guy I assumed Watson met with at The Enchanting. I'm not the best in the world at remembering faces, but I'm almost certain I'd encountered him on several occasions. There weren't that many vehicles out at 1:13 in the morning. However, when I glanced into my rearview mirror for the umpteenth time, I saw the headlights of the same car that had been behind me from the moment I entered onto the expressway. Actually I spotted it beforehand. I just didn't think the driver would continue trailing me for this long, at about a thirty-yard distance.

Reaching the Smyrna exit, I looked up, and saw that the occupant seemed to have the same destination. By this time, my survival instincts kicked in. Making it to the main road, instead of taking the usual left turn that leads to my home, I made a right. My visitor did likewise. That's when I was finally able to recognize the car as a white Mercedes-Benz, occupied by a white male, whose features I couldn't make out.

Nearing the first traffic light that was red, I grabbed my Glock off the seat beside me, clutching it in my right hand, while keeping my left on the wheel. When I stopped, the Benz stopped directly behind me, which immediately let me know I was not being trailed by a professional. Had it not been for the eyeglasses, and round-brimmed hat, I'd be able to get a good look at his face.

When the light turned green, I accelerated, with my gun resting on my right leg, while forming an immediate plan of action in my head, because I was a little too tired to play the cat-and-mouse bullshit. I'm no coward, so whatever this fucker had in store for me, I was about to expedite that shit.

Seeing a residential street coming up on my right, I initiated my right turn signal, and glanced into the rearview mirror. Of course, this guy followed suit. I released the grip on my gun, just long enough to unlatch my seatbelt, and free myself. Finally making the turn, I drove about five yards, before slamming down on the brakes, throwing the gear into park, and lunging from the car. I moved swiftly, with my gun aimed like I was on tactical duty, toward the Mercedes. Just as I reached the driver's door, the driver slammed on the brakes, and threw both hands up in surrender. I was pissed when I realized I was being followed, but not as pissed as I was when I realized who I was being followed by.

"What are you, a statue?" I voiced through clenched teeth to the older man. "Roll the window down!" His left hand trembled as Attorney Peter Hines lowered the window, before placing both hands on the wheel. "You have got to be suicidal," I went on, gun still aimed. "How long have you been following me?"

"I'm here on behalf of—"

"I know who you're here on behalf of," I cut him off. "How long have you been following me?"

"For a while," he answered, making it sound more like a question. "Like I said, I'm only doing what I was paid to do."

"Is she paying you enough to lose your life?" I questioned. "I can murder you right now in self-defense."

"Georgia doesn't have self-defense laws," Hines argued, like a true defense attorney.

"I'm FBI," I countered, as if to say I can do whatever the hell I wanted without punishment. Then, after a moment of staring the old man down, I glanced around at the still houses lining the street, before lowering my weapon. "Look," I went on. "I am not in the mood for this game you and Plummer are hell-bent on playing."

"Why don't you just go and visit her?" he pleaded, sounding like he was also fed up with doing his client's biddings.

"What if I continue to decline?" I posed. "Are you gonna continue to stalk me?"

The attorney shrugged. "I'm only doing what I was paid to do."

"Yeah, I'll make sure they put that on your tombstone," I told him, thinking if he said this one more time, I'd go ahead and shoot him, and take my chances with Georgia's no-self-defense laws. "What does she really want? And don't give me that crap about you not knowing."

"I really don't know, Mr. Bishop. Sure, we have the attorney and client confidential thing between us, but I swear she told me nothing pertaining to what she seeks your presence for. Whatever it is, it has to be of great importance, considering the kind of money she's paying me to hunt you down in the middle of the night, like I have no life of my own."

"You're a better man than I am," I expressed. "Tell your client that if I catch you following me again, you two will be cellmates."

# Playa Ray

## Chapter 19

The following day, I got my highly dedicated ass out of bed a little earlier than I had to. Being overly supportive of my occupation, Monique had already conspired with Carmen, to take the children to see some Disney movie, being that my assignment, and new swift, wouldn't allow me to be there.

I ended up leaving the house a little past 10:00 a.m. after having a lengthy conversation with Monique about our impending wedding date that was currently set for the first of January, and where we'd be spending our honeymoon, something we're still indecisive about. Only staying inside the James P. Russell building long enough to fill my thermos with coffee and turn over my report from yesterday to Agent Powell, I collected the keys to the burgundy Kia Sorento, and was on my way to Norcross, Georgia.

Homicide Detective McCoy sent me a text, that I didn't see until this morning, informing me that Olivia Whitley's funeral was today, and she would be voluntarily heading the security detail. I wanted to snoop around, but I was too anxious to find out about the guy Shonda had dinner with last night, bringing me back to the telephone number I discovered in Mario Ballard's criminal file. Before leaving the house, I text the digits to my dear friend Chad Hoffman asking if he would sneak down to the basement of the James P. Russell building, and log them into the wire-tapping device. I'm looking to hear something back from him later on.

Upon entering Palmer Street, I was a bit surprised to see that The Queenz' guardsmen were already parked outside the house, in the Denali truck parked behind that of The Queenz. As I drove by, I noticed Theresa Joiner and Ebony Davis were already on board, clearly awaiting the other two. Agent Pierce nodded at me when I passed the Chevy Silverado, he was occupying. I didn't want to drive too far, so I made a U-turn and ended up parking two houses from Pierce's rear. Just as I was about to put the car into park, I saw Sheila Griffin and Shonda Watson emerge from the house. I quickly pulled Pierce's number up on my cellular.

"Pierce," he answered, momentarily.

"Fall back!" I told him.

"Do what!"

"I'll keep you informed of their movement, Pierce," I promised. "I doubt if they'll separate, but if they do, I'll keep eyes on your subject, and document everything."

"I don't know, Bishop," Pierce lingered. "I don't think Agent Powell—"

"We don't have to report *everything* to Agent Powell," I cut him off, surprised that he was acting like a rookie. By this time, The Queenz were pulling off with their guards trailing behind. "Our assignments are clear," I pressed. "But we have the authority to alter them, and to improvise when necessary."

"I already know this, Bishop."

"Then, act like it!" I snapped. "Stay your ass right there and watch the house! I'll keep you posted."

I didn't give him a chance to retort. Concluding the call, and tossing the phone onto the seat beside me, I pulled from my spot. I didn't even look in Pierce's direction as I passed him, in pursuit of the convoy that I couldn't see, until I turned onto Branch Avenue. They were entering onto the expressway.

Although it was Saturday, the expressway was packed like a regular weekday, providing me with enough cover to keep from having to play dodgeball, in order to keep from being mad. Reaching Atlanta, their first exit was Bankhead Highway. I was three cars behind them, as we traveled the famous Northwest Atlanta Road. I didn't think anything of it, until I saw their turn indicators come on as we neared Grove Street, the same street Mario Ballard and Olivia Whitley were murdered on.

At that very moment, I was beginning to feel the same way I was feeling when I was investigating The Kingz, and Shonda Watson definitely reminded me of James Young, who carried on like he was above his comrades, the same exact deportment Watson seemed to be displaying. Hell, I guess every organization needs someone of such a bearing within their circle.

Up ahead, I saw the SUVs drive past Grove Street, but entered the next one, Cedar Avenue. By the time I made the turn, I saw the trucks pulling over to the right side of the street. I wanted to speed up, and pass them before they got out, but the doors on the first SUV came open, and The Queenz were dismounting. Therefore, I pulled over, and brought the car to a halt in front of a house that had a red conversion van in its driveway.

Looking ahead, I saw Watson stop, and say something to the driver of the second truck, before she and her girls crossed the street to a house that had a gray, four-door, Oldsmobile Cutlass in the driveway. At about seventy yards away, I could see a bright orange sticker on the windshield of the car, which could very well mean that its owner had recently attended a funeral. Olivia's, perhaps? This had me curious about the residents of the home. Did either of them fit the description of the men Olivia Whitley gave of the ones responsible of murdering Mario Ballard, and subsequently herself?

Of course, from where I was stationed, I couldn't see who it was that answered their knock and allowed them entrance into the house. Not knowing how long they'd be, I put the car in park, but left the engine running. A part of our duty while doing surveillance on someone is to identify a large number of people they come in contact with. So, I'd have to report this location to the lead investigator. Well, I'd do my own investigation first. If it turned out that the residents were the guys responsible for the Grove Street murders, then that would be another piece of evidence Special Agent Dan Powell wouldn't be receiving.

"Bishop," I announced through my cell phone.

"Are you sure you gave me the right phone number?" Hoffman inquired.

"As far as I know," I told him. "What's wrong?"

"It's been changed to a private number," he apprised. "Well, that's what the automated operator told me. I'm still down in the basement, so if you have another number."

"No, Chad," I interrupted. "That was the only one. Thanks! I'll call you if I come up with anything."

"Okey dokey," my friend replied, before hanging up.

Well, the phone number was a dead end. I just wish I knew of somebody who had direct connection to one of The Queenz, so I could harass and threaten the phone number out of them. Spencer Kelly was supposedly dating Theresa Joiner, so her number would be logged into his contacts, but the GBI may have already released his property to his family by now.

Just then, I saw The Queenz emerging from the house. When they climbed back into their truck, and rode off, I remained where I was, just in case they decided to turn around, and come back this way, instead of exiting the other end of Cedar Avenue. When I saw them make the left, I pulled from my spot. Passing the house that they visited, I made sure to memorize the address by the numbers on the side of the mailbox.

We ended up entering the other end of Grove Street, which came as a surprise. Maintaining my distance, as I trailed them toward Bankhead Highway, I came upon the spot where the abandoned house used to be. The same house that Ballard and Whitley were murdered in. Now, there was only an indication that the house once occupied the area.

As it went, The Queenz only had two more stops, which were also in Atlanta. I assume they dismissed their guards, because they broke formation shortly after the last stop, and went their separate ways. Shonda ended up pulling into a Zaxby's restaurant. I was glad they decided to dine in because I had a call to make. However, right after I parked, I made sure to check in with Agent Pierce first to brief him for his written report. Then, I called the Decatur Chief of Police, John Moody.

"What is it?" Moody answered his phone, sounding agitated.

"Did I catch you at a bad time?" I inquired, looking out at the restaurant, though I couldn't see inside for its light-tinted windows.

"No really," he pressed. "I'm just tired of every time I turn around, there's some kind of budget cut. Right now, we're looking to lay off twelve officers within the next three weeks. It's not confirmed yet, but that's what we're looking at. Anyway, enough about my pitiful life. How's it going on your end? I hope you have some good news for me."

"Not yet, old timer," I replied. "I'm actually seeking information on a female group known as The Queenz. Have you heard of them?"

"Surely, you're not talking about a street organization headed by women, are you?"

"What about your CI?" I pushed, already figuring Moody hadn't heard of the group. "The one who was close to the D.J. at the club. Do you think you can trust me to question him?"

"I haven't even heard from the piece of shit," Moody grumbled. Then, after a beat, he asked, "What kind of information would you expect out of him, anyway?"

"Just basic stuff about Kelly," I answered, sensing how protective he'd become of his informant, just as Detective McCoy had become of hers. "I understand that he was dating one of these women in question and figured your informant could assist me a little."

"Um," the older man lingered. "I'll see what I can do, Bishop."

"Thanks, Moody!"

I hung up, with the notion that Chief John Moody was not going to keep his word. Sure, I could've called McCoy, and inquired about Spencer Kelly's cellular phone, but I was pretty much trying to dodge her, after the stunt I pulled to obtain the projectiles in the highway shooting case. I consider the homicide detective a friend, but even she knew there was a thin line between friendship and career.

# Playa Ray

## Chapter 20

### *Monday*

Even in a red, jail issued jumpsuit, forty-three-year-old Shirley Plummer aka Phoenix, still exuded sex appeal with her wide hips, and Double D breasts that pushed against the fabric of her attire. As she was being escorted into the booth opposite of the one I was seated in, by two female detention officers, I expected her to regard me with a look that would indicate she was glad I finally decided to show up but her expression was unreadable.

Once her wrists were free of the manacles, Plummer extracted a cigarette from its container, and obtained a light from one of the officers, before they secured the door, and moved along. I waited patiently as she gracefully planted her bottom onto the steel stool, placed her pack of cigarettes on the concrete slab in front of her, and took a long drag on the one in her hand, while staring into my eyes.

This is the closest I'd been to her since that night in her hotel room. Now, regarding her through the large and impeccably clear glass, I was surprised at how beautiful she was without makeup. Plus, her naturally dark hair was clipped, and slicked back, putting me in the mind of Jamie Lee Curtis, when she did the hotel scene in *True Lies*.

"I got your message," Plummer finally spoke, after exhaling a large amount of the smoke that she'd inhaled. There was no phone like most institutions, so her voice carried through the two vents up under the window. "I wouldn't mind having Hines as a cellmate, but he's a little too old for my taste, even though a cat will play with anything you throw at her."

Not caring to reply, I pulled my recorder from the inside pocket of my coat.

"No recording," she protested, pointing her cigarette at the device.

"It's the only way this conversation will take place, Ms. Plummer."

Her eyebrows went up. *"Ms. Plummer?* Is that what you call me, now? You can't call me *Phoenix?"*

"I can call those guards, and have you escorted back to your cell," I threatened, raising my eyebrows for emphasis.

"Geez!" the older woman let out, thumping ashes on the makeshift desk. "Who put coffee in *your* Corn Flakes this morning?"

I pressed the play on the recorder, then sat it down in front of me. "Ms. Plummer," I spoke slowly and clearly. "I'm here at the Federal holding facility, on the third of November, at your behest. Can you, please, explain your reason for calling upon the presence of the Federal Bureau of Investigation?"

"I was something like a matron of a child prostitution ring," she said blandly before lighting another cigarette with the first one, then grinding the first one out on the counter. "I mean, you already know this—" She paused to take a long drag on her cancer stick. "Anyway," Plummer resumed. "On top of being a scout for our headquarters in Sandy Springs, Georgia. I also ran a personal, and smaller operation from the basement of my own home."

"Is this a documentary?" I asked, feeling more like a news correspondent, than an FBI agent.

"One day," she went one, fixing me with a leery look. "I met this guy. There was something about his demeanor that drew me to him and compelled me to open up to him about what I did, and just like that—" she snapped her finger. "—he became one of my personal customers. His preference was little boys. Although he came by faithfully and never gave me any problems with payments, there was still something uncanny about him, which led me to believe that the name he'd given me was fictitious."

"My partner and I gave you fictitious names," I reminded her, now thinking about how I inadvertently played a part in Rhonda Thomas' death.

"Of course," Plummer replied with a smile. Then, she took another long pull on her cigarette. After exhaling the smoke, she resumed. "However, I wasn't in charge of doing background checks for the administrative center of the organization, but I ran my personal business with an iron fist. He didn't provide me with a photo identification but I did manage to take a picture of him, before making copies with my printer. I usually don't video record my clients while they're fulfilling their sexual fantasies, but I made an exception with this one. It took some time, but I eventually found out his true-identity and began logging it into my logbook whenever he showed for an appointment, though he was unaware of it."

"There was no record book of any sort found at your residence," I told her, remembering what Dan Powell had reported to me.

"It was on my kitchen counter," Plummer contended. "In plain sight, like I intended it to be."

"Maybe they overlooked it," I offered, shrugging.

Keeping her eyes drilled into mine, Plummer slowly shook her head. "You're too intelligent to pretend to be naive, Special Agent Bishop."

I was ready to conclude this frivolous meeting. "What's so special about this guy?"

"Oh, he's definitely *special*," she said. "I'm telling you this, because I think he may be a friend of yours."

"Give me a name!" I demanded, now feeling like this woman was playing some psychological game with me.

Plummer chuckled, then commenced to enjoying her cigarette, as if I was no longer there. Then, after lighting another one, and adding a second butt to the concrete counter, she asked, "How much would a name be worth to you?"

"Not one cent," I replied, pushing myself up from the plastic chair I was sitting in. "I don't know what your expectations are, but the FBI can't save you from whatever prosecution you're facing. Your attorney should've—"

"When I heard about the raid on our complex," she cut me off. "I should've shut down my operation by disposing of the children and burning everything that would've linked me to it. Instead, I photocopied my records book with my cell phone, and stored everything in a tackle box."

"So, you chose to get caught," I stated, realizing that she really could have gotten away.

"Not exactly," Plummer argued, thumping her ashes. "I kept my operation going, under the promise that I had nothing to worry about. I stored those things away because I've always found it hard to trust human beings."

For some reason, I found myself retaking my seat. "Who made you this promise?" I wanted to know.

Again, she wasted more of my time by taking an extremely long drag on her cigarette, holding the smoke in for what seemed like forever, then exhaled slowly from her nostrils. "You'll find the tackle box buried in my backyard."

"What makes you think I believe you enough to even go on this witch hunt?"

At that time, a broad smile spread across her face. "Curiosity killed the cat, remember?"

\*\*\*

I still couldn't believe how I let the Queen of Seduction trick me into driving out to Sandy Springs, Georgia. It was already 11:23 a.m. which was thirty-seven minutes until I was to be on my assigned post. Well, lucky for me, I don't have to relieve anyone, because there's no telling how long I'd be out on this wild goose chase. Plus, there was no telling what I might find—*if* I find anything.

When I made the Sandy Springs exit, I moved in the direction of the house, as if I'd been there before, while pondering why Plummer chose to inform me about one particular sick bastard that frequented her even sicker establishment. I don't know how she thought he was a friend of mine, but that assumption alone had me under the impression that I was either walking into a trap, or being used as a puppet, because I don't recall socializing with anybody who'd even *look* at a child, sexually.

The pink house, was the only pink house on this street and didn't look like it had been stormed by agents over two months ago. The curtains still hung in the windows and it looked like the place was still lived in, though there were no vehicles present. If someone was living inside the home, they would be squatters, because there was still a federal hold on the place.

Choosing to pull the government issued Buick Skylark into the driveway, I put the vehicle in park, and waited. For what? I don't know, but I was attentively watching the curtains in the windows for any kind of movement, still feeling like this could be a trap, though I didn't tell Plummer I'd come by here. At the same time, I didn't tell her that I *wouldn't* come by here either.

After a few minutes of watching the house, I concluded there was no imminent threat, and killed the engine, before stepping out into the light September breeze. It wasn't freezing out, but I still wore my FBI windbreaker more so for whatever nosey residents that may spot me and report my suspicious activities to the locals.

Holding my camera that hung from its strap around my neck, I took a picture of the front of the house, before moving around the side of it. There was no fence lining the place, so I entered the wide back yard with no impediment. Just as I figured, the lawn was unkempt, the grass too tall to tell where something had been buried. However, after taking pictures of the back of the house, and the yard in full view, I kind of tip-toed around, until I came upon a very small tract of land that differed from the rest, whereas the grass was shorter, and matted down, as if something sat in that particular spot for a long period of time.

Based on common sense alone, I could tell something was buried there. Once I snapped a shot of it, I looked around to see if I was being watched from one of the neighbors' houses. Then, finally realizing Plummer had to have had a shovel in order to inter the tackle box, I eyed the wooden deck, but saw nothing that would avail me. Now, I was thinking about my investigation kit, where I had plastic scoops that I used to collect trace evidence. It was either use one of those, or search for something semi-reliable.

Choosing the former, I made my way back to the Buick. My kit was on the front passenger seat. I opened the car's door, and donned a pair of latex gloves, before selecting the scoop I felt was the most sturdy. Just as I was about to shut the passenger door, a squad car from the Sandy Springs Police Department rode by. However, I didn't stand there as if trying to see who was driving it. I spun on my heels and continued. Surely, they'd see those large-ass letters on the back of my jacket and find themselves something safer to do.

Making it back to the area of interest, I squatted and felt the earth with one of my gloved hands. Thankful for how soft it was, I first, experimentally breached the moist dirt, chipping extremely small chunks away at a time. At this rate and considering how far the box may be from the surface, I could be at this for hours. I'd driven all the way out here, so there was no turning back now.

According to my watch, I'd been working for more than forty minutes, before discovering some kind of hard substance that was ensconced beyond what appeared to be a black trash bag. By this time, I was perspiring, and my knees were aching from maintaining this position for entirely too long. Satisfied with how close I was to attaining the buried content, I took a moment to stand, and walk around a bit, to stretch my limbs, for a good three minutes.

More than anxious to get back to what I was doing, I snapped a picture of the spot as it was, then got back down in my uncomfortable position, and commenced to free the trash bag from its shallow grave which took another fifteen minutes, or so. Then, I was able to pull the bag out, and set it aside. After securing a shot of it, I ripped the bag open, and snapped a shot of the gray tackle box.

Knowing I had to photo-document everything inside the box, I took ahold of the bag with the box still inside it, collected my scoop, and made my way back to the Buick. I tossed the bag onto the ground, and set the box on the hood. Releasing both latches, I lifted the top, and took a picture of the contents as they were, before strategically placing the items about, which consisted of a pink cellular phone, a compact recording disc inside a clear case, a syringe that appeared to contain some DNA sample, housed inside a small Ziploc bag, and a large manila envelope that was stuffed with God knows what.

After photo-documenting the items as I had them, the first item I picked up was the phone that had a piece of paper taped to its back with four digits on it. Taking it to be the passcode, I held the power button to activate it. It seemed like the phone took forever to advertise its brand before informing me that the battery was down to one percent. When the lock-screen finally popped up, I typed in 1-2-1-2, gaining access to the device. Not really knowing which application to choose, I selected the photo app, and the screen went completely blank, ending my snooping, before I could even get started.

Being that I had no access to a DVD player at the moment and had no interest in toying around with the tainted syringe, I placed the phone back onto the hood of the car and tried my luck with the manila envelope. It wasn't sealed, so I was able to slide the papers out. Right then, at that very moment, my whole body tensed up. On top of those papers, was a printer-copied facial shot of someone I did not expect to see. We're not *friends* as Shirley Plummer assumed, but I was highly familiar with the sick son of a bitch.

# Playa Ray

# Chapter 21

"Why didn't you report this to Hall?" asked Assistant Director Calvin Swint, as he eyed the content on his monitor with disgust.

Upon leaving Sandy Springs yesterday, I reported to my post in Norcross, to resume my surveillance on Shonda Watson. Lucky for me, she remained inside all day. I was so anxious to further explore the contents of the tackle box, I left my post at 11:28 p.m. and headed back to the James P. Russell building, where I clocked out, and retrieved my BMW.

Monique and the kids were asleep, so I made the living room my temporary laboratory, first plugging Plummer's cellular up to my phone's charge. Then, I extracted the documents from the folder again. Only taking a few seconds to regard Dan Powell's employee's identification photo. I went right into the following documents, which were photocopies of the pages from the logbook Plummer admitted to having in her home on the day she was arrested, and copies of identification cards used by her clients. I took my time scanning each one for any familiars but didn't recognize any.

Remembering what Plummer said about recording Powell, during one of his illicit sexual intercourses with one of the children, I intentionally circumvented the DVD, and tried the cellular again. Memorizing the four-digit passcode, I typed it in, and went straight to the photo gallery. It was full, mostly with replicas of documents I just perused from the manila envelope, including the photo of Dan Powell. After viewing a large number of photos of a family of four and drawing the conclusion that they were Plummer's daughter with her husband and two children. I closed the app and went into the video player.

Well, damn! Seeing a sole video clip that displayed the still image of a bedroom, pretty much let me know I really didn't have much of a choice but to go ahead and endure the inevitable. So, after taking a highly necessary deep breath, I pressed my thumb onto the video to start it.

At first, the screen jostled around a bit, as though someone was trying to secure a proper view of the small bed that was covered in a velvet-looking bedspread. A few minutes after the image stopped shifting, a young Caucasian boy of no more than eleven years old entered on-screen, clad in a pair of blue boxer shorts, and a white tank top that was entirely too big for his boney frame. Fidgeting with his fingers, he moved timidly to the bed, where he obediently sat down on the edge of it and looked off in the direction from whence he'd come. Then, he nodded his head up and down, clearly responding to someone's question, or demand. Plummer's, I assumed. That's when I realized the volume was down and turned it up.

The boy went back to fidgeting, with his head down. After another moment, his head slowly raised, and he looked warily at the door. It didn't take long for Dan Powell to come into view, dressed in a gray suit, and sit extremely close to the child. He said a few inaudible words, but when he began running the back of his hand along the boy's jawline, I disengaged the entire application, not willing to go through with the entire scene.

"I think there's something going on between those two," I now answered the assistant director's question. "It's like she has a soft spot for Powell and would probably sweep this thing under the rug. This is not something that should be ignored."

"I agree," said Swint, who was forty-seven years old, dark-skinned with a box-like crew cut, sprinkled with gray strands of hair. "I guess I'm authorized to submit this to the Justice Department myself. In the meantime, I'll send the specimen to forensic."

"I don't think that would be wise," I stated.

Swint stopped the video on his computer, then leaned forward, interlocking his fingers on his desk. "Why?" he asked. "You don't trust Vaughn, either?"

"Right now," I replied. "I don't trust anybody here. Who's to say Vaughn after making her discovery won't notify Powell? That would give him enough time to cover whatever tracks he's left behind and come up with a plausible excuse as to how his semen ended up inside the syringe."

"What about the video?" the older man posed, leaning back in his chair. "There's no way he could alter what's on that disc, or even fix his mouth to say that the person in it isn't him."

I only nodded my agreement.

"If it makes you feel any better," he went on. "I'll drop the syringe off at Grady Memorial Hospital on my way home today. Now, before I submit anything to the DOJ, I'll need the identification of those children, especially the one in the video."

"Can I run point in this investigation?" I asked, as a mental picture of me shooting Dan Powell between the eyes, entered my mind.

"You already are," Swint said. "Get me those names!"

*** 

"Back so soon?" Shirley Plummer asked, upon taking a seat in the booth opposite the one I was already seated in. "Did you get my present?"

"I found the box," I told her.

"So, you *did* go on the witch hunt?" she said, giggling, taking a short drag on her cigarette. "Curiosity is always a cat's downfall. However, I assume you're here to question me about your friend?"

"He's not my friend," I made sure to clarify. "But I am here to ask you some questions."

"What if I refuse to answer?"

"You have a right to refuse," I told her. "As I said, there's nothing I or the bureau can do, to reprieve you of whatever punishment you're facing. There really isn't anything I could offer as a reward for your compliance."

This time, she took her precious time finishing off her cigarette, and using it to light her second one. "You're lucky, I have nothing else to do."

"Thanks!" Taking that as my cue, I pulled out my recorder, pressed play, and sat it down before me. Plummer only gave it a mere once over before casting her eyes to the ceiling. "When the main operation was busted," I dove in. "Why did you continue with your side operation instead of shutting down? Did someone promise you that you had nothing to worry about?"

A smile spread across the woman's face. "You're very clever, Mr. Bishop. I'll give you that. Of course, someone promised me that my side operation wouldn't suffer the same fate as the main operation."

"Does this person have a name?"

"You should already know his name," Plummer answered, then looked down at the recorder. "Or am I to say it for the record?"

"If you don't mind, Ms. Plummer."

Her eyebrows shot up. "Who!"

"Phoenix," I corrected, knowing she was going to play this card with me. "If you don't mind, Phoenix."

"Now, was that so hard?" There was an even broader smile on her face now. She ground out her cigarette. "His name was Special Agent Dan Powell. Do you want his address?"

"I want to know about the children."

"What about them?" she asked, a confused look on her face.

"What were their names?"

"I thought that kind of information would be in the FBI's files."

"What about the child in the video?" I switched my tact. "Could you, at least, provide me with *his* name?"

"I called them what they were," Plummer offered, with a shrug.

"I'm not sure I follow you," I told her. "Are you saying you addressed them by their gender?"

"That's exactly what I'm saying," she answered. "*Abduction* is way different from *adoption* when these children are snatched, they don't necessarily come with birth certificates."

"What about the syringe?" I inquired, disregarding her quip. "I assume it contained semen? Could you tell me who it belonged to?"

"Do I have to say his name again?"

"How did you obtain the DNA?"

"You make it sound like I'm a forensics analyst, or something," Plummer replied, smiling. "Maybe, I chose the wrong profession."

I tilted my head to one side but said nothing.

"Okay, Mr. All-Too-Serious," she gave in. "I extracted the semen from the boy's rectum myself. You know, just in case *somebody* didn't keep their promise." Then, as if a lightbulb came on in her head, she asked, "Do you think he still has my record book?"

"Why would he have your record book?"

Shirley Plummer only responded by regarding me with a knowing look, which immediately made me feel like an idiot. Of course, Powell would've been the one to collect the records book, but why would she ask if he *still* has it? I'm quite sure he set fire to it the first chance he got. Or did he?

Playa Ray

# Chapter 22

## *Sunday*

## *October 16, 2005*

It had been twelve days since my last visit with Shirley Plummer. A man of his word, Assistant Director Swint worked the investigation without the knowledge of Director Hall. As we expected, the DNA experts at Grady Memorial Hospital confirmed that the syringe indeed belonged to Dan Powell. Adding that report with everything from the tackle box, Swint made his submission to the Justice Department, who faxed their approval back in less than a week. Also, to be more inconspicuous, they flew six District of Columbia federal agents in for the take-down.

Of course, being that I was the only agent in our department who was aware of the situation, and more knowledgeable than the visiting agents, I was appointed Commander of Operations, and chose to brief them inside the room they'd been sharing at the Marriott hotel downtown for three days. Though most agents are deliberately irreverent toward non-domestic agents, these guys were surprisingly docile. They gave me their undivided attention, never interrupting while I explained the plan of action, and had no questions when I was done.

Being that Dan Powell always took his Sundays off, the assistant director pushed me to move in on him today, which is why I was now seated in the front passenger seat of a black Chevy Suburban that was parked several houses away from the one belonging to the sought-out agent. Accompanying me were three of the six D.C. agents, who were all outfitted in tactical gear that I must admit made ours look like children's Halloween costumes. Hell, even their handguns seemed futuristic.

"Bravo Team is in position. Over," came through my earpiece, confirmation from the remaining agents, who were now stationed at the back door of Powell's home.

"Copy that," I responded. "Stand by."

"Standing by."

I looked over at the driver. "Let's do it!"

Giving just a slight nod of the head, the driver put the truck in gear, and drove casually toward Powell's house, where his motorcycle and Rodeo truck were sitting in the driveway. It was 7:12 a.m. and dusk was still amongst us. Considering that Powell liked to play cards, and drink on Saturday nights, I figured he'd still be in bed with a possible hangover.

Once the truck was docked in front of the house, the four of us dismounted, and moved cautiously toward it. I didn't have my gun out, nor was I dressed in tactical gear. In fact, I was dressed in one of my favorite gray suits for this occasion. Their protective helmets were now on and the flanking agents made me feel like that white guy on the movie, *Equilibrium*.

I stopped at the bottom of the steps and allowed them to step onto the porch. After receiving a nod from me, the one with the steel breacher, began expertly detaching the hinges on the burglar bar door, which was subsequently propped against the railing. Then, the other two positioned themselves in front of the main door, holding onto a battering ram.

"All units," I said through my transmitter. "Prepare to breach in five—four—three—two—one."

*Boom!*

The wooden door caved in much easier that I thought it would. However, I didn't move until the third man entered the house. I still didn't have my gun out as I took my time trailing the agents I'd instructed to head straight for the bedroom, feeling like a mob boss on my way to dispose of some disloyal motherfucker. Hell, all I was missing was a round-brimmed hat, and some awful-tasting cigar hanging from my mouth.

By the time I made it to Powell's bedroom, all six agents had already surrounded his bed with their guns aimed. With the covers pulled up to his waist, and wearing a gray t-shirt with FBI in black letters, Dan Powell was sitting up in his bed, regarding the six agents with a look that could've been a cross between surprise and fear. Let me tell it, it was pure fear. Especially the look he gave me when I came into his sight.

"Bishop!" he voiced, breathlessly. "What the hell's going on here!"

"Don't sit there and act like you don't know why I'm here, you poor excuse for a human being!" I said as cool as I could. "You know what? I'm not even gonna waste my time with reading you your rights because as far as I'm concerned, you have no rights. Detain this piece of shit!" I added, gesturing to the agents.

I didn't even wait around to supervise the restraining of the subject. They already have my authoritative order to toe-tag Powell if he attempts to put up a fight. The house had to be searched, so I left the room, to get a jump start on it. Whatever evidence they collected would be of no value to me, personally. I was only after one thing. I mean, that's only if it still existed and if Powell was stupid enough to stash it on his property.

Entering the living room, I pretty much stopped, and just looked around as though what I was looking for would automatically appear. However, as one of my methods, whenever I searched for something in particular, I conduct a visual overhaul of my surroundings first putting myself in the mind of a criminal, which helped me conjure up possible hiding places.

For instance, in this case, I considered the size of Plummer's records book. So, as I slowly spun around, I tried to assume the mind of Dan Powell and ponder where I would hide such an item, if I was stupid enough to bring it back here, instead of destroying it.

After doing a complete three-sixty, I concluded that the book was not in the living room. Therefore, I made for Powell's first guest room, which resembled a small office; a computer and all its accessories were set up on a small table, accompanied by the same exact kind of chair that Powell had back at the office. There were no file cabinets, only several documents cluttered the table. One of the agents with his helmet clutched in the fold of his arm, seemed to be taking his time sifting through the mess. He looked up as I approached.

"Carry on," I said, nodding. "Make sure you commandeer that computer, and every disc you come across."

Re-entering Powell's bedroom, I saw that two of the agents were still there. One was searching the room, while the other stood guard over Powell, who was lying on his stomach, atop the bed, with a black zip-tie binding his wrists. Disregarding the three of them, I did my visual survey of the room, as I'd done with the living room, highly aware of the awkward stares I was getting.

"So, you're not gonna tell me what this is about?" Powell questioned, just as I was about to exit, after coercing myself to believe that the records book wasn't in this particular room.

Stopping in my tracks, I retraced my steps, and stood over the big guy who seemed surprisingly calm. "I'm not gonna play this game with you," I told him. "You already know what kind of activities you've been engaging in. Now, you have to figure out how you're gonna spend your time in prison because you're definitely taking that ride."

I exited, making my way to the last guest room where two more agents were pretty much tearing up the place with their helmets sitting on top of the dresser. Without crossing the threshold, I only took a brief moment to survey the place, before moving to the kitchen, where the remaining agent was going through cabinets and drawers. Placing a hand over my mouth, as I yawned, I entered the kitchen, pacing myself while darting my eyes back and forth.

While absently moving toward the back door, I thought about where I found Plummer's tackle box, but when I got to the door, I reached for the knob, and paused mid-air. Something wasn't right about the notion I was feeling at the moment. Letting my hand fall back to my side, I slowly spun on my heels, conscious of how the agent was now watching me, though I was looking at the steel, double door refrigerator.

Like my feet had a mind of their own, I found myself moving in the direction of the box. This time, there was no hesitation. I pulled both doors open and eyed the beverages and comestibles from top to bottom. Leaning over, I pulled the vegetables drawer open. Just as I was about to close it back, a green color that contrasted with that of the bag of green apples caught my attention. Taking hold of the bag, I lifted it, and smiled. *So, Powell wasn't as smart as I thought he was.*

Playa Ray

# Chapter 23

"Okay, all units!" I said through my transmitter, as people began exiting the church. "It's showtime!"

It had been a whole month since the arrest of former FBI agent, Dan Powell who was still being held at the federal holding facility downtown. Of course, when Director Amy Hall found out about this she immediately called me into her office and appointed me head investigator of The Queenz investigation. She didn't know of my involvement in the takedown, because Assistant Director Swint who was backed by the Justice Department, insisted that I refrain from making any kind of statement in reference to it.

Right now, I was leaning against the black Crown Victoria that was parked on the other side of the Atlanta Police Department's escort detail and black Cadillac hearse sitting directly in front of the church, where a funeral service was being held for Ebony Davis' sister, Erica Davis who was murdered a week ago in East Atlanta right along with her boyfriend Teddy Jefferson.

The moment I heard about the crime from Detective McCoy, I rushed down to the M.E.'s office, where I learned that Davis and Jefferson both sustained individual stab wounds to their necks from a knife with a possible six-inch blade. I was also able to gain access to Davis' belongings that were found at the scene, which were her Gucci purse, a jean suit with matching boots, cell phone, and a diary once homicide investigators were done with them.

These items weren't really essential but being the true Federal agent that I am, I took my precious time reading every passage in her diary, all the way up to the day she was murdered. According to her daily book of events, Erica Davis had visited a clinic on the last day of her natural life and discovered that she was pregnant. She wrote, saying that she was on her way home from the clinic and couldn't wait to tell her baby's father, claiming she'd come back and explain how happy he was of the news. Either she didn't get the chance to tell him, or she didn't get the chance to jot down his response, but the passage remained incomplete.

However, what I saw at the bottom of that same page, sparked my interest. In the same handwriting, Davis wrote: *Rico Drop Sq*— Then, as if interrupted, a crooked line seemed to run off the page. I still didn't really know what to make of this, but I didn't need a scientist to tell me that she intended to write *Rico Drop Squad*, before something, or someone, prevented her from doing so. I hoped like hell Ricardo Willis, a.k.a Rico had nothing to do with this. I still ended up setting up an around-the-clock surveillance team at his mother's home. Till this day, there had been no sign of him.

Now, clad in dark-gray jeans, my blue windbreaker, and my sunglasses propped up on my nose. I watched the pallbearers slowly exit the church, three on each side of the oakwood casket. Once I saw the family and friends of Erica Davis emerge, I waited a good fifteen seconds allowing my band of agents to snap pictures of everyone in attendance from where they were positioned before grabbing the brown paper bag off the hood of the Ford and crossing the street.

"Ms. Ebony Davis?" I said, approaching the woman, who was being consoled by her boyfriend none other than Philip Lakes, one of the three head members of Drop Squad. "These are Erica's things," I went on, handing the bag over to her. "They were at Teddy Jefferson's place. And I offer my condolences."

"Thank you," she replied, her voice barely a whisper.

Giving a slight nod, I spun on my heels, and headed back to my car, climbed behind the wheel and drove on. The other agents were instructed to wait until the funeral attendees cleared out, before leaving the scene, and meeting me back at the James P. Russell building.

The agents I had on Sheila Griffin both reported that she'd recently started dating some guy, who resided in Canton, Georgia, but they had yet to photograph or I.D. him. What gets me about the whole thing is that he was reported to have his own driver who chauffeurs him around in a black Lincoln Navigator, which is no fucking coincidence! There was no doubt that this was the same fucker Shonda Watson met at The Enchanting restaurant on the night I followed her there. He was also the same fucker who'd accompanied Griffin to the funeral, I couldn't wait to get back to the War Room so I could get a better look at the son of a bitch.

"Talk to me!" I answered my phone that vibrated in the cupholder.

"I just received a call from the commissioner," Detective McCoy informed. "He wanted to know how the highway shooting case was coming along. You know, the same case I was duped into believing the FBI has jurisdiction over?"

Shit! I kept my eyes on the road but said nothing.

"You've really crossed the line, Bishop," she resumed. "Not only did you lie to me, you falsified federal documents, in order to steal essential evidence in the case." There was a brief pause, before she went on, "In the beginning, I thought nothing of it, when you seemed overly interested in the case. Now, I'm under the impression that you know the shooter, and you're trying to protect them."

Lieutenant Kowanda McCoy was beyond hurt, it was evident in her voice. Still, I said nothing.

"For your sake," the detective went on, "I hope you didn't dispose of those projectiles because I want them back like yesterday!"

"Name a time and place," I finally spoke, noting the bit of hostility that now laced her tone.

After committing the time and location to memory, I concluded the call, and realized that the friendship between McCoy and I was no more. Well, that's one of the many sacrifices a person has to make, in order to become successful. Oh well.

Getting off the elevator on the sixth floor, I stopped at my cubicle long enough to see that I had no messages. Then made for the War Room, took a seat at the rear of the empty room and thought about how my last encounter with Homicide Detective Kowanda McCoy would be.

Another thirty plus minutes had gone by, before my team begun to show up. I was quite sure they'd stopped to grab a bite to eat, but I was more concerned about the photos I was so anxious to get a look at. Once everyone was accounted for, except for the two agents

I ordered to remain out in the field, I chose Agent Pierce to share his pictures first.

After loading the projector, he extinguished the lights, and switched the machine on. The first picture was of the six pallbearers, preceding the attendees while carrying Erica Davis' casket at waist-level. From where Pierce was positioned, I could only see the right side of their faces, though these guys were of no factor.

"I think these guys were hired by the church," I spoke up. "Show me something else."

Pierce pressed the select button on the remote, when the next picture entered onto the screen, I found myself slowly rising from my seat, removing the sunglasses from my face. I couldn't believe I was looking right at this piece of shit who seemed to be looking right back at me, through the dark lenses of his ever-present sunglasses. I rarely forget a face, and this was one of those faces I didn't even think I was capable of forgetting. Even without the long hair, he still looked the same, but how was it that I was seeing him walking and breathing amongst the living, when I'm sure he was doing anything other than?

"I think I've seen enough," I said, now moving toward the door. "Everyone, return to your posts."

Making it to my cubicle, I flopped down into my chair, and switched my computer on. While waiting for the device to become fully active, I used my desk phone to place a call to the records department.

"Records," a female's voice flowed sweetly through the earpiece.

"This is Agent Bishop," I announced, typing my password into my computer. "I need a file retrieved from the archives."

"Has there been a request submitted in reference to said file, sir?"

"No," I answered. "And there won't be any submitted."

"Well—"

"Arguing back and forth about this silly—ass policy won't get us anywhere," I cut her off. "All I'm trying to do is look over an old case I worked on years ago. That's it."

I heard the woman take a deep breath before asking me, "What's the file number?"

"Eighteen, twenty-seven, fourteen, nineteen, zero, eight," I recited from memory.

"And you will like the file to be delivered to which floor?"

"I'll pick it up on my way out," I answered.

Hanging up, I logged into Criminal Records, then typed in the name of Ray Young. Already knowing who I was looking for, I scrolled down until I found him staring back at me from the only mugshot he'd ever had taken of him. Logging into his file, I went straight to the address, and saw that it was the same as it was, prior to his supposed death, although there was no mentioning of his expiration.

Considering this, I backed out, and typed in *James Young*. To my surprise, the first word that popped up in bold letters was: *DECEASED*. Then, it went on to explain the cause of death. This was confusing, because on the night The Kingz' limousine was ambushed, Agent Towns reported seeing four bodies pulled from the vehicle, all clad in fashionable robes, before being stuffed into body bags. Plus, I saw the news footage later that night, and the following day. The anchorman announced that all four men that headed the street organization known as The Kingz were dead, but, yet and still, I'd seen Ray Young, a.k.a King Ray, with my own two eyes. Who doesn't trust their own two eyes? I'd watched them close enough to know if either one of them had an identical twin walking around.

Prior to leaving the James P. Russell building, I retrieved the awaiting file from the Records Department. As I drove, I could not stop thinking about Ray Young. If he was still alive, then who was the fourth man murdered alongside James Young, Frederick Mills, and Keith Daniels? Surely, Ray Young hadn't been dethroned, and replaced by another, because I would have known this. A fifth King was definitely out of the question. However, there was still a fourth body unaccounted for. I planned to find out who it belonged to, which is why I was now pulling my car onto the property of the cemetery on Martin Luther King Drive.

Before exiting my car, I shed my FBI windbreaker, to minimize unwanted attention, though there were only a handful of people present. After taking in the massive rows of tombstones, I set my feet in motion, and made my own pattern, so not to miss any. Momentarily, I came upon Keith Daniels' grave, but saw no reason to stop. Another three minutes into my hunt, I came upon the one belonging to Frederick Mills, and felt I would soon be able to put the pieces to this puzzle together.

However, when I came upon the plot belonging to James Young, I stopped, wondering if I should continue, being that I was almost certain I wouldn't run across one with Ray Young's name on it. Well, giving in to my impulse, I continued, keeping to the pattern, while searching for a name that may stand out to me, when I did come across a familiar name, I'd made it all the way to the other side of the cemetery. I was definitely familiar with the name Raymond Bailey who according to his tombstone, had expired on the same date as Young, Mills, and Daniels.

Making it back to the warm confines of my BMW, I started the engine, then grabbed the large file off the seat beside me, placing it in my lap. Searching through the known associates of The Kingz it didn't take long for me to come across Raymond Bailey, who I now remembered used to date April Moore the sister of James and Ray Young. Why was he inside the limousine that night instead of Ray Young? Fuck it! I may never know the answer to that but I knew one thing. Now that Ray Young was known to still be alive, I could re-open The Kingz investigation and see to it that he was punished for every crime committed by his organization, whether he was personally involved, or not.

\*\*\*

"Do you need anything else, sir?"

"No, thank you!" I said to the Caucasian waitress that approached my table, carrying a glass coffee pot.

It was 9:37 p.m. and I'd been at The Common restaurant for a little over twenty minutes, pretending to pick over my meatloaf and mashed potatoes, while chewing on six pieces of Wrigley's chewing gum. This was my second visit at the restaurant. On my first visit, I noticed it didn't have interior, or exterior cameras which is why I chose to come here tonight.

The place wasn't packed, however after glancing around to make sure I wasn't being watched, I began ripping pieces of the gum, attaching them to the backs of my cell phones lying face down on the table. Then one by one, I stuck them to the underside of the table. Once I felt they were both secure, I consumed a great portion of my meal, before making my exit.

I agreed to meet with Detective McCoy at 10:00 p.m., but it was twenty-one minutes after, when I made it to our meeting place, a deserted dirt road, just outside the city limits. Extinguishing my headlights and leaving the alternate lights on, I parked with the front-end of my car at about four yards away from the driver's side of her Range Rover truck that was still running, with the alternate lights also on and her sitting patiently at the wheel.

Not wanting to make her wait any longer than she already had, I donned my black gloves, grabbed the box off the passenger seat, and dismounted, moving toward the SUV. McCoy rolled her window down. The boxes didn't have any flaps, so as I neared, I reached my hand into it, and took hold of the .38 Revolver. Just as I looked up, I found myself staring down the barrel of the detective's handgun that was hanging from the window.

I feinted to the right, just as a succession of three rounds exploded from the weapon. My box fell to the ground, but I was in great possession of the Revolver as I took refuge behind the Rover. At that moment, I heard the transmission shift, and saw the back-up indicator lights come on. Wasting no time, I made a dash for the right side of the truck, just as McCoy slammed down on the gas pedal. I barely cleared the rear of the SUV, when it plowed into my left shoulder.

I must've spun twice, before collapsing to the ground. Realizing the truck had come to a halt, and was about to charge at me again, I mustard up all the energy and strength I could to quickly pull myself off the ground and secure an aim at McCoy through the windshield. As she charged at me again, I was able to get off three shots, before having to dive out of the way, landing in some under-brush.

Still feeling like my life was in danger, I drew into a crouching position, aiming my gun at the Range Rover, just as it crashed into a tree, and the airbags deployed. On instinct, I jumped up, and ran over to the driver's side. McCoy's face was buried in her airbag. Reaching in, I pulled her head back, and saw that one of my bullets had penetrated her right eye socket and her whole face was covered in blood.

"If I had a chance of getting into heaven," I said to the dead woman. "I'm quite sure I just fucked that up."

Then, I turned on my heels, and headed back to my BMW, where I retrieved the gas can from the trunk, and doused the SUV with the gasoline. Lighting a cigarette, I took a long drag on it as I reflected on how bad I felt having to do this to my friend, although I knew it would happen, once she found out what I'd done.

*Oh well*, I thought as I tossed the burning cigarette through the driver's window and walked away, hearing the *whoosh* sound of the gasoline igniting and flames immediately consuming the expensive vehicle.

***

It was 11:28 p.m. when I made it back to the restaurant. To my surprise, the place was deserted. The parking lot was empty, and there were no one inside the establishment, but I wasn't hearing this. There was no way I was going to leave here without my phones. Pulling out of the parking lot, I cruised slowly down the dark road, amidst the handful of motorists who were probably retiring to their homes from a long day at work.

Coming upon a car repair shop that had what seemed to be un-repaired vehicles in its lot, I pulled in, and parked amongst them to blend in. Retrieving a lug wrench and ballcap from the trunk, I donned the cap, tucked the wrench into the waistline of my pants, and began moving in the direction from whence I'd come, on foot.

214

Reaching the restaurant, all I took was one glance around, before approaching one of the large windows, with the steel wrench in my hand. All it took was one swing, and the window came crashing down. I didn't have to enter, because I was already at the table. Tucking the wrench, I extracted both my phones from under the table, and moved on, heading for my car, while peeling the gum off.

Returning the wrench, I climbed behind the wheel, and powered my phones on to check for missed calls, only to see there were two from Agent Catherine Perry, who was assigned to Theresa Joiner. Seeing that they were thirteen minutes apart, I immediately called her back, while pulling out of the body shop's lot.

"I figured you were asleep," Perry said, answering her phone.

"Yeah, I did doze off for a few," I lied. "Do you have something to report?"

"Yes, sir," she replied. "I trailed Joiner and Watson to Watson's home, where the local authorities were waiting to report a break-in."

*"A break-in!"* I exclaimed. "Their home was broken into?"

"That's what I gathered in the beginning," said the agent. "However, I was able to question the responding officers. Once I flashed my credentials, they were more than willing to tell me everything, which wasn't much."

"Did Watson write a report, explaining what was missing?" I wanted to know.

"She wrote a report, but claimed nothing of value was taken."

Bullshit! This wasn't just the house where Watson and Griffin laid their heads. This was The Queenz' stash house, where they kept their product, and incontestably their company's account. So, if the home had been burglarized, then there were definitely valuable items missing, such as drugs, money, and jewelry. The big question was, *who was bold enough to violate The Queenz in such a manner?* Of course, it was someone close enough to them, to know that everything was stashed at this house and not the one in Riverdale, Georgia.

# Playa Ray

## Chapter 24

### *Eight Days Later*

The alley was spacious enough for the three SUVs to enter, and not be seen by motorists traveling along the main road. Shortly after being informed by Brenda Lane of the alcove Vincent Calhoun had in his office, that led to this side of the building, Agent Knight and I made sure to check it out, before turning the information over to the lead GBI investigator. Being that we were the only two FBI agents involved in the investigation, Knight and I were enlisted for the Task Force operation, which is why we were now seated in the rear of the second SUV of the convoy that came to a halt on the side of the Worldwide Insurance Agency building.

As planned, we all quickly dismounted, first conducting a weapons and communications check. Then, we gathered around the front-end of the first truck as Agent Rommel, the lead GBI investigator, spread a drawn blueprint of the building out on the hood of it. Other agents had to assist with keeping the drawing from being carried away by the wind that was doing about sixty-five miles per hour.

"Okay, men," he started, though there were three women in attendance. "For the last and final time, once we reach the top floor, Alpha, Charlie, Delta, Echo, Foxtrot, and Golf Units are to make for the elevators. Foxtrot, you'll take the Ground Floor. Echo, you'll take the first. Delta, you'll be securing the second. Charlie, I want you raising hell on—"

He stopped mid-sentence, upon the sound of keys being fussed with from beyond the metallic door. Automatically, we all went into defense mode, assault rifles aimed at the door, while unceremoniously setting up a perimeter with some agents using the first two SUVs for cover, and the rest of us forming a semi-circle before the entrance.

Just then, the door swung open, and I'd be damned if Vincent Calhoun's fat ass didn't come tumbling through it as if being pursued. Seeing us, he stopped in his tracks, and threw his hands up. I don't know about the others, but I saw fear in the man's eyes the moment he emerged from the building, which was now replaced with relief.

"Get on the ground, now!" the commander barked, maintaining his position, as we maintained ours. Once the man complied, he said, "Bravo unit, secure the subject, and stand sentry! Everyone else, move in!"

Of course, Bravo Unit consisted of Knight and myself, so, while the rest of the team filed into the building, we got Calhoun into a zip-tie, and placed him in the rear seats of the truck we rode in. A part of me was glad we no longer had to go inside, but another part of me felt I really deserved to see the interior of the building I spent many weeks conducting surveillance in front of.

"We're approaching four, ten fifty-fours in the corridor," one agent announced over the radio. "All male."

Knight and I, were both still standing outside the SUV, exchanged a glance.

"I'm going inside," I told him. "Can you handle the babysitting detail without me?"

"Sure," Knight said, coolly, pulling out his pack of cigarettes. "You got a light?"

I tossed him my lighter, before dashing inside the building with my M-16 at the ready. There were no windows, so I activated the lamp on the front of my helmet, as I climbed the endless, winding concrete staircase. At the same time, I wondered about the information that came over the comset about the four possible dead bodies. Did Calhoun murder four men, and try to make a break for it, which is how he just landed in our laps? No, that made no sense at all. Why would he be running from *dead* men? Unless someone else liquidated the men, and he was eluding his own fate which counts for the fear I saw registering in his eyes. If this was the case, then it was possible that we were entering hostile grounds.

I finally reached the breach in the wall that was standing wide open, entering Calhoun's office that was just the way Brenda Lane described it. The first thing I noticed was the array of monitors sitting off to the right of the desk. Giving only a quick glance at them to see where the team was located, I entered into the hallway where the four dead men were sprawled about in puddles of blood before the elevators. Stopping, I took in the four weapons, and spent shell casings, as an idea came to mind.

"Fifth floor is clear!" someone from Golf Unit apprised.

"Copy that," came the commander's response.

Retracing my steps, I re-entered the office, and stepped behind the desk. After another look at the monitors, I began toying around with the keys on the computer's keypad. Not knowing how far to rewind the footage, I just tapped the back key, until I got the confirmation I was looking for.

On the monitor showing the corridor on this particular floor, I saw the two women, cloaked in caps and trench coats, moving backward from Calhoun's office, carrying assault rifles. Still pushing the footage in reverse, I watched as the women backed onto the elevator, and the four deceased men, rose off the floor, and back into the chairs they were occupying, before the interruption. Two of them were playing Checkers, and the other two were just sitting around. This is where I eased off the back key, leaving the images at a standstill.

Shifting my gaze to the image of the elevator, I found myself looking at the backs of the women's heads. Hell, even with the ball caps and trench coats, I could tell they were Theresa Joiner, and Shonda Watson who'd visited the place last Sunday, the day after Watson and Griffin's home was broken into. At that time, I theorized that they were seeking a loan from the shark, to get back on their feet. Now, I wasn't so sure of their motive. Robbery, perhaps?

"Fourth floor is secured," Alpha Team reported. "We have zero subjects."

"Copied."

Unpausing the footage, I watched as Watson and Joiner emerged from the elevator like a pair of female mercenaries. Before the men could get their weapons out, they were immediately gunned down. Wasting no time, the women marched toward Calhoun's office, which was a blind spot. Figuring this was around the time the loan shark was hauling his Humpty Dumpty—looking ass down the stairs to save his worthless life, I waited until I saw the women emerge, and get back on the elevator.

Surely, they were aware of the electric eye on the shaft, because neither one of them made the amateur mistake of looking up at it. When they got off on the Ground floor, that's when I finally thought about Vincent Calhoun's secretary, Brenda Lane and looked over at the monitor. Lane was standing behind the receptionist desk, but she was not alone. Another female, cloaked in the same fashion as Watson and Joiner had her at gunpoint. Of course, she was none other than Sheila Griffin.

"Ground floor is secure!" Foxtrot Unit checked in. "We have zero-one casualties. Female. Causcasian."

"Received."

I heard the call, but I was confused, because the only Caucasian female present on the Ground floor was the secretary, and she wasn't—

Oh shit! Seconds after Joiner and Watson exited the elevator, Griffin shot Lane in the face, and pretty much watched her collapse to the floor. Making it to the front desk, Watson grabbed what appeared to be a logbook off it, and the three of them marched through the front door, climbing into an awaiting black SUV. *Their SUV!* The same fucking GMC Denali I spotted sitting at the entrance when we arrived!

I almost felt sorry for the secretary. Out of everybody that were present, she was the only one that was going to leave the building without restraints, but now she'd be carted out in a body bag. Remembering that I was not supposed to be inside the building, I hung my M-16 over my shoulder, then donned a pair of latex gloves over the ones I already had on. After extracting the surveillance disc, I stuffed it inside my vest, then stepped back out in the hallway, where I brandished a plastic evidence bag, and secured the spent shell casings, being careful not to step into the puddles of blood.

Concealing the bag into one of the side pockets on my pants, I made it back outside, where Knight was still standing beside the truck we arrived in, smoking a cigarette. Saying nothing to him, I snatched the rear door open, grabbed Calhoun by the lapel of his dress suit, and yanked him toward me, where our faces were inches apart.

"Your men are dead," I hissed. "Your secretary is also dead. The only reason you haven't joined them is because you fled the scene. Now, who is after you?"

"I wanna talk to my lawyer."

"Fuck your lawyer!" I spat, shaking him a bit. "Who's trying to kill you?"

"I am a man of many enemies," Calhoun spoke, maintaining his composure. "Hell, as far as I know, it could be the Grim Reaper."

I wanted to headbutt this fucker with this hard-ass helmet I had on, but I was glad he wasn't the type to fold under pressure. He knew damn well who was after him, but he wasn't going to give them up to the authorities. No way. Vincent Calhoun was going to keep this beef in the streets, which had me a little worried about the fate of The Queenz.

# Playa Ray

## Chapter 25

"I still can't believe you stole evidence from the crime scene?" Director Hall said, after diverting her eyes away from her monitor. She looked down at the ziploc bag containing the bloodstained shell casings atop her desk, as though they were highly contagious. Pointing an ink pen at them, she said, "I'm quite sure they saw those."

"Oh, I can assure you they saw those," I replied from across the desk. "Rommel mentioned it, but what can he do? It's not like he can actually prove what happened to them."

Hall leaned back in her chair. "So, what do you plan on doing with those items, Bishop?" she posed. "You stole them from an active crime scene, so you know you can't present them in a trial against The Queenz. If you ask me, I think you should either dispose of them, or find a way to anonymously get them into the hands of Agent Rommel. I mean, disposing of them would be a better option, considering your current investigation."

"Yeah, you're right," I lied, knowing damn well I wasn't about to commit to any of her suggestions. "Has Powell contacted you?"

"No!" She made a face. "He has no reason to contact me. I still can't believe we had somebody like him working in our division."

"You never know these days," I offered, glad to know how she felt about the situation, which meant she would probably never hear of my involvement.

"The Flennory investigation was a success," my superior changed subjects. "They arrested one brother in Texas, and the other in St. Louis. Twenty-five members of their organization were also indicted. Agent Count claims it's the most fun he's had since being on the force."

"Well, it's too bad I missed out on that one," I said, getting to my feet. Seeing that I was ready to leave, Hall ejected the disc I'd stolen from Calhoun's office, and handed it to me. "I guess I'll dispose of these and get back to work?"

Making it back to my cubicle, I placed the disc and shell casings inside a manila envelope, sealed it, and placed it at the back of my bottom drawer. Then, I lifted the receiver of my desk phone, and placed a call to a dear old friend of mine.

"Manning," the Atlanta Chief of Police grumbled through the device.

"How's it going, champ?" I inquired, leaning back in my chair.

"I feel like the ringleader of a damn circus!" he replied. "I'm starting to adopt the notion that some of my subordinates paid their way through the Police Academy. Hell, these days, you can pay for a medical degree, and perform open-heart surgery on some poor bastard the same damn day!"

"I see they got you working like a Hebrew slave," I commented. "Perhaps, I called at a bad time?"

"Not really," my friend assured. "You're probably calling me about the progress of Detective McCoy's case."

"I am."

"We're still coming up with nothing," he told me. "She was burned beyond recognition and could only be identified by her dentals. Any fingerprints or trace evidence that may have been found on her vehicle were destroyed by the fire. Her husband was out of town, so that excludes him from being a cardinal suspect, and I doubt if she had some boy toy on the side. However, it still remains a mystery, why she was in such a secluded area. My theory is she was murdered somewhere else, then driven to that location."

"It's crazy," I offered. "I'd just spoken to her that day."

"I know," Manning replied. "I saw your number on her call print out. Of course, I drew a line through it, excluding you as a suspect."

"I got my ears to the streets, also," I told him. "If I hear something, you'll be the first to know."

"Thanks, Bishop!"

Concluding that call, I knew I had to call and check on Agent Shayla Wright to see if she was well enough to work her shift tonight, being that she'd come down with a cold a couple of days ago.

"Hello?" Wright answered, sounding hoarse, then went into a coughing spell.

"I guess you pretty much answered my question," I said, once she was done. "Take as long as you need off. I'll take your shift tonight, and figure something out until you get back."

Truth be told, I didn't mind taking her shift tonight. I'd already put a rotation on Shonda Watson once I accumulated enough agents to do so, which left me free to orchestrate this investigation like I wanted to. So, I didn't mind driving out to Canton, Georgia, and watching Ray Young's house for tonight. Maybe, things would get interesting for a chance.

I ended up making it to Canton a little before 8:00 p.m. in a blue Dodge Magnum. Agent Alton Mason, who was occupying a gray Chevy Silverado was parked up the street from Young's house. Upon passing him, I made a U-turn, and pulled to the bumper of the truck, then dismounted, approaching the driver's window.

"Tell me something good," I said to the forty-two-year-old Caucasian agent, when he let the window down.

"He's home," Mason said, with a shrug. "Griffin's with him."

"Yeah, I'm quite sure she is," I said, reflecting on what The Queenz had done at Vincent Calhoun's establishment earlier. "Go on home to the wife and kids," I told the agent. "I'll see you in the morning."

"You can count on it."

Climbing back inside the Dodge, I watched the pick-up pull off, but I was thinking about how things would have played out, had I not given the agents on The Queenz detail the day off. The shooting would've been the most talked about event at the bureau which would've given me no choice but to go ahead and turn all my findings over to Hall, so she could expedite them to the DOJ, which would've pushed the Justice Department into pressing me to set an immediate takedown date for the women and their organization. My vibrating cell phone broke me from my thoughts.

I retrieved it from the cupholder. "I'm listening," I said, answering it.

"I'm calling in with the current location of Ricardo Willis," offered the female agent I had trailing Rico.

"Okay," I urged.

"He's at Gibson's residence again."

"He'll probably stay over," I said, almost to myself. "Go ahead and call it a night, Brantly. We'll reconvene tomorrow morning."

"Yes, sir."

I'd finally picked up on Rico last week, while stopping at a gas station to put a little more air in my tires. The place was so crowded, he didn't notice me, or my familiar BMW, as he pumped gas into the tank of a turquoise Chevy Monte Carlos on gold Datons, while boldly sporting his Drop Squad chain outside his buttoned-up coat. I ended up trailing him to some apartments out in East Atlanta, while getting a read on his license plate. Of course, the car was registered to his mother, Connie Willis.

A pair of headlights caught my attention, and I could tell it was a taxi-cab, before it pulled up to the gate of Young's house. I assumed Young was about to send Griffin on her way, until Blake Jones climbed from the back seat, and began waving his hands at the camera, as if he expected Young to be watching the monitor, instead of sexing with Griffin's fine ass. I grabbed my camera off the seat beside me and snapped a couple of shots of Jones just before the mechanical gate slid open.

Jones climbed back inside, and the cab driver drove on up to the house, where Young stepped out onto the porch, wearing a pair of pants and t-shirt. I snapped more shots as Jones dismounted and joined him. They spoke for a few seconds, before Young stepped back inside, returning minutes later with a handful of bills. He handed them to the awaiting cabby. Then, the two of them went inside.

Now, as I yawned, I was thinking about this impromptu visit from Blake Jones. I'd wager anything that Young was not expecting him. The fact that he arrived in a taxi, and not his own car, was enough for me to gather that something wasn't right. He would be a fool to murder Young and Griffin, when the cab driver could identify, and place him at the scene of the crime. Then again, he did murder Mario Ballard in front of Olivia Whitley before subsequently eliminating her at a much later time.

226

Another seventeen minutes had gone by, before there was any other movement. The door on the car garage, raised up. The gate was still open, so when the black Mercedes-Benz pulled out, it drove right through it, and moved toward the main road.

Of course, I was right behind them, leaving my lights off, until I reached McConnell Highway, where there was a good flow of traffic that provided me with sufficient cover to maintain a good distance behind the dark-tinted vehicle. However, it was a whole lot better, once we got onto the expressway, and seemed to be heading to Atlanta. That's when I was able to discern there were three occupants inside.

While trailing behind them, I mentally toyed with the notion that Ray Young could be LKS, though I still had no clue what it meant. However, he definitely fit the bill, because, since running surveillance on him, I couldn't help but think about what I'd heard about how this three-letter character moves. Nobody's ever seen him, but they're purchasing drugs from him, through his lieutenants, who I'd already pegged as Joseph Rhodes, and Michael Peterson the two guys he started the customs shops with when the other Kingz were still alive. Plus, Young hadn't been anywhere near any kind of drug transaction.

Yes, he definitely fit the bill!

Getting off on the McDaniel Glenn exit, I made sure to maintain a distance of about one hundred yards behind the Benz. Shortly, Young turned into the lot that provided parking for the Pretrial Detention Center, Garnett Transit Station, and the Greyhound bus station.

This is where I had to make a quick decision, because I was not trying to pull into that same exact lot, and I was definitely not trying to drive back and forth like some pervert, stalking an elementary school. My decision wasn't made, until I reached the street that had over a dozen signs, warning motorists that only Greyhound buses were allowed to pass through it.

Well, I made the illegal turn. As I passed the lot, I glanced over to see that Young was parking, which let me know he wasn't just dropping someone off. I passed three already docked buses, before coming out on Gwinnett Street, and making a right, plus another right, entering the sole parking lot of the Greyhound station.

Not wanting to miss a thing, I docked in the first available slot I saw, killed the engine, and dismounted, tugging at the bib of my ballcap. Moving in the direction of the operational part of the bus station, I pulled at my leather coat for the sake of the cold air, and to make sure the butt of my gun wasn't sticking out from my shoulder holster.

Just then, I saw Young and Jones moving amongst the vast crowd of people, alongside the buses. This is where I slowed my momentum, in order to see exactly what they were doing. I mean, I'm assuming Young was accompanying Jones, until he got on whatever bus he had a ticket for. But why is he getting on a bus? Why did he have Young drive him here instead of the taxi driver? Something wasn't right about this scenario.

At this time, Young stopped, and watched Young continue to the ticket booth, indicating that the fucker didn't have a ticket, and this was some *spur of the moment* shit. He's running from something, or someone. The first person that came to my mind was Miles Whitley. Perhaps, word had gotten around that Drop Squad was looking for Young's two henchmen, for the death of Olivia Whitley, and Young was trying to protect Jones. But what about Richard Nelson, Jones' partner in crime, has he already decamped?

Now, I kept my eyes on Young as I neared the schedule board. He seemed to be endeavoring to keep a watch over his friend, and Griffin who was still in the car. Shifting my gaze over to the ticket booths, I considered the distance between them, and where Young was standing, then pretty much moved on impulse, in Jones' direction, pulling my credentials from my pocket.

"Mr. Jones?" I spoke, flashing my badge, as I stood on the left side of him, keeping Young on the far right. "I'm from the Federal Bureau of Investigation. You can either come quietly, or we'll use force, and take your friend Ray Young with us. Trust me, we have the green light to use our firearms on you both if you resist."

I was expecting him to hit me with a barrage of questions, but he cast one last glance at his friend, then gave me a look that was a mixture of defeat and sleep deprived. Considering this, I took one step back, and gestured with my hand. Like an obedient hound, he stepped out of line, and began walking toward the lot I was parked in. I made sure to walk directly behind him, in an attempt to block Young from spotting the light-blue coat Jones was wearing. I noticed the dark stain on the right arm. *Blood, perhaps?*

"Sit up front!" I told Jones when we reached the Dodge Magnum. Once we were seated beside each other, I started the car, then looked over at him. "I see you were on your way out of town. Where to?"

He gave me a leery look but said nothing.

"There's a reason why you're not in handcuffs, yet," I resumed. "Especially when we already know about you and Richard Nelson murdering Mario Ballard and Olivia Whitley in that abandoned house on Grove Street, amongst other things. Where's Nelson, anyway?"

Jones furrowed his eyebrows. "Don't you already know?"

"If I knew, I wouldn't be asking."

"It was all over the news."

"Stop beating around the bush, Jones!" I demanded. "What was all over the news?"

"The accident," he answered, now directing his attention out his side window. "We were on our way to Nevada. It was me, my girlfriend, Rick, his girlfriend, and their two-year-old son. We weren't on the expressway for two minutes, when somebody pulled up beside us, and started shooting up the camper."

"Wait!" I said, knowing he was lying, because I heard nothing pertaining to this incident. "When did this happen?"

"Tonight," he confirmed. "I couldn't outrun the car, so I rammed it. The whole damn camper flipped over."

"You got hit in the arm," I assessed, figuring it was Drop Squad. Did anybody else survive?"

This time, he gave me a knowing look. I directed my attention over to the Greyhound station and saw Young retreating to his car. Surely, he assumed his friend had intentionally eluded him, and would probably put a hefty bounty on Jones' head.

"How far back does your friendship with Ray Young go?" I changed the subject.

"We're childhood friends."

"Would you testify against him?" When Jones didn't respond, I said, "All I need you to do is write a statement, saying that you'll testify against him in a court of law, if called upon to do so. Hell, if you want, I can make a call, and have you placed in a witness protection program, right now. You won't have to worry about Young, or whoever he may send looking for you. You also wouldn't have to worry about the authorities or Drop Squad coming after you for those murders on Grove Street. It's an easy, and smart decision to make."

Blake Jones directed his attention out the side window, again, biting on his bottom lip. While he was mentally debating if he should betray his childhood friend, a lightbulb came on inside my head. It was hit or miss, but I had to try.

"Another thing," I finally spoke gaining his attention. "Why does he call himself *LKS*?"

# Chapter 26

## *Two Weeks Later*

"My next client should be here at any minute now," Felicia Gibson a.k.a Duchess announced when she re-entered the bedroom, wearing nothing but the knee-high boots that she insisted keeping on while we had sex.

After weeks of monitoring Rico's movements, and breaking his appointments with Gibson down to a science, I without the knowledge of anyone at the bureau, made it my business to accost the dancer at Club Strokers one night. True to what she does outside of dancing, Gibson gave me her card, and insisted I call for an appointment. Well, tonight made our third *meeting*, and I still hadn't run into Rico, which is the objective I was trying to obtain. Honestly, I was also enjoying my sessions with Felicia's fine ass, being that the money was coming out of my own pockets.

Ever since the night I trailed Young to the Greyhound station, I'd concluded my surveillance on him. I actually didn't have much of a choice, because Director Hall started snatching agents right from under me, saying they were needed for other assignments, and furtively throwing hints that I was taking too long with my investigation. So, before she conducts any more deductions, and leaves me agentless, I plan on wrapping this thing up within the next three weeks. After this, everybody could kiss my ass, because I'm taking at least a month off.

Now, I was sitting on the edge of Gibson's bed, clad in my jeans and tennis shoes which is what I took my time putting on, while she was out of the room, disposing of the condom, and freshening up for her next client. I pretty much took that time to visually snoop around. I really didn't know what I was looking for. Getting off the bed, I grabbed my shirt off the floor, while she retrieved my coat off the coat rack, holding it in one hand, with the other poised on her hip. After I slipped on my shirt, she helped me into my coat, then donned her pink housecoat.

I don't know why, but I could not walk past her built-in-the-wall fish tank in the living room, without marveling at the various multicolored fish. By the time she opened the front door for me, I already had the five, one-hundred-dollar bills in my hand. This would make fifteen hundred dollars of my own money I'd spent on this high-priced prostitute.

"Thank you!" she said, receiving the bills. "I hope you enjoyed me and consider calling on my services again."

"Of course," was all I said, before stepping past her, and out the door.

As if it was timed, the moment I stepped onto the porch, the turquoise Chevy Monte Carlos, belonging to Rico pulled up in front of the house, parking behind the GMC Envoy I was driving. Maybe, three times really is a charm, because this piece of shit couldn't have picked a better time to cross my path.

I didn't just stand there. I descended the steps and traveled the short walkway toward the vehicles. Rico killed the engine but didn't budge. Of course, he was eyeing me, just as I was eyeing him. Unlocking the doors by remote, I walked between the vehicles, and approached the driver's door. Pulling it open, I looked back at my old friend, locking eyes with him. Back then, he'd regard me with all pleasantness, but right now, his expression was anything other than that.

Well, figuring I'd done my job of letting him know that I recognized him, I climbed in, started the car, and drove on, wondering what Felicia Gibson thought of our awkward exchange as she looked on from the threshold of her front door. Making it to the end of Burns Drive, I took this time to check both of my phones for messages. There were no messages, but a missed call from John Moody, the Decatur Chief of Police. Being that the call had come in seven minutes ago, I immediately called him back.

"I figured you were asleep," Moody asserted, answering.

"Did something come up?" I got straight to business, turning onto Sylvan Road, headed for the expressway.

"You bet your ass something came up!" The Chief got animated. "I'm in Roswell with Chief Williams. There's been another gang-related shooting, involving members of Drop Squad. This time, I think one of the head honchos got it. Some Williams person."

"Kenny Williams?" I asked, knowing damn well he was the only head member that resided in Roswell, Georgia.

"Yeah, that could be him," he answered. "It looks like—"

I cut him off. "Is the scene still active?"

"Like a damn electrical fly trap!"

"I'm on my way."

\*\*\*

There were so many emergency vehicles, I had to park about three hundred yards away from the actual crime scene and make my way to the hot zone on foot. After flashing my credentials to one of the officers, I was allowed beyond the barrier, where I immediately spotted five dead men lining the street, in front of Kenny Williams' home, all sporting Drop Squad chains.

I don't know who this gang had pissed off, but whoever it was, had been wiping them out by the numbers. Just a couple of weeks ago, there was a home invasion in Decatur, Georgia, where five of their members were found murdered. On the same night in East Point at another home two more of their men were liquidated. Of course, this was sure to spark a street war, once Drop Squad pinpointed their nemesis, or just decided to take it out on whoever they felt responsible. When this does happen, the locals will surely have their hands full.

"Bishop!"

I pulled my eyes away from the crime scene technicians, who were drawing a sketch of the corpses and multiple shell casings, to see Chief John Moody approaching from the driveway, clad in a brown trench coat, and matching Stetson.

"This way," he said, gesturing with his hand. "Your guy is over here."

As I followed, I cast one last glance at the white mid-size SUV parked at the curb, that was being dissected by forensics, then to the

black Porsche truck in the driveway, behind the white Chevy Cor-
vette that was also being examined. That's when I noticed a dark-
haired white woman, lying in a pool of blood on the right side of it
who I figured to be Williams' girlfriend, Reese Blanchard, though
I couldn't see her face, being that it was covered in blood. Before
we even reached the side of the house, my eyes were already taking
in the sight of a well-dressed Black man, lying face-down in the
grass with the back of his head blown out. The high intensity Klieg
lights made it very easy to see the blood and brain matter that splat-
tered all over the grass, and stained the white sidings of the house,
leaving that horrid smell of death lingering in the air.

This was, indeed, Kenny Williams.

## Chapter 27

"I don't really keep up with the news," Director Hall said, leaning back in her chair. "The only articles in the newspaper I'm interested in are the weather, and horoscopes. However, are you one hundred percent sure that one of the guys was the leader of Drop Squad?"

"*One* of the leaders," I rectified. "There's no doubt in my mind that the other two will soon suffer the same fate, which is why we should pull Agent Kent out."

"That's Agent Houser's case, right?" she asked. "I'll get with Swint about this first. If he shares your sentiment, we'll order Houser to pull Kent out. Now, about *your* investigation."

Damn! I knew this shit was coming.

"As of today," she began. "You have approximately one week to turn over your findings, or I'm terminating the entire investigation."

"Does this mean you'll stop kidnapping my agents until then?"

"Of course not," Hall replied, displaying a mischievous grin. "If I find myself needing agents for other assignments, I'll gladly deduct from your harvest. Please, shut my door back on your way out."

Hell, I saw no need to argue with her, so I did as I was told. Getting back to my cubicle, I took a seat and retrieved my accordion folder from my bottom drawer which contained all my findings for The Queenz investigation and even from The Kingz investigation. Being that the DOJ had already approved The Kingz investigation, years ago, all I had to do was prove that Ray Young, a.k.a King Ray was still alive and they'd be more than happy to grant me permission to move in on him, The Queenz and whoever else's name I drop onto their desks.

Considering this, and realizing I didn't need another week, I begin dissecting and organizing my findings, starting with Young which only took a little over forty minutes. My file on The Queenz is what took almost three hours in which I ended up taking two brakes from. Despite what Director Hall said about the shell casings and surveillance disc from Calhoun's establishment, I still mentioned the items, making sure to add the projectiles from the highway shooting, hoping the director would just skim over my draft, before submitting it to the Department of Justice. Hey! You can't get by if you don't try, right?

# Chapter 28

## *December 25, 2005*

"Don't let him fall, Mel!" I yelled out to Melody, who was teaching Brian Jr. how to ride his new bike with training wheels.

Well, it was finally Christmas Day, and I still had yet to hear anything from Director Hall, in reference to my recent investigation. It had also been surprisingly quiet, though every governmental agency in Georgia were bracing for an all-out street war to break out between Drop Squad and pretty much every other street gang in our region. So far, no new surveillance had been orchestrated on their behalf. Also, Hall and Flint had gotten up with Agent Houser, and he'd decided to leave Agent Kent undercover, but warned the Denver agent to watch himself, since he was still one of the bodyguards of Miles Whitley.

"Okay, guys," I said to my children, as they were making their way back to me, Brian laughing gleefully as he pedaled his bicycle without the help of his older sister, who was jogging behind, ready to catch him if she saw him about to fall, or crash into something. "It's time to head on in," I announced.

"Already?" Melody whined.

"Your mom told me to have you guys in by seven-thirty," I told her, looking at my watch. "It's seven thirty-five. She's gonna have a fit about those extra five minutes."

"Daddy, I can do it by myself," My two-year-old son said, stopping in front of me. "Can you take the other wheels off?"

"Not until you turn twenty," I told him, pulling him off the bike, and into my arms. "You won't be jumping over school buses on my watch."

Melody collected the small bike, and we entered the house, where Monique was still in the kitchen, cleaning up our mess from tonight's dinner. After sending the kids to their rooms to prepare for their baths, I went into the living room, where the stereo was playing one of our Christmas C.D.s at a low volume. I switched the track to our favorite song, *Silent Night* by *The Temptations*. Shedding my overcoat, I hung it on the coat rack, then entered the kitchen, where Monique was placing dishes inside the dishwasher. Sneaking up behind her, I wrapped my arms around her waist, pulling her close.

"I should hit you in the head with one of these plates," she said, indicating the items she held in each hand.

"Why?" I asked, planting a kiss on her nape.

"Because you brought the kids in seven minutes late."

Damn! She was actually timing me. "It wasn't my fault, babe," I offered, nibbling on the lobe of her left ear. "You know how children are. Especially on Christmas."

"Mm-hmm!" she expressed, bending over to place the plates into the washer. "How long do you plan on letting them stay up?"

"Until they're done with their baths," I replied. "Should I meet you under the Christmas tree then? I mean, that's where common folk like to unwrap their presents."

She turned to face me, still wrapped in my arms. "As long as you promise to unwrap me slowly and play with this toy like you've never played with it before."

"That's exactly what I intend to do," I told her, kissing her in the mouth.

"I can't believe we have seven more days," Monique asserted, her smile broadening by the second. "I'll finally be Mrs. Bishop."

"Then, you can parade around with a copy of our marriage agreement like it's some kind of bill of sale."

"You're starting to sound like Dorian," she said of my father, making a face.

"Um, let me go and check on the kids," I said, kissing her on the forehead, then making for the exit.

I don't know where that statement had come from, but I could tell it really struck a nerve with Monique. We were set to be wedded on the first of January, and me reminding her of my father, who's blatantly bitter toward the M-word, is one of the last thoughts she'd want floating around in her head right now. Yeah, I know we're not a match made in heaven, and that our marriage won't be all peaches and cream, but it's something we'll have to keep building on, in order to make it work.

Being that Monique had her hands full in the kitchen, I took it upon myself to help Brian Jr. with his bath, then tucked him in. As always, Melody took her precious time, so I returned to my bedroom to prepare my own bath. After placing my keys, and both phones on the nightstand, I moved over to the dresser for a fresh pair of boxer shorts, but before I could pull the drawer open, one of my phones began vibrating behind me. Crossing back over to the nightstand, I collected the device.

"I hope you called to wish me a Merry Christmas," I said, upon answering.

"Of course," Atlanta Chief of Police, Darrel Manning, replied. "I also have a gift for you. No, make that, two gifts."

"I'm listening."

"One of your Drop Squad friends was just found murdered," he went on. "Multiple gunshot wounds to the face and upper torso."

"Is that all?" I asked, feeling a bit relieved that it wasn't a multiple homicide. "What's the other gift? Did you finally get a suspect?"

"I guess you could say that," answered Manning. "He was murdered, right after committing the act of murder against the female whose yard he was found in. According to my investigators, he entered her home through the front door, fatally wounded the woman by use of a six-inch blade knife to the larynx, then fled out of the back door, where he was immediately gunned down by *God knows who.*"

Why did this shit sound familiar?

"The emergency operator received two calls on the incident," the Chief continued. "One from a neighbor, and the other from the female victim's six-year-old son."

"What's the location of this crime scene?" I finally asked.

"Burns Drive," he answered. "Right off Sylvan Road."

Oh Shit!

\*\*\*

Once again, I found myself moving along the dim-lit, quiet, and highly disinfected corridor of the morgue, in the bowels of the Grady Memorial Hospital building. Oh, you better believe I caught hell from Monique when I told her that I had to leave. To say she was mad would be an understatement. Hell, she'd even went as far as threatening that if I walked out the door, she and the kids would pack up and leave, never to return. Of course, I explained how important this case was, letting her know that I was almost at the end of this investigation. To be honest, I was actually looking forward to us sexing under the tree, all night, and waking up to Christmas tree ornaments sticking out of our asses, but like I told her, this was important.

Reaching Examination Room Seven, I pushed one of the double doors open, and entered as if I owned the place. Chief Manning said he wouldn't be able to meet me here, but the medical examiner, Mr. Alvin Wells was definitely present, though he wasn't alone. Seated across from him, at his steel desk, was a sandy-blonde-haired woman in purple scrubs, and a white lab coat, like the one he had on. They looked up from whatever card game they were playing, upon my rude intrusion.

"Manning told me you were on your way," the M.E. spoke, placing the cards he was holding, down on the desk, before standing, and shaking my hand. "Despite the circumstances, welcome back."

"Thanks for having me," I told him. "Did you—"

"Manning instructed me not to touch anything until you were done," Wells cut me off. "All I did was roll them into the intake cooler and lock it."

"Great!" I said, looking around. "I take it that the intake cooler is not in this room?"

The old man fixed me with a benign smile, "Of course not. Follow me!"

After letting his company know that he'd be back in a jiff, Wells led the way out into the corridor, and down to the next set of doors, where he pushed both doors open, and entered like a cowboy entering a saloon to see who he was going to challenge to a showdown at high noon.

This was my first time being in this room that boasted of what seemed like a gigantic cooler, with the largest padlock I may have ever seen in my life, as if the box contained gold bonds, instead of newly expired human bodies. As we neared it, I powered up my camera hanging about my neck, while the M.E. fumbled with the multiple keys on his ring. After removing the lock, he turned to me, not missing a beat to marvel at my camera again.

"I have a card game to get back to," he said, with a smile. "Take as long as you need."

"Thank you, sir!"

Giving only a slight nod, he disappeared through the double door, leaving me alone in this horror film-like setting. Ready to get this over with, I tugged at the release handle of the large, steel door, pulling it open. If the atmosphere wasn't enough to spook someone, then the creaking sound coming from the hinges as the door opened up, was sure to do the trick.

Just like a refrigerator, the extremely bright interior lights came on. To my surprise, there were only two gurneys sitting side by side, several feet from the entrance, each containing a black body bag with a corpse. The extremely cold air welcomed me as I entered, donning a pair of latex gloves. There were no labels on the bags, but I chose the one on my left, moving around to the left side of it.

Taking hold of its zipper, I began unzipping it, and was immediately hit by the odor of post death excreta, which was common, being that, upon death the muscles of the body involuntarily relaxes, causing the pent up bodily fluids to flow freely from its temple, hence the reason for the material of these bags.

Getting the zipper down to the thigh section of the corpse, I peeled it back, and instantly knew I was looking at the body of Ricardo Willis a.k.a Rico, even without regarding the Drop Squad chain around his neck. His face was partially disfigured from the barrage of bullets he'd taken to it.

Playa Ray

*Why do people feel they have to inject so many bullets into a person's skull?* I wondered, propping the Drop Squad medallion up on his chest, before taking pictures, then zipping the bag back up.

Moving over to the other bag, I didn't deem it necessary, or appropriate, to pull the zipper down to her thigh, so I stopped at the waist area. In spite of the foul body odor, even in death, Felicia Gibson was still a sight to behold. What tainted this image, was the knife wound in the right side of her neck that still seemed to gurgle blood. Her eyes were wide open, stuck in a state of shock, and she had on the same robe she was wearing the night I last visited her. Pulling her garment, to conceal her bare chest, I even took the initiative to make sure that her blonde, blood-stained extensions were a little more presentable, before snapping shots of her. Then, I stood there, staring at her, while trying to make some sense of the incident between the two.

The crime scene itself already proved that Rico had murdered Gibson, just before he was found dead in her yard, still in possession of the knife he used, but why? Why did he murder her? Could it have been hatred, fueled by him encountering me at her home that night? What about his own murder? For some reason, I feel like The Queenz had come across the passage in Erica's diary, where Rico's name appeared, and put two and two together. If this was the case, then could it be possible that these women are responsible for the deaths of Kenny Williams, and those other Drop Squad members?

The creaking sound of the cooler's door pulled me from my abstract musing. I looked over, and saw it slowly moving forward, as if it was about to close shut, but it stopped. Then, I saw a shadow flash along the far wall, at the opposite side of the room. I was exhausted, which could account for what I thought I saw, but there wasn't enough wind blowing throughout this building to move that heavy-ass steel door. Maybe, it was just a sign for me to get the hell up out of there.

## Chapter 29

"I haven't heard anything yet, Bishop," Director Hall offered, when I took it upon myself to enter her office, where she was seated behind her desk, looking over a newspaper that was spread out in front of her. "Hell, considering the volume of your submission, I wouldn't be surprised if it took half a year for them to respond."

"Very funny!" I was now standing in front of her desk. "So, what's your take on it?"

"On what?" she asked, looking up from her paper, agitation written over her face.

"My submission."

"It was like one of those boring-ass action films with an oblique storyline," Hall replied, then returned to her reading.

She didn't have to say it, but I'm almost certain she didn't view the whole brief before submitting it to the Department of Justice, which is good.

Now, it was time I changed the subject. "What kind of nonsense do they have in the paper this morning?" I ventured.

"Ms. Joseph brought this to me," the director answered, not looking up. "She was telling me about a woman being murdered last night, in a neighborhood she used to live in."

"Where?" I inquired, feeling I already knew the answer.

"Somewhere off Sylvan Road," answered Hall. "I think she knew the woman. They say something about the woman's murderer being found in her backyard, right after murdering her. They even mention Drop Squad."

Hearing this gave me an idea. "Well, I was just checking to see if you'd heard anything from the DOJ. If you need me, I'll be out in the field."

She looked up. "You wouldn't be secretly building a case on another organization, would you?"

I couldn't help but smile. "If I told you, it wouldn't be a secret, right?

I turned and exited the director's office, only stopping at my cubicle to grab my overcoat, then got onto the elevator, making sure to sign out one of the unmarked, before heading for the parking garage. While letting the engine warm up, I dialed Chief Manning's number on my cell, hoping he wasn't too busy to entertain my nosiness.

"Manning," the Chief's grumpy voice came through.

"Hello, old man!" I greeted. "Am I bothering you?"

"Yeah, you know you've always been a pest," he shot back. "What can I do for you, son?"

"In that double homicide case from last night," I began. "You said there were two calls placed to the emergency operator. Do you have intel on the neighbor?"

"I'll have to beat the information out of the responding knucklehead," he said. "Once I have it, I'll text it to your phone."

"Thanks, Manning!"

"Don't mention it."

I pulled the Ford out of the garage, and was en route to Sylvan Road, wondering about this perpetual feud between Drop Squad and The Queenz. Well, I don't have substantial proof that these women are the gang's primary nemesis, but I intend to find out, which is why I'm taking this drive now.

I was on the expressway, about ten minutes out from my destination, when I received Manning's text, which provided me with a full name, and address of the female who'd reported the shooting at Felicia Gibson's residence. Reaching Burns Drive, I saw that the address was to the house right next door to Gibson's. I docked the Crown Victoria in front of the home that had a blue Chevy Astro van in its driveway.

Killing the engine, I looked over at Gibson's house that was still a hot zone, whereas GBI, and local crime scene investigators were still all over the place like a colony of ants, making sure they left no stones unturned. Even in the daytime, the decoration of active Christmas lights seemed to exude a sense of happiness, but the yellow crime scene tape was like a storm cloud looming over a recreational park on Independence Day.

Exiting the car, I left my overcoat unfastened, so my windbreaker would be on display, as I approached the front door of the home, where I rang the doorbell.

"Who is it?" said a female's voice that I was hoping belonged to the woman I was here to see.

"Special Agent Bishop," I replied. "From the Federal Bureau of Investigation."

There were no sounds of any kind of locks being disengaged, before the door slowly opened up to a woman who looked to be in her late thirties, clad in blue jeans and a gray sweater, with a multi-colored scarf wrapped about her head.

"Are you, Ms. Regina Dorsey?" I asked, showing her my credentials.

"Yes, I am." There was a skeptical look on her face.

"I'm only doing a follow-up on what you told the responding officer pertaining to the incident that took place at your neighbor's residence last night," I assured, putting up my credentials, and brandishing my small notepad and pen. "If you don't mind, can you please run me through what you saw or heard?"

"Well," the woman said, folding her arms over her chest. "I was just getting out of the shower when I heard the first shots. They sounded so close, I went to my bedroom's window, to see if I could see where they were coming from. That's when I saw three people standing over some guy, with guns. They seemed to be talking to him, until one of 'em shot him in the face a bunch of times—" Pausing, she took a deep breath, and looked past me to the house in question. "The Police didn't tell me that Duchess was dead," the woman went on. "I just learned that by watching the news."

"Did you know her?" I inquired, pretending to jot something down.

"She was my neighbor," Ms. Dorsey offered matter-of-factly. "What about her son, Kevin? Who will take care of him?"

"That's up to the Department of Child Services," I told her. "I know it was dark out, but were you able to get a look at any of the suspects' faces?"

"No, I couldn't see their faces."

"What about gender?" I tried. "Could you tell if they were male, or female?"

"They were all female," she said with absolute certainty.

"Are you sure?"

"Of course." There was a hint of attitude in her voice. "Unless they were drag queens in wigs, which I seriously doubt. These were definitely women."

***

Upon leaving Sylvan Road, I journeyed out to Riverdale, Georgia, pondering this chaotic vortex that The Queenz were leaving in their wake. Some damn women! Hell, The Kingz had a nice size body count, but they were assisted by the Kingzmen. However, this small-ass band of women had probably already topped that record, which is why I felt like it was a must that I take them off the streets, immediately.

Turning onto Lawrence Street, I drove past the house belonging to Ebony Davis, and Theresa Joiner which is where Sheila Griffin and Shonda Watson had been staying ever since the day they went after Vincent Calhoun. There were no signs of the new conversion van they'd purchased, or Shonda Watson's Ford Mustang, which pretty much indicated that the women weren't there at this present time, being that neither one of them rode alone now.

Considering this, I decided to drive out to the house in Norcross. Neither one of their vehicles were present, but I did notice someone staked out in a blue Nissan Altima that was parked several houses up from the home. As I drove by, I gave the occupant what may appear a casual glance to him. Even with the ball cap pulled low over his eyes, I was able to identify him as Anthony Moody, a former Queenzman. I didn't know what happened between the women and their guards but that was beneath me right now. At that very moment, as I made a U-turn, and parked in front of another house, I was wondering why Moody would be staking out his ex-employers' residence. Well, I didn't plan on leaving this spot until I found out.

Leaving the engine running, I adjusted the heat, and took off my overcoat, being that I'd started to perspire. Just then, a sedan pulled into the driveway of the house I was parked in front of. I did my best to ignore the couple and their brood, as they all gawked at me like I was some kind of extraterrestrial. What drew my attention away from them was the vibration of one of my cell phones.

"Bishop," I answered, now seeing the yellow Mustang enter onto Palmer Street.

"Congratulations!" Director Hall's voice pierced my ear. "The fax just came through from the DOJ. You now have the green light to move in on The Queenz."

"Great!" I was now watching Shonda Watson enter her home.

"You don't sound so enthused," Hall pointed out.

"Oh, I am *very* enthused," I told her. "Thanks for the update, Director!"

Ending the call, I looked up to see Moody exiting the vehicle, and casually moving in the direction of Watson's house. Though he seemed normal to the naked eye, I noticed something disturbing about his posture, like he was driven by some kind of motive. Revenge, perhaps?

Reaching the front door, he placed one hand at his waist, and grabbed the doorknob with the other, experimentally turning it. Discovering it was unlocked, Moody looked around, before easing the door open, and entered. Right now, the bells in my head were going haywire, but why wasn't I making any effort to get my ass out of the car? Surely, something terrible was about to take place, and all I could do was sit there. I mean, what the hell—

*Pow!*

Oh shit! Despite how muffled the sound was, I'm no fool to think it was anything other than the report from a gun, and that it didn't come from Watson's house. I'm not gonna even share the mental picture I have in my head. However, I was expecting to see the ex-Queenzman fleeing from the place at any moment now. Then, there came the sound of multiple gunshots that suddenly sounded like an exchange of gunfire, before ceasing.

I waited, listening, looking around! I saw people coming out of their homes. After another minute or so, there was the sound of two more shots. Call me crazy, but I was entertaining the silly idea that these two actually met up here, just to shoot it out inside the house. Still, I was expecting to see Moody hauling ass back to the Nissan, but there was no movement.

"Fuck it!" I gumbled, killing the engine.

Grabbing only one of my cells, I dismounted, and quick-stepped to my destination, stuffing the phone into one of my pockets, then extracted my gun from its holster.

Reaching the front door that was ajar, I paused for a moment, to listen for any sound of movement. Hearing nothing, I used my foot to thrust the door open, aiming my gun in every direction of the empty living room. Entering, I was about to peer into the kitchen, when I spotted Moody's body lying motionless in front of one of the bedrooms. Stopping, I listened some more. Then, there was a thud sound, like something falling to the floor, which came from beyond the closed door of the bedroom Moody was lying in front of.

I made sure to do a quick survey of the other two empty bedrooms, as I approached the last one. Looking down at Moody's corpse, I saw that he'd sustained multiple gunshot wounds to the upper chest, and two to the skull. His handgun lay beside him. Though he was visibly deceased, I still kicked the weapon away from him, which is standard protocol.

Then, I studied the bedroom door that had been riddled with bullets, which gave me a clear understanding as to how this shootout went. Hearing no other movement beyond the door, I moved closer, and chose one of the many holes to peer through. I almost swore out loud, when I saw Shonda Watson sitting on the floor, with her back against the dresser, and her head drooping downward. The top of her coat was drenched in blood, though I couldn't tell where it was coming from. However, I was able to tell that she was also deceased.

Though I didn't have on any gloves, I still tried the knob that was locked. For some reason, I felt that I had to get inside the room, but breaching the door was out of the question. Hell, I was already contaminating a crime scene, although I was still legitimately investigating Watson. Then, I made for the kitchen, where I surprisingly found a butterknife in one of the drawers.

Making it back to the bedroom, I jimmied the door open, and entered, blindly stepping on Watson's handgun that was right at the entrance. The only furniture was the dresser. On the floor was a black trash bag with clothes in it, and Watson's purse with its contents dumped out. Moving closer, I looked down at her cellular, with its screen still bright, but my eyes shot over to her left hand that was covered in blood. That's when I saw the wound in her neck.

Hearing the sound of squeaky brakes out front, alerted me that the local authorities had shown up. I picked up Watson's cell phone and saw that she was on an outgoing call with *LKS*. How about that shit! Not wanting to be inside the bedroom when the cops came in, I stuffed the phone and knife into my pocket, and exited, pulling the door back up, making sure to lock it, and wipe the knob with the tail of my shirt. Then, holstering my gun, I pulled out my credentials, and stepped out of the front door, where two police officers were cautiously approaching with their weapons drawn. Seeing me, they stopped in their tracks, pointing their guns directly at me. I threw my right hand up, and slowly approached with my credentials in my left.

"FBI," I said, though I didn't have to. "I was just about to call you guys."

*** 

It only took about thirty-five minutes for me to fill out incident and statement forms, to exclude myself as a suspect in this new double homicide case that included a subject I just so happened to be investigating. This had me beyond angry, because I wanted to be the one to personally slap the restraints on Shonda Watson's wrists, and I actually wanted to talk a little shit to the four of them while taking them down. I guess I'll just have to make due with the remaining three Queenz and the last King standing.

Playa Ray

Suddenly, I was hit with deja vu. My mind automatically went back to the night the Kingz were murdered, which seemed like a premonition. Honestly, ever since that day, I'd reprimanded myself for not moving in on the organization earlier than the date I'd chosen. Surely, I would have gotten to them before their enemy had. I wasted time, which has me wondering if I was doing the same thing at this very moment.

Now, as I pushed the Crown Victoria along the highway, I emptied my pockets of the butterknife, and both cell phones. Tossing the knife and Watson's phone onto the passenger seat, I logged in the number to the James P. Russell building, making sure to use the correct extension.

"Director Hall," my superior announced.

"It's Bishop," I said. "Hear me out."

"Aww, do I have to?" she whined, clearly mimicking one of her children.

"Watson was just murdered."

"Watson—who!" Hall immediately became serious.

"Queen Shonda," I told her. "By one of their ex-guards."

"You're joking, right?"

"I really don't have a plan of action at this moment," I went on, disregarding her question. "However, I do wanna move on the other three as soon as possible. I'm talking about within the next two or three days."

"Have you been drinking?" the director posed. "Don't you know how much of an impossible task that is?"

"It won't be too impossible," I contended. "Normally, the women shack up at the same house."

"Normally?"

"Well, Griffin is the one exception. She periodically sleeps over at Young's place. We can storm the girls' home on a late-night extraction mission."

"Negative!" Hall blurted out. "We're the FBI—not the damn U.S. Special Forces!"

The Director just flat-out hung up on me, pretty much letting me know that she wasn't authorizing anything irrational, even if she's the only one who thought it was irrational. I was about to toss my phone onto the seat, when it vibrated, indicating an in-coming call.

"Bishop."

"It's Barnes," the Riverdale Chief of Police announced. "I just received word from Alpharetta that another Drop Squad member was just gunned down at the Royal Suite Hotel. A Philip Lakes, I think."

*"Lakes?"* I questioned, knowing damn well he was right, considering the hotel was owned by the guy, and was, indeed, in Alpharetta, Georgia.

"Yeah, that's his name. Hell, I was out on an errand, so I'm on my way to the scene."

"So am I."

Tossing my phone, I activated the emergency lights and siren, and punched the gas pedal to the floor, while thinking of all the deaths I've witnessed throughout this year, which is probably more than I've witnessed in my entire career. Today seems to be taking the cake as the most I've witnessed in one day, although I was still finding it hard to believe that somebody had actually caught Lakes slipping like that. Then again, if a motherfucker can assassinate John Fitzgerald Kennedy, the thirty-fifth president of the United States, then it's highly possible to wipe out some street punk, who'd made himself a head member over a bunch of other street punks.

Despite the large array of streetlamps, the red and blue lights of what seemed like every emergency vehicle in the world, lit the night sky up like fireworks on the Fourth of July. I found a spot, parked, and lunged from my car, moving with a purpose, flashing my credentials to every government worker I encountered, until I reached the front of the building, where pictures were still being taken of Philip Lakes' body that was lying on its back, directly in front of the entrance, which put me in the mind of how I found Anthony Moody, just over an hour ago.

Careful not to step on the numbered indicators that pinpointed the abundance of shell casings, I moved closer, until I was able to identify Lakes, lying in a puddle of his own blood, staring up at nothing.

"You must be Special Agent Bishop?"

I looked up to see a GBI agent standing before me, holding a camera in his hand. "I am," I answered.

"I was told to escort you to the manager's office," he told me. "As you can see, the front entrance is off limits until further notice, so we'll have to use the side door."

"Okay."

As he led the way to the side of the building, I wondered if Chief Richard Barns was already here, and if he and Alpharetta Chief of Police, Elaine Smith, were awaiting me.

"Is the building on lockdown?" I asked my escort.

"Yes, sir," he answered. "I think they're viewing the surveillance footage to see if the suspect, or suspects, are still in the vicinity."

Reaching the side door, he did some special knock, and the steel door was pushed open. I followed him into the stairwell enclosure that was guarded by three, heavily armed GBI agents. He only nodded at his comrades, before leading me out onto the first floor that was pretty much deserted with the exception of a handful of employees who were huddled in two groups. Of course, talking about what transpired tonight with the owner of the place.

"We've asked everyone to remain in their rooms until we get things sorted out." the agent offered, as if he knew I was going to question the emptiness of the establishment. "Here we are."

The manager's office was just beyond the front desk. My escort rapped on the door twice, then opened it up for me. I thanked him, then entered to see Chief Richard Barns, Chief Elaine Smith, the GBI director, whose name I'm not familiar with, and two GBI Task Force agents. The woman sitting at the desk, clad in the hotel uniform, I assumed to be the manager. They were all gawking at the array of monitors, while the manager controlled the reels from her computer.

"Well, hello, Mr. Bishop!" Elaine Smith beamed at me as I entered.

The fifty-eight-year old, dark-skinned woman, was cloaked in a long, black leather trench coat with her predominantly gray hair neatly cut into a bob.

"Hello, Ms. Smith," I returned her greeting, crossing over to shake one of her gloved hands, before shaking Barn's.

"How's everything going at the Bureau?" The older woman inquired. "Is Director Hopkins still giving you a hard time?"

"Hopkins was transferred a couple of years ago," I answered, directing my attention to the monitors. "Have you all discovered anything yet?"

"Rewind it back a bit, Ms. Foskey," Chief Smith said to the manager, who did as she was told. "Right there. Run it from there."

Considering where Lakes was found, my eyes searched the monitors, until I found the one of the parking lot and front entrance. Just then, I saw Lakes exiting the building. Almost instantly, I saw a man in a ball cap, step from the front-passenger side of some dark SUV and move toward the building with his head slightly down, cutting through other parked vehicles.

Suddenly, there was a flash of lights from a car the man was passing. When he turned his head in that direction, Lakes did a quick spin, and was headed back toward the entrance of the building, indicating that he'd recognized this person, who was clearly a threat, which is why he distracted the guy by deactivating his car alarm. I always knew he was a clever son of a bitch!

Then, the unidentified subject quickened his steps to catch up with Lakes, while pulling a handgun from the back of his pants. At that same moment, Lakes spun back around, with one hand out. I didn't see the gun, until sparks spat from the barrel of it, causing his pursuer to take shelter behind a car.

Letting up off the trigger, Lakes turned, and broke into a run towards the entrance. For a brief second, it looked like he was going to make it, until the other guy came from behind the car, secured a proper aim, and fired a salvo of rounds into Lake's back. It seemed animated how his body just slammed right into the glass doors, shattering them, then fell backwards to the ground. The culprit climbed back into the SUV, and its driver cruised off as if nothing happened.

I turned to the manager. "How long was Mr. Lakes inside the building?" I asked her.

"I had no idea he was even inside the building," she answered, with a shrug.

"The footage shows him exiting the front entrance."

"I saw that, sir," she offered. "But he doesn't always stop by the office. He didn't stop by the office tonight."

"What are you getting at, Bishop?" Smith butted in, coming to the other woman's rescue.

"I know I'm just a visitor," I made sure to point out. "However, I still share the same interest as the rest of you, which is to find out who this gunman is."

The Chief folded her arms over her chest. "So, what are you proposing?"

"That the manager run the footage back to the point where Lakes first pulled into the lot," I told her. "From there, we'll be able to see if this SUV followed him here, and which way it came from, in order to know which traffic light cameras to use to identify its occupants."

"Impressive!" The older woman's expression matched her tone. After a moment of pensiveness, she looked over at the hotel's manager. "Go ahead and run it back, Ms. Foskey."

The manager did as she was instructed. I watched the shootout in reverse. When Lakes backed into the building, I looked over to the monitor that had a better view of where the truck was parked, until it backed out of the lot. Shifting my gaze back to the entrance, I expected Lakes to come right back out, but he didn't. The place was a buzz like a hotel in Las Vegas, but I still foolishly searched other monitors to see if I could spot him amongst the interior crowd, to no avail.

Suddenly, he came back into view on the exterior monitors. I don't know why I was surprised to see he'd shown up with one of his *girl toys*, but I was very surprised. Maybe, it was because I first saw him leaving alone, right before encountering the gunman in the parking lot, prior to the shooting, as if he'd left her inside, and went out to grab something from his car.

"Play it from right there," I told the manager.

She stopped the footage, and resumed play, right where Lakes was backing his gray Aston Martin into a slot. When the doors opened, I was all over his female acquaintance the whole time. Thanks to the brightness of the lamps, it wasn't hard for me to identify her, which made me want to kick myself in the ass. I couldn't believe I'd totally forgotten about the fling Lakes has with Ebony Davis. Hell, considering what's been going on with the Queenz and Drop Squad, one would automatically assume these two were long done, but apparently not.

Well, I guess this made it easier for Davis to lure Lakes here, where it would be a piece of cake for Ray Young to catch him in a vulnerable state, knowing he wouldn't have a security detail trailing him. Yes, I've already deduced it was Young. There are certain things you won't forget about certain people, and I'll never forget his build or the way he walks.

"Did anyone notice this before?" I asked, watching Lakes and Davis near the hotel's entrance.

"I don't even think we went that far back," Chief Barns admitted.

"We definitely didn't go this far back," Chief Smith offered, a hint of disappointment in her voice. She looked over at the manager. "Did he take her to his personal suite?"

There was a puzzled look on the woman's face. "I have no idea," she answered.

"Well, find out!"

Ms. Foskey began tapping on her keys, changing the images on the monitors. On one particular monitor, she tracked the movement of the two, switching views as they moved about the building. We watched them enter the establishment, and walk right past the front desk, unnoticed by the desk clerks, and the crowd of people moving about. It seemed like an elevator was already waiting. As soon as they entered the shaft, the monitor switched to its camera view, whereas we could clearly see the faces of the seven passengers, as they all regarded the floor indicator above them.

"They're getting off on the fourth," the manager informed, when Lakes, Davis, and another female exited the shaft.

"Where's the suite?" I inquired.

"Eleventh floor," answered Ms. Foskey. "Third monitor."

I shifted my gaze to the third monitor, and only saw the image of a door to a hotel room. No action there. Reverting my attention back to the one we were all engrossed in, I saw Lakes and Davis enter a room, then turned to the manager.

"What number would that be?" I asked her.

"Twenty-seven," she answered.

"Does he have, like a master key to every room?"

"I doubt it. He usually doesn't use any room other than his personal suite. However, I could check with one of the clerks to see if he'd checked into that one."

"Smith," the Alpharetta Chief said into her cellular. "At least until the coroners have secured the body." Concluding her call, she said, "The news jerks are here, and Lord knows I'm not in the mood to be interviewed!"

"Here's Lakes," I said, upon seeing him leave the hotel room, alone.

Getting to the elevator, instead of pressing the service button, he pulled out his cell phone, dialed a series of numbers, and put it up to his ear. The call didn't last but a few seconds, whereas he said something, then slid the device back into his pocket, before ringing for the elevator.

"Maintain eyes on the room" I instructed, curious about the call Lakes made.

Almost five minutes had went by, when Lakes appeared on the third monitor, which indicated that he'd taken a trip up to the eleventh floor, to his suite. When he entered, there was another fifteen minutes before we saw any movement worth noting.

Two men in ball caps approached room twenty-seven. I don't know if the others noticed, but the first guy just pushed the door open, as if it was already ajar. They entered, closing the door behind them. Roughly seven minutes later, they exited the room, headed for the elevators.

"Keep those two in sight, Ms. Foskey!" I said, once they'd stepped onto one of the shafts.

"Yes, sir!"

The manager used the fourth monitor for this purpose, tracking them all the way out to the parking lot, where they climbed into a white pick-up and made off. Shortly afterwards, Lakes exited his room, got onto the elevator, and got off on the ground floor, on his way to his final destination.

I turned to the manager. "I need to get into room twenty-seven."

"I can have one of the housekeepers let you in," she told me.

"Great!" I turned to the GBI director. "May I borrow these two guys for a few?" I asked, indicating the two Task Force members.

"By all means," he answered, with a nod.

"If you're planning to arrest this woman," Chief Smith began. "Maybe you should take someone from *my* department."

"That won't be necessary," I told her, realizing she was unaware of what may have transpired inside that room. "I just wanna take a look around."

The manager stepped out of the office, and instructed one of the housekeepers standing around, to assist me with accessing room twenty-seven. So, with her, and the GBI agents in tow, we climbed onto an elevator, just as my phone vibrated in my pocket.

"Talk to me!" I answered.

"I heard about the double homicide in Norcross," Decatur Chief John Moody asserted. "I also heard you were the first on the scene. One of yours?"

"Yeah," I answered, now thinking about how I found the bodies of Shonda Watson and Anthony Moody.

"Well, there was another one similar to that one, in Gwinnett County, at the Glamor Girlz beauty salon. Male and female."

"Do you have an identification on the subjects?" I asked, as the elevator reached the fourth floor, remembering that the Queenz owned the aforementioned salon.

"I have an identification on the female," Moody replied. "A Theresa Joiner of Dallas, Texas."

"And, how sure are you of that?"

"One hundred and twelve percent, Bishop."

Shit! I couldn't believe how fast karma had come back and bit these women in their asses. All on the same fucking day! How is it that I'm having the same luck with the Queenz, that I had with the Kingz? Perhaps, I should take this as a sign to find myself another profession. A security job, or something.

"We'll have to discuss this some other time, Moody," I told the Chief, as we approached room twenty-seven. "In the meantime, see if you can get an I.D. on the male subject."

Stuffing my phone back into my pocket, I nodded to the house-keeper, who seemed to be awaiting further instructions, with a worried look on her face. After accessing the door with her keycard, she quickly moved out of the way, assuming we weren't in any immediate danger, I left my gun in its holster, as I pushed the door open, and entered the room that was extremely clean, except for the wet impressions of shoeprints in the carpet, that led from the bathroom.

Taking only a mere glance at the GBI agents, who were standing just inside the threshold, I crossed over to the bathroom, intentionally avoiding the prints. The door was standing wide open stopping in the threshold, I'm not even going to act like I was surprised to see Ebony Davis, a.k.a. Queen Ebony, lying dead inside the bathtub, with her private parts visibly on display through the water that looked like it once contained some kind of solution.

I saw her purse on the floor, closer to the sink, as if it was jostled during a struggle. I could see the barrel of a handgun sticking from its opening. Well, there goes another investigation up in flames. The next person I'm expecting to get a call about, is Sheila Griffin. Then, I'll have to concentrate all of my effort into apprehending Ray Young. Hell, I may just kill him myself, since he's supposed to be dead already.

## Chapter 30

### *January 1, 2006*

"I now pronounce you husband and wife," the Reverend announced. "You may now kiss the bride."

It seemed like it took forever for the old man to get to that part. I know it's my wedding day, and I was more than happy to take Monique as my lawfully wedded wife, but I was ready to get this over with. I mean, I tried not to show it as I turned to her and saw tears of joy cascading down her cheeks, making me feel a tinge of selfish guilt. Monique had been waiting her whole life for this moment that will remain a special part of her life forever, and my selfish ass was hoping to get it over with as soon as possible.

As the Reverend insisted, I wrapped my arms around my woman's waist, and kissed her like I've never kissed her before. Everybody in attendance cheered and applauded. After breaking the kiss, I looked into Monique's eyes, while using my thumbs to wipe her tears that never seemed to stop. She was happy, and so was I.

"Are you ready, Mrs. Bishop?" I asked.

All she could do was nod. I grabbed her hand, and we made our way down the aisle of the church, accepting congratulations from our friends and family members in attendance, who all followed us outside, where our decorated limousine awaited. Of course, I stood by while she tossed her bouquet of flowers over her shoulder and was surprised to see that they were unintentionally caught by Director Amy Hall, who was clad in a beige, three-piece pants suit. The baffled look on her face was definitely something to remember. After waving at everyone, the driver let us into the limousine.

"We finally did it!" Monique expressed, squeezing one of my hands.

"Yes, we did." I couldn't help but smile at how happy she was. "You look wonderful!"

"Thank you, baby!" She blushed. "You know we can't stay at the reception too long."

"We've already been over that," I said, as the car pulled away from the curb. "Everybody else knows this, also. We'll make a toast, cut the cake, dance, then be on our way to South Beach."

"Our first time on a yacht," she acknowledged, dreamily. "One day, we'll have to set up another cruise, and take the children with us."

"That would be nice," I told her. "First, we'll have to hit the lottery."

***

"Last, but not least," I said, turning to Monique, who was standing beside me, clad in a white skirt she'd doffed her wedding dress for. "I wanna toast to my lovely wife, whose been a handful, but a great force behind me for many years. May she continue being the woman I need her to be, for many more years to come."

I lifted my wine glass to finalize the toast, prompting everyone else to do the same. As orchestrated, the D.J. put on *Luther Vandross Here and Now* and everybody made room for Monique and I to make our debut on the dance floor of the small club. While we embraced each other in this intimate moment. I couldn't help but intermittently glance over at Amy Hall, who was watching us like the others, though her eyes seemed to hold some kind of ancient secret.

Right at the conclusion of our song, *Usher's Yeah* came pumping through the speakers, and the floor instantly became packed. As if switching dance partners, Monique and I separated, though I did not intend to dance with anyone else right now. I danced through the crowd, until I made it to the table, where my father was seated with Carmen.

"Get out on the floor, old man!" I told my father. "I wanna see you do the wheelchair bounce."

"How about I bounce this wheelchair upside your head?" he replied, smiling. Then, he held his hand out. "Congratulations, my son!"

"Thanks, Pops!" I responded, shaking his hand. "Just make sure I'm the best man, when you two decide to tie the knot."

Leaving those two blushing like high schoolers, I made it over to the beverage table, where I scooped up two, already-filled wine glasses, then circled the dancing crowd to where Hall was standing alone.

"The invite said you could bring a wedding date," I said, handing her one of the glasses.

"Oh, I've never been too fond of bringing sand to a beach," she said, smiling. "Besides, don't worry about me. This is your wedding day. You should be having a blast. We'll talk work when you get back from your honeymoon."

"What makes you think I came over here to talk work?"

She took a sip of her wine then leered at me. "Because I know you. You're the most tenacious and dedicated agent I've ever known. You eat, sleep and breathe this profession. *That* is how I know you came over here to talk work."

"I guess I'm guilty as charged," I admitted. "So, when do you think we'll hear something?"

Hall took another sip of her drink, and seemed to hesitate a little, while glancing around the room. "I got a call from Washington yesterday," she finally announced.

"On a Saturday?"

"We have the same office hours," Hall went on, with a shrug. "They're doing a recalculation of the case."

"Why would they be doing a recalculation?" I inquired into something I've never heard of. "That doesn't even—"

"Bishop!" She cut me off. "With the exception of one, every subject they gave you the green light to take down, are dead."

"Make that two," I rectified. "Ray Young is also still alive."

"Whatever," The Director said, waving a dismissive hand. "The point is, they wanna make sure the charges brought against the remaining subjects are exact."

"That's usually left up to the courts to decide."

"Who knows? Maybe, they're trying to protect the bureau from civil ramifications. They also want you to resubmit your brief, but in reference to the remaining subjects, and existing affiliates."

# Chapter 31

## *February*

As of today, it's been almost six weeks since I resubmitted amore edited brief, in reference to Sheila Griffin, and Ray Young, to Director Hall, and I still haven't heard a thing.

After reaching a crescendo in the middle of January, the crime rate had slowly dwindled to its sporadic, *run of the mill* bad acts, though the enforced curfew was still active through Georgia. Ever since coming back from my week-long honeymoon, I've pretty much been doing a lot of paperwork, including the documents re-submitted to the DOJ. However, being that I'm still the lead investigator of this recent case, I'd periodically spy on Ray Young and Sheila Griffin, who'd both pretty much been cooped up in Young's home in Canton, Georgia. From the looks of Griffin's stomach, I could tell that she's now with child, and Young must've dismissed his lieutenants because he now rides solo or with Griffin in tow. Plus, I haven't heard a word about the notorious *LKS*.

It was a little after 4:00 p.m. when I left the barbershop. Being that I had nothing to do and no more agents to boss around, I decided to drive out to Canton, Georgia and watch Young's home for a bit. I know the Crown Victoria stuck out like a sore thumb, but from where I always parked, I didn't expect him to notice it. At the same time, I didn't give a damn if Young did spot me. His ass was toast, and his little girlfriend was going down with him.

After a couple of hours of boredom, I felt it was time to stretch, and relieve myself. Considering the distances between the houses on this particular street, I could pretty much hear a vehicle approaching, before seeing it. So, upon dismounting, I immediately began relieving myself in the grass.

Hurriedly fastening my pants, before the cold air could damage my precious jewels, I went into stretching my limbs, while looking around. That's when I noticed one of my phones lighting up on the front passenger seat. Thankful for some kind of action, I didn't hesitate to get my ass back into the car and answer it.

"Bishop," I announced.

"I'm in the basement," Chad Hoffman said, sounding like he'd been running. "Young just received a call. You need to hear this!"

Recorder:

*Young: "I hope you have a good explanation for all this."*

*Man: "Of course, she does."*

*Young: "Who the fuck is this?"*

*Man: "You might wanna calm down a little. I have someone I assume you care about. No, make that two, because she's with child. You may want to think about that. In fact—"*

*Young: "How much?"*

*Man: This is not about money, King Ray. This is far bigger than money. I thought my mission was complete when I was told the Kingz were dead. Then, two years later, I find out that one survived. That pissed me the fuck off! And trust me, pissing me off should be the last thing anybody wants to do."*

*Young: "I see. Since it's not about money. What do you want?"*

*Man: "I thought you were the smartest King in the deck. But since I was wrong, I'll break it down for you. Considering the baby is not born, I'll refer to your pretty little girlfriend as one. What I want is an even swap. Your life for hers. King for a Queen. You show up, I'll let her go."*

*Young: "And I'm supposed to believe you'll let her go when I show up?"*

*Man: "No, you shouldn't believe that. I'll admit that I'm known to play dirty, but tonight, since it's you, I'll keep my word. If anything happens to her after tonight, it won't be by me, nor the hands of my men. That's my word."*

*Young: "How do I know she's still alive?"*

Seconds later.

*Griffin: "Don't do it, Ray!"*

*Young: "When and where?"*

*Man: "There's an old Sears warehouse."*

*Young: "I know where it is."*

*Man: "Good! I'll see you at twenty-one-hundred-hours. Drive around to the back. If you're more than five minutes late— well, let's just hope you're not more than five minutes late."*

*Click!*

Holy shit! Had I not heard the conversation for myself, there wasn't enough money on this side of the planet that would make me believe this exchange actually took place. From what I gathered, the man responsible for the deaths of the Kingz over two years ago, had kidnapped Sheila and wanted Ray to trade his life for hers, in which he readily agreed. This would definitely be one of my favorite stories to tell the guys at whatever assisted living facility I'll be confined to, in years to come.

"When did this call come in?" I asked Hoffman.

"About four minutes ago," he answered. "I came down to see if the tape needed to be changed, before heading home, just as the call came in. I listened to the whole conversation, before immediately calling you."

"I have to act on this, somehow," I said, almost to myself.

"Did you hear about Agent Kent?" Hoffman inquired of the agent loaned to us from Colorado, who'd infiltrated Drop Squad.

"What about him?" I asked.

"He was one of the casualties in last night's shooting."

"What shooting?" I was now thinking about Miles Whitley, the remaining head of Drop Squad, who Kent was a personal bodyguard to.

"It happened at the Twin Lanes bowling alley, owned by Miles Whitley. Whitely, and other members of Drop Squad, were pronounced dead on the scene."

"I told Hall they should pull him out," I said, staring at my watch. "In fact, I'm about to call the director, right now. Let me know if anything changes."

"Okay."

Concluding that call, I dialed Director Hall's cell phone number, then put the Ford into gear, and pulled off.

"Hall," The director announced.

"I heard about Kent," I made sure to start with.

"Yeah," she replied with a sigh, "We're making arrangements to have his body flown back to Denver once the ME's finished with it. "I hope you didn't call to rub it in."

"Not at all," I said, though I really wanted to. "I have a much more delicate issue on my hands. In fact, I need an emergency extraction team assembled, like yesterday!"

"Excuse you!" my superior exclaimed. "Bishop, we've already been through this. How many times do I—"

"This is a matter of life and death, Director!" I cut her off, then explained the reason for my request.

"Are you serious?" she asked once I was done.

"I hope that's a rhetorical question," I replied.

"I think we should, at least, get the GBI involved."

"Ray Young belongs to the FBI," I pointed out, not willing to let my subject fall into the hands of any other governmental agency.

"Well, let me see what agents I can rustle up for you," she finally gave in." This means I'll have to leave the comforts of my bed, to find my Rolodex and rouse other agents from the comforts of their homes."

"You'll be saving lives, Director."

"Yeah, whatever."

\*\*\*

"Delta Unit, I'll need you moving from your positions like the speed of sound, when I call the scene to action," I said to the four agents that made up the Delta company.

I was surprised to see seven tactical-dressed agents waiting for me in the parking garage of the James P. Russell building, when I arrived. It took me a good twenty minutes to enter the building, suit up, and make it back down to them. I was even more surprised to see that nine more agents had made it. Chad Hoffman ended up staying late, making sure that our communication implements, and other items, were ready for use, which were loaded up in the three SUVs we'll be piling into.

"Echo Unit," I went on. "You all are to remain out of sight. Keep the vehicles hidden, until further notified. As I said before, there is no telling how many hostels we'll encounter at this rendezvous but all weapons are free. The thing is to come out alive and try not to harm the hostages. Now, I hope there are no questions because we don't have time for any. Let's mount up and roll out!"

With the sirens was blaring, and the emergency lights illuminating the dark expressway, we made it to the abandoned Sears warehouse, with under twenty minutes to set up. Once we climbed from the vehicles, the three drivers made off, to take up positions further up the road. There was no kind of lighting in this area, so we all had to immediately activate our night-vision goggles, in order to see what we were doing, while setting up for this impromptu extraction.

We got the three snipers set up on the roof, with their rifles and spotlights, before the rest of us entered the windowless building, and improvised, with me giving out last-minute instructions. At thirteen minutes until nine, I did a communications check, then we all settled in.

"You have a dark vehicle approaching," One of the snipers announced over the wire, at ten minutes till nine. "Mercedes-Benz. One occupant."

"Copy that," I responded, already figuring it to be Young, who was making sure to not test the abductor, and his five-minute-late rule.

We'd left the side door, and the doors to the loading docks open, but stayed clear of their entrances especially being that we didn't know exactly where the subjects were going to park. Momentarily, Young's Mercedes rounded the building, it's high beams activated for the sake of the darkness, which also caused a distortion to our goggles, being that they were impaired by any fraction of illumination.

I deactivated, and lifted the goggles from my face, as Young brought his car to a halt, just beyond the door I was positioned on the side of. Thankful that he parked horizontally to the building, whereas his beams weren't aimed in our direction, I cast a furtive glance out at Young's car, but could only see traces of his silhouette through the dark windows, which was produced by the luminous digital display of the vehicle's dashboard. He seemed to just be sitting there waiting.

"You have three SUVs seventy-six," came from the same sniper, almost ten minutes later, which made it approximately nine p.m. on my watch.

"Roger that," I responded over the line. "All units in position!"

I nodded to the agent across from me, on the other side of the door, who was kneeled down over the *Sonik Wave* recorder. After sliding the headphones over his ears, he powered it up. Seconds later, probably after picking up the barely audible sound of Young's engine, he gave me the thumbs up, letting me know that the device was fully active. This was to record whatever final exchange they'll have, prior to whatever outcome the abductor had in mind for his guests, even though our body cams will document the scene once it's active.

Just then, three black H-2 Hummers, rounded the building in tandem, circling the Benz, before parking across from it. Young didn't waste time climbing from his car and standing in front of it. Also, ready to do business four, military-dressed figures, emerged from the first truck, carrying Ak-47s, with the same amount climbing from the third one in the same fashion. From the middle SUV, emerged three more figures, but only two of them resembled the others, whereas the third one was clad in a long trench coat.

It didn't take but a few seconds for me to recognize this piece of shit. Had I not notified the locals that day, this fucker would most likely be dead. The Kingz definitely did a number on him and his military goons in that secluded area of Lithonia, Georgia, over two years ago, but they made a critical mistake by not making sure he was dead, which cost them their own lives. Hell, maybe I played a big part in that also.

"I didn't think you would show," Franco said to Young, as he and his men stood before him with no sign of Griffin.

"Fuck the small talk!" Young retorted. "Where is she?"

"Oh, I'm sorry!" he said, making some gesture with his hand.

At that moment, the rear door of the second Hummer opened and out stepped another goon, who had Griffin by the back of her coat, pushing her forward.

"Team," I said through the com-set," we have approximately twelve hostels and zero-two neutrals. Stand by for extraction."

"You can let her go now, Grip," Young said to Griffin's handler.

Upon hearing the name, I studied the guy's face, and wasn't at all surprised to see that it was none other than Maurice Griffin, an ex-Kingzman. Especially after the highway shooting that claimed the lives of Cecil Henderson, and Jesse Bridges, two former Kingzmen. Plus, the one that was murdered by Theresa Joiner while in the process of murdering her, at the Glamour Girlz salon. Hell, it didn't take a scientist to explain that these guys had went rogue or was working for someone else.

Now, Maurice Griffin looked to Franco for further instructions. Franco nodded, and the ex-Kingzman released Sheila who rushed over to Young and wrapped her arms around him. I couldn't hear what the two were saying but it appeared that Griffin was refusing to leave him. Young escorted her to the driver's side of his car, opening the door for her, as Franco and his men looked on.

"Get your ass in the car, Griffin!" I muttered, keeping a wary eye on Franco, ready to call my team to action if he made any kind of weird gesture.

Griffin accepted a brief kiss on the lips, before climbing into the car, and driving away. Young turned to face the awaiting mob ready to accept his fate.

"We have zero-one neutral eighty-eighty," I said over the wire. "Twelve hostels, and zero-one neutral remains. Stand by."

"That was quite touching," Franco now said. "If it was me, my wife would be one dead bitch. Child or no child. And let me make one thing clear for you—I hired the Kingzmen after the death of your comrades. They had nothing to do with that. I know what you're thinking, right now. Let me clear that up for you, also."

He made some gesture with his hand, and guns erupted amongst his men, before three of them fell to the ground. I immediately recognized Griffin as one of them.

"All units, stay frosty!" I said through the set for the agents that heard the shots but couldn't see the scene. "It was hostile on hostile. We are now zero-nine hostels, and zero-one neutral. Stand by."

"The hit came from the Kingz," Franco continued. "But the Kingzmen were the ones who pulled the trigger. Had I not had this metal plate in my head, I wouldn't be here today, huh?" He pulled out a chrome revolver, aiming it at Young. "Any last words?"

Shit! I pressed the talk button on my com-set. "Team, prepare to breach in three—two—"

"What made you go after the Queenz?" Young questioned Franco. "They haven't done anything to you."

"Bravo to Commander," came over the line. "Could you ten-nine that last command?"

"Ten twenty-two that last command," I responded, when I saw Franco lower his weapon. "Standby"

"Strip!" Franco ordered.

"Do what?"

"Take off your clothes."

"Fuck that!" Young protested. "I'ma die with some kind of dignity."

"You asked me a question," Franco told him. "If you expect me to answer your question, I have to make sure you're not wearing a wire. It's your call."

This shit was getting weird. Franco worried about Young wearing a wire, but he didn't think to check this building, to make sure it wasn't full of agents from every agency in the United States, or aliens from Planet Wutdafuk. It was already in the mid-thirties, so I was hoping Young wasn't considering dying of hypothermia, just to have a few questions answered.

Well, obviously, I was wrong, because he began by taking off his coat. I know I should've just called the scene to action, so my team and I could get back to our cozy homes, but, for some reason, I didn't. Who knows? Maybe, Young had a trick up his—well, you know.

"Before I answer your question," Franco said, once Young was down to nothing but a pair of socks, "I have a question for you. What made you go at Drop Squad like that?"

"They were the first ones I suspected," Young answered, folding his arms over his chest.

"I commend you for the job you did on them. You really did a number on them. But, to answer your question, it started off as a scare tactic. When I heard there was a group of women trying to take on a male-dominated game, I figured I could scare them into returning to household chores women are supposed to be doing. But, when I found out they were the Kingz widows, it turned real. They were tougher than I thought. They wouldn't go down without a fight."

"What about Curt?" Young asked

I sighed inwardly, while gandering at my watch. This was definitely like a scene in a movie, where the bad guy confesses to a gang of misdeeds, before being murdered, or hauled off to jail in the end. This actually went on for another thirteen minutes, before I realized Young didn't have any tricks wherever a naked man would hide any. Perhaps, he was just seeking closure, before taking his last breath.

"Bullshit!" Young now blurted. "Why the fuck would he have Sylvia knocked off?"

"I already told you what I know," Franco said, raising his gun. "You wanna die with your clothes on, or not?"

Despite the freezing weather, I began to perspire, and my heart rate seemed to increase beneath the multiple layers of clothing I had on. As I anticipated Franco's Revolver to spark without warning. However, no matter how sadistic the older white man has proven to be, he was decorous enough to let Young put his clothes back on.

"All units," I said over the line, just as Young picked up his coat, which was the last article of clothing he had to put on. "Prepare to extract in three—two—one. Go!"

## Chapter 32

The following day, I ended up making it to work at 7:36 a.m. being that I couldn't sleep after finally taking Ray Young into custody. Well, the real reason why I couldn't sleep is because, as of now Young was being held at the federal facility downtown, under no charges while Franco and his men have already been booked on charges ranging from murder, kidnapping, extortion, and other related offenses. According to our policy, we could only hold Young for twenty-four hours without cause. Therefore, if Director Hall didn't make something happen soon, the son of a bitch will be free to roam the streets again, and I may never get another chance to nab him.

Usually, when I get off the elevator, I'm greeted by the aroma of freshly brewed coffee, put on by Mary Joseph, the director's secretary, but all I smelled was the faint aroma of whatever chemical agents the janitorial service personnel used last night. I did hear noise coming from the break room, which indicated that the older woman was in the process of livening up the place.

Making it to my cubicle, I sat my briefcase on top of the desk, grabbed my thermos, then made for the break room. Seeing the secretary with her back to me, pouring beans into the Coffee Maker X-12, I stopped in the threshold.

"You're early, Mr. Bishop," she spoke, without looking back.

"How'd you know it was me?" I entered and took a seat in one of the four plastic chairs at the small table.

"You've been wearing the same cologne since you've been here," Joseph acknowledged, moving over to the box of pastries she'd brought in. 'Trouble at home?"

"Not that I know of," I replied, not really knowing how to answer such a question.

Turning, she placed a bear claw on a napkin down in front of me, then drilled her dark-brown eyes into mine. "You're carrying around something real heavy on your heart," she told me. "Dark secrets, maybe. All I know is that your spirit is off-balanced. If you've never sought God a day in your life, I advise you to do so

273

today." Heading for the door, the secretary stopped in the threshold to regard me again. "I bless this room every morning. Feel free to use it as your sanctuary."

*What the fuck just happened!* I wondered as the woman moved on.

No disrespect to my elders, but old people always find a way to creep me out with that ancient shit about knowing how misaligned a person's soul is. All I wanted to do was grab some coffee, return to my cubicle, and wait for the director to get in—not to be spooked by the *Return of Nefertiti*.

I had no appetite, so I put the bear claw back into its box, filled my thermos with the steaming hot coffee, then exited the break room.

To my surprise, Mary Joseph was seated behind her desk, paying me no attention. However, what she was doing caused me to stop in my tracks. There was a lit candle before her, in which she seemed to be talking, or praying to, with a beaded necklace draped over her hands that were clasped together. I could only see the side of her face.

When her lips stopped moving, she opened her eyes, and blew out the candle. The moment that the flame went out, the lights faltered twice, putting me in the mind of my last trip to the morgue. Like any other normal human being, I looked around the still empty place. When I directed my attention back to Ms. Joseph, I almost gasped. She was now looking at me, but her facial features had taken on another form, and I could spot the facial features of the late Kowanda McCoy from many miles away.

"God knows what you did, Bishop," she spoke, though her voice sounded distant. "You'll get what's coming to you. Just give it time. Do you hear me, Bishop? Bishop!"

"Huh!" I broke from my abstract musing, to see that I was seated across the desk from Director Hall.

"Give it time," she said, a concerned look on her face. "Swint and I, both have faxed requests over to these guys, explaining everything. If they feel that Young should be held, they'll fax the hold over to the jail."

I looked at my watch.

"We still have enough time," Hall offered. "Just make sure you don't—"

*Beep!*

We both shifted our gazes over to the fax machine on the stand beside her desk, and watched the document slowly spew forward from it. Hall reached over, snatched the paper from the device, and began reading it. As she did, I studied her expression. Seeing her eyebrows furrow, I sensed something was wrong and wanted to leave her to whatever issue she was silently taking in at the moment.

"Congratulations!" she finally said, handing the document over to me. "He's all yours."

# Playa Ray

# Chapter 33

## *August 23, 2008*

### *Saturday*

"The eagle has landed," I said over the com-set, when the black BMW belonging to Ray Young, pulled through the entrance of the building across the street, thought it was driven by Sheila Griffin.

Over the past two and a half years, the industrial building had been converted into a nightclub, dubbed *The Palace* by Griffin, who is the owner of the place, just as she was the owner of the Glamour Girlz salon, and Posh BMWs in Marietta, Georgia. Though she hadn't been engaging in anything illegal, I still maintained my investigation, being that the Justice Department rebutted my findings in The Queenz investigation but granted me a continuance to gather fresh intel on Griffin in particular.

However, figuring the *big guys* were only playing hardball, I took the file I have on The Queenz, dissected it, rearranged it, then resubmitted it to them eighteen months later. It was the same exact file but worded differently. Hell, I was actually expecting them to chew me out for trying to pull the wool over their eyes, but the fuckers granted me permission to engage, which is why I and a nineteen man tactical unit, was parked in the Colonial parking lot, just across the street from The Palace.

Almost five minutes after Griffin entered the club, I spotted a male figure exiting, though I couldn't make out his features, without my binoculars that were hanging about my neck. Putting them up to my eyes, I saw that the man was Andre Hunt a.k.a Ace who was one of the bouncers of the place. He's also the husband of Nicole Lane, the baby's mother of the late Keith Daniels, a.k.a King Black.

As I watched Hunt move toward his champagne-colored Toyota 4-Runner, I thought about how I had to twist Chief John Moody's arm to introduce me to his confidential informant, especially after informing me that he'd gotten married, which was right at the same time I heard about Lane tying the knot. I needed someone closer to

Griffin, who could feed me personal information about the former Queen, and Hunt turned out to be a great asset, though he hadn't turned over anything criminal on her.

"I'm listening," I answered my vibrating phone, after extracting it from a pocket on my vest.

"Sheila's just got in," Hunt informed me of something I already knew. "She was headed for her office as I was headed out. Like I said, she'd sit in there for a good thirty minutes, before inspecting the place."

"What's the location of the others?" I inquired.

"Precious has everybody on the loading dock, unloading the truck. Star is the only other person inside, stocking the bar. I only got away, because Precious needed somebody to go to the store for items ordered by the artists."

"What artists are performing tonight?" I asked out of curiosity.

"I don't know what order they'll be performing in," Hunt answered. "But it'll be T.I., Young Dro, Gucci Mane, and Crime Mob. Some underground Atlanta group by the name of *Southern Comfort* will be doing opening."

I looked at my watch. "Well, I think you need to get going, if you don't wanna get caught up in this raid."

"I'm leaving now," he replied, ringing off.

"Okay, team," I said over the transceiver, as I watched Hunt's SUV approach the main road. "Prepare to roll out. Charlie, Delta, and Echo Units, I want you all to storm the loading dock. Bravo, you'll be breaching the entrance with us. Let's do it!"

I nodded to my driver, who responded by pulling the Chevy Tahoe from its parking spot. The five SUVs lined up at the entrance of Colonial's parking lot, then in formation, the drivers initiated emergency lights and sirens to bully their way across the always-busy Fulton Industrial Road.

Finally making it across, the vehicles branched off on the large parcel of The Palace. Three of them sped towards the right side of the building, where the loading docks were, and Bravo Unit trailed us to the front. Before our truck could come to a complete stop, I was lunging from it, with my Glock .40 at the ready.

Yes, I was the commander, but that didn't mean I had to send agents ahead of me. I pulled the door open with my free hand and entered. Just as Hunt said, Star Mason was the only somebody inside, while the others were out on the dock. She immediately threw her hands up, though she wasn't one of the ones who'll be arrested today.

This was my first time being inside the place, since the day I found Charles Steven's body here, years ago. Trust me, I was awed by the reconstruction, but I was too focused on the door to the main office, to give you a full description. Reaching the door, I unnecessarily kicked it open, scaring the daylights out of Sheila Griffin, seated behind her desk, now holding one hand over her chest, with her eyes the size of saucers.

"FBI!" I voiced with much authority and my gun aimed at her. "I'm only gonna ask you one time to get on the floor."

# Playa Ray

## Chapter 34

### *May 6, 2009*

### *Wednesday*

"Please, remove your sunglasses, sir!" Judge Belinda Harmon, an older black female asserted.

Obliging, I removed my 'Highway Patrols', and slipped them into the interior pocket of my blazer.

"Raise your right hand and place your left hand on the Bible!" The bailiff instructed, holding the book out to me.

I obeyed.

She continued, "Do you swear that the testimony you're about to give, is the truth the whole truth and nothing but the truth, so help you God?"

Yeah, right. "I do," I responded.

"You may be seated," she told me, before walking off.

I sat down.

"Special Agent," Judge Harmon took the reins. "Please, state your full name, and spell your last name out for the court."

"Brian Bishop," I said. "B-I-S-H-O-P."

"State," she regarded the prosecutor. "Your witness."

Federal Assistant District Attorney Ethan Banks, a Caucasian man in his late-forties, stood and rounded the state's table, then planted himself about six feet away from the witness stand, regarding me through the lenses of some very expensive-looking eyeglasses.

"Mr. Bishop," he spoke, clasping his hands together. "I'm Assistant District Attorney Ethan Banks. How are you?"

"I'm fine," I replied. "How about yourself?"

"I'm blessed," he offered with a nod. "For the court, how are you employed?"

"I'm an FBI agent," I answered with pride. "Atlanta Division."

The ADA continued, "In the investigation into the street organization known as The Kingz that resulted in the arrest of several of its members, were you the chief of operations?"

"Yes, I was the chief of operations."

"Arrested in this investigation," the older man went on. "Was Ray Young one of its leaders who goes by *King Ray*, am I right?"

I nodded. "Yes."

"Do you see the defendant Ray Young in this courtroom today?"

"I do."

"Could you point him out and tell me what he's wearing?"

I pointed at the defendant in question. "He's right there, at the defense table wearing a gray suit. Blue tie."

The prosecutor looked over to the judge. "Let the record reflect that the witness has identified the defendant, Ray Young."

"Reflected," the judge acknowledged.

"Mr. Bishop," he turned back to me. "This same investigation yielded the apprehension of a Joseph Rhodes, correct?"

"Yes."

"Do you see the defendant, Joseph Rhodes in this very courtroom?"

It took a couple of seconds but I was finally able to spot Joseph Rhodes, and also Michael Peterson a.k.a Poppo, seated on the very first bench, behind the defense table with their own attorneys.

"I do," I assured.

"Could you point him out and tell me what he's wearing?"

"First bench," I pointed. "Brown shirt, and tie."

"Let the record reflect that the defendant Joseph Rhodes has been identified."

"Reflected," came Judge Harmon's response.

"During this same investigation," the prosecutor resumed. "A Michael Peterson, a.k.a Poppo was also taken into custody. You can correct me if I'm wrong."

"You're right," I offered. "He's also seated on the first bench. Burgundy button-up shirt."

"Let the record reflect that the defendant, Michael Peterson has also been identified."

"Reflected."

"Now, Mr. Bishop," Banks went on. "I may need you to elucidate this a little for me. This is a joint trial but there were two separate investigations, correct?"

"Correct," I answered, casting a glance over at Sheila Griffin, who was also seated at the defense table, accompanied by her own lawyer. "The other investigation was into another street organization known as The Queenz."

"Which was spearheaded by a group of women?"

I nodded. "Yes."

For the record, were there any arrests made in that investigation?"

"Yes," I answered. "Sheila Griffin, a.k.a Queen Sheila was taken into custody."

"Is this person in the courtroom today?"

"She's seated at the defense table, wearing a light-blue dress suit."

"Let the record reflect that the witness has identified the defendant, Sheila Griffin."

"Reflected," said the judge.

"One minute, Mr. Bishop," The prosecutor said, before returning to his table to retrieve a manila folder filled with documents. Regarding the judge, he asked, "Your Honor, may I approach the witness?"

"Are there any objections from the defense?" she asked, looking over at the defense table.

"None, Your Honor," answered Attorney Melissa Griggs who was representing Griffin.

"You may approach," Judge Harmon permitted.

Banks walked over, placed the folder down in front of me, then stepped back. "Mr. Bishop," he started. "What I just placed in front of you is a folder. Please, take a moment to skim through its contents."

I opened the folder, and instantly noted that it was the file I submitted to the court clerk, which contained documentations of my findings in both investigations. I really didn't need a moment to *skim* through it, so I closed it, and looked back up at the prosecutor.

"Are you done?" he asked.

"Yes, I am."

"Can you tell the court what you were looking at?"

"It's the file that I built on both organizations," I answered. "This is the actual copy I submitted to the clerk of court."

"Thank you!" Retrieving the folder, he turned to the judge. "Your Honor, copies of this entire file has been distributed to defense attorneys. With that said at this time, I would like to publish this file into evidence, as State's Exhibit one."

"Any objections from the defense?" Judge Harmon inquired.

"Yes, Your Honor," Attorney Griggs answered getting to her feet with Young's attorney following suit.

"Ground?" asked the judge.

"Under the grounds that aforementioned file is erroneous, and not proper before the court."

The judge leered at her. "Could you, please, elaborate, counsel?"

"The agent was sworn in to tell the truth," Griggs went on. "However, to allow his documented findings into evidence, would totally contradict this oath and constitute perjury."

Judge Harmon shot a confusing look over at me, then back at the attorney. "Come again!"

"We can substantially prove that a large portion of the agent's findings were illegally obtained," Young's lawyer offered his two cents. "Therefore, at this time we would like to move for a Motion for Limine."

"We also join in on that motion, Your Honor," Peterson's lawyer stated, getting to his feet. Rhodes' attorney also stood, indicating his partaking in the same request.

"And what portion of the file are you all trying to exclude?" Harmon wanted to know.

"Every part that pre-dates signed consequent forms by the agent's superiors," Attorney Griggs offered.

After an exasperated sigh, and one last glance in my direction, the judge said, "I want all parties up here, right now!"

She turned off her microphone, as all four attorneys, and the prosecutor, moved toward the front of her desk. The court room was quiet. Besides the stenographer on the opposite side of the judge's bench, I was close as hell, but still couldn't hear the conversation, as the six of them physically dissected the contents of the folder.

Suddenly there was a loud pounding on the entry doors of the courtroom, which is prohibited and deemed disrespectful to whatever judge presiding. Alarm was on the faces of the eleven appointed bailiffs, as three of them, including the one that swore me in, moved toward the entrance with their hands rested on their service weapons. Hell, I would've had my hand rested on mine, had I not had to adhere to the courthouse's policy of no guns being allowed inside unless by authorized personnel.

"It's a band of agents from some kind of federal agency, Your Honor," the female bailiff informed.

"How do you know they're agents?" Judge Harmon inquired.

"This guy is holding his credentials up to the window."

"I hope they have a perfectly good reason why they're disrupting my courtroom," said Harmon. "Let them in!"

The bailiff opened the door and stepped aside. To my surprise, the first person that marched through the door was Assistant Director Swint, followed by Director Hall and a handful of tactical-dressed agents I'd never seen before. If the abrupt presence of both my superiors wasn't questioning enough, then the presence of my former superior, Manny Hopkins, who brought up the rear certainly was. Plus, he was accompanied by the blonde woman from the CIA, who helped me solve the Bernadine Yarborough's case by showing me satellite footage of where the parents dumped her body.

"I'm sorry for the intrusion, Your Honor!" Swint spoke, as he approached, holding up his credentials. "But we have official business with Mr. Bishop here. I promise it won't take long." He turned to me. "Mr. Bishop, you are under arrest for the murders of Leonard

Watts and Atlanta Homicide Detective, Kowanda McCoy. Please stand and allow these men to take you into custody."

Instinctively, I looked at the CIA agent, and pretty much knew how they were able to tie me to these murders but I may never know what tipped them off, being that I was very sure I'd covered my tracks. However, yet and still, I find myself having to answer to my wrongdoings. No matter how smart we think we are, there's always someone out there much smarter. Then, there's karma and God. I'm not sure if those two go hand in hand but I believe in them both. Especially now.

Now, signing quietly, I stood, retrieving my *Highway Patrols* from my inner pocket, and put them on my face. Then interlocking my hands atop my head, I stepped around the witness stand and turned my back to the first Task Force agent, to be handcuffed while noticing that neither one of them had their weapons drawn. Just as the agent grabbed one of my hands. I spun around quickly, snatched the Glock from the holster on his vest, and pointed it at his chest with no intention to do him any harm.

Gasps and screams sounded around the courtroom. The other Task Force agents were quick with the drawing of their weapons and just as quick with eliminating the immediate threat. Their guns went off, simultaneously, and their rounds hit home, knocking me back onto the floor between the witness stand and the jury box.

As darkness slowly overtook me, I thought about how I failed as a father to my children and a husband to my wife. However, this was my life, and I chose to end it at this chapter of the book. Goodbye world! Before they lower my casket into the ground, I want to leave you with a few words of encouragement, "Go fuck yourselves!"

# Chapter 35

### *Two Year Later*

"Make sure you take the trash out before you leave, Ray," The manager said, before walking off.

Ray shot daggers at the man's back, until he'd disappeared inside his office. Disposing of the trash, before clocking out, was something he'd been doing for the past seven months, but this clown always made it his business to remind Ray to do something that a dog would be conscious of doing repetitiously.

Refusing to let this idiot get to him Ray who was the first-shift grill man at Checkers, continued cleaning his area for the next grill man. Once he was done, Ray made for the back door, looking around for Sheila who was nowhere in sight. Reaching the back door, where all the trash from the day shift was piled up on the floor, he disarmed the alarm, and propped the door open, before filling the only trash cart with as much trash as he could, to limit his rounds.

"I can't believe I'm still doing this slave-ass shit!" Ray grumbled, as he wheeled the car across the lot, to the dumpster that had a concrete structure around it, with a wooden door.

Although it was only 4:37 p.m. and the restaurant had only been robbed twice on night shift, Ray was always vigilant. Plus, he was forever looking around for parked vehicles with someone sitting in them. Especially after the episode of him getting arrested and finding out there was a full-scale investigation going on with his organization, as well as the one Sheila was a part of.

What happened in that courtroom, two years ago, still seemed surreal. That FBI agent had gone to all that trouble, hard work, and dedication to bring the roof down on both groups, only to have his life taken that day, in order to escape prosecution for his own evil deeds. Well, it all worked out in the favors of Ray and Sheila because the judge immediately dismissed all charges, before excusing herself from the courtroom, for the sake of the dead body lying before her. Although he escaped that snare, Ray still felt he was being

watched by another enthused, cowboy-of-an agent, who was determined to finish what Special Agent Brian Bishop started.

It had only taken three trips to complete the trash run. Returning
to the building, Ray re-activated the alarm, then retrieved his leather
coat that he donned over his Checkers windbreaker and was ready
to get out of there. The assistant manager, who was the wife of the
manager was in the office when he went in to clock out. As usual,
there were only a few words exchanged between them. Although
the woman, who was only a few years older than him, always had a
sly way of letting it be known that she was into him. Leaving the
office, Ray looked around for Sheila once more, to no avail, then
approached Calvin, who was putting on his coat.

"Yo, Calvin?" Ray spoke, approaching. "Have you seen
Sheila?"

"I saw her going into the freezer with Jerry," he answered.
"That was about five minutes ago."

Ray didn't like Calvin's tone of voice. In fact, he always used
that same tone, whenever a conversation involving Sheila and the
manager came up, as if insinuating there was something going on
between the two. Not caring to respond, Ray turned, and was about
to head for the cooler, when the door came open, and Sheila
emerged, followed by Jerry, who was carrying a clipboard.

"Thanks again, Sheila!" The manager said.

"You're welcome," Sheila replied, then made her way over to
Ray. "Are you ready, baby?"

Ray didn't answer. He shot a menacing look over at Jerry, who
had a sneer on his face, as he ducked inside the office. Without a
word to Sheila, Ray spun around, and walked away. Of course, she
was right on his heels, saying her goodbyes to everyone, as they
made their way out of the establishment. They climbed into their
burgundy, 2006 Cadillac CTS.

Sheila put on her seatbelt, and waited for Ray to start the engine,
in anticipation of the heater to warm the console, but he just sat
there, staring out of the windshield, without even sticking the key
into the ignition. Instantly, Sheila knew something was wrong. Ever
since they'd been back together, things hadn't exactly been *peaches*

*and cream*, and Sheila could only blame it on the night she was kidnapped, and Ray traded his life in order for her and their son to live. He prepared for his death, so he expected to die that night. Or maybe he was hoping he'd died that night which was probably why he didn't attempt to reach out to her the whole time he was sitting in that jail, awaiting trial.

"Ray?" Sheila finally spoke. "What's the matter, baby?"

"This shit has to end!" he spoke through clenched teeth, still looking ahead.

Sheila's heart stopped. "W-what has to end?" she stammered.

"We built an empire," Ray went on. "The Kingz had this shit on lock. We ate out here in these streets. My brother lost his life for this shit, and here I am, living like a fucking peasant! Busting my ass at a fucking fast foods joint!"

"You're earning a decent living, Ray," Sheila pointed out, hating to hear him talk like this. "We both are."

Ray finally faced her. "Well, you can continue earning a decent living. You and Jerry."

"What the fuck is that supposed to mean?" she argued.

"I'm going back," Ray told her. "The streets owe me!"

To Be Continued…
Kingz of the Game 7
Coming Soon

**Lock Down Publications and Ca$h Presents** assisted publishing packages.

**BASIC PACKAGE** $499
Editing
Cover Design
Formatting

**UPGRADED PACKAGE** $800
Typing
Editing
Cover Design
Formatting

**ADVANCE PACKAGE** $1,200
Typing
Editing
Cover Design
Formatting
Copyright registration
Proofreading
Upload book to Amazon

**LDP SUPREME PACKAGE** $1,500
Typing
Editing
Cover Design
Formatting
Copyright registration
Proofreading
Set up Amazon account
Upload book to Amazon
Advertise on LDP Amazon and Facebook page

***Other services available upon request. Additional charges may apply
**Lock Down Publications**
**P.O. Box 944**
**Stockbridge, GA 30281-9998**
**Phone # 470 303-9761**

# Submission Guideline

Submit the first three chapters of your completed manuscript to ldpsubmissions@gmail.com, subject line: Your book's title. The manuscript must be in a .doc file and sent as an attachment. Document should be in Times New Roman, double spaced and in size 12 font. Also, provide your synopsis and full contact information. If sending multiple submissions, they must each be in a separate email.

Have a story but no way to send it electronically? You can still submit to LDP/Ca$h Presents. Send in the first three chapters, written or typed, of your completed manuscript to:

**LDP: Submissions Dept**
**Po Box 944**
**Stockbridge, Ga 30281**

*DO NOT send original manuscript. Must be a duplicate.*

Provide your synopsis and a cover letter containing your full contact information.

Thanks for considering LDP and Ca$h Presents.

## <u>NEW RELEASES</u>

AN UNFORESEEN LOVE 2 by MEESHA
KING OF THE TRENCHES by GHOST & TRANAY
ADAMS
A DOPEBOY'S DREAM by ROMELL TUKES
MONEY MAFIA by JIBRIL WILLIAMS
QUEEN OF THE ZOO by BLACK MIGO
MOB TIES 4 by SAYNOMORE
THE BRICK MAN by KING RIO
KINGZ OF THE GAME by PLAYA RAY

# Playa Ray

STREET KINGS III

PAID IN BLOOD III

CARTEL KILLAZ IV

DOPE GODS III

**Hood Rich**

SINS OF A HUSTLA II

**ASAD**

RICH $AVAGE II

**By Troublesome**

YAYO V

Bred In The Game 2

**S. Allen**

CREAM III

**By Yolanda Moore**

SON OF A DOPE FIEND III

HEAVEN GOT A GHETTO II

**By Renta**

LOYALTY AIN'T PROMISED III

**By Keith Williams**

I'M NOTHING WITHOUT HIS LOVE II

SINS OF A THUG II

TO THE THUG I LOVED BEFORE II

**By Monet Dragun**

QUIET MONEY IV

EXTENDED CLIP III

THUG LIFE IV

By **Trai'Quan**

THE STREETS MADE ME IV

By **Larry D. Wright**

IF YOU CROSS ME ONCE II

# Playa Ray

By **Anthony Fields**

THE STREETS WILL NEVER CLOSE II

By **K'ajji**

HARD AND RUTHLESS III

THE BILLIONAIRE BENTLEYS II

**Von Diesel**

KILLA KOUNTY II

By **Khufu**

MONEY GAME II

By **Smoove Dolla**

A GANGSTA'S KARMA II

By **FLAME**

JACK BOYZ VERSUS DOPE BOYZ

A DOPEBOY'S DREAM III

By **Romell Tukes**

MURDA WAS THE CASE II

**Elijah R. Freeman**

THE STREETS NEVER LET GO II

By **Robert Baptiste**

AN UNFORESEEN LOVE III

By **Meesha**

KING OF THE TRENCHES II

by **GHOST & TRANAY ADAMS**

MONEY MAFIA

By **Jibril Williams**

QUEEN OF THE ZOO II

By **Black Migo**

THE BRICK MAN II

By **King Rio**

## Available Now

RESTRAINING ORDER **I & II**
By **CA$H & Coffee**
LOVE KNOWS NO BOUNDARIES **I II & III**
By **Coffee**
RAISED AS A GOON I, II, III & IV
BRED BY THE SLUMS I, II, III
BLAST FOR ME I & II
ROTTEN TO THE CORE I II III
A BRONX TALE I, II, III
DUFFLE BAG CARTEL I II III IV V VI
HEARTLESS GOON I II III IV V
A SAVAGE DOPEBOY I II
DRUG LORDS I II III
CUTTHROAT MAFIA I II
KING OF THE TRENCHES
By **Ghost**
LAY IT DOWN **I & II**
LAST OF A DYING BREED I II
BLOOD STAINS OF A SHOTTA I & II III
By **Jamaica**
LOYAL TO THE GAME I II III
LIFE OF SIN I, II III
By **TJ & Jelissa**
BLOODY COMMAS I & II
SKI MASK CARTEL I II & III

## Playa Ray

KING OF NEW YORK I II,III IV V

RISE TO POWER I II III

COKE KINGS I II III IV

BORN HEARTLESS I II III IV

KING OF THE TRAP I II

By **T.J. Edwards**

IF LOVING HIM IS WRONG...I & II

LOVE ME EVEN WHEN IT HURTS I II III

By **Jelissa**

WHEN THE STREETS CLAP BACK I & II III

THE HEART OF A SAVAGE I II III

MONEY MAFIA

By **Jibril Williams**

A DISTINGUISHED THUG STOLE MY HEART I II & III

LOVE SHOULDN'T HURT I II III IV

RENEGADE BOYS I II III IV

PAID IN KARMA I II III

SAVAGE STORMS I II

AN UNFORESEEN LOVE I II

By **Meesha**

A GANGSTER'S CODE I &, II III

A GANGSTER'S SYN I II III

THE SAVAGE LIFE I II III

CHAINED TO THE STREETS I II III

BLOOD ON THE MONEY I II III

By **J-Blunt**

PUSH IT TO THE LIMIT

By **Bre' Hayes**

BLOOD OF A BOSS **I, II, III, IV, V**

SHADOWS OF THE GAME

# Kingz of the Game 6

TRAP BASTARD

By **Askari**

THE STREETS BLEED MURDER **I, II & III**

THE HEART OF A GANGSTA I II& III

By **Jerry Jackson**

CUM FOR ME I II III IV V VI VII

An **LDP Erotica Collaboration**

BRIDE OF A HUSTLA **I II & II**

THE FETTI GIRLS **I, II& III**

CORRUPTED BY A GANGSTA I, II III, IV

BLINDED BY HIS LOVE

THE PRICE YOU PAY FOR LOVE I, II ,III

DOPE GIRL MAGIC I II III

By **Destiny Skai**

WHEN A GOOD GIRL GOES BAD

By **Adrienne**

THE COST OF LOYALTY I II III

**By Kweli**

A GANGSTER'S REVENGE **I II III & IV**

THE BOSS MAN'S DAUGHTERS I II III IV V

A SAVAGE LOVE **I & II**

BAE BELONGS TO ME I II

A HUSTLER'S DECEIT I, II, III

WHAT BAD BITCHES DO I, II, III

SOUL OF A MONSTER I II III

KILL ZONE

A DOPE BOY'S QUEEN I II III

By **Aryanna**

A KINGPIN'S AMBITON

A KINGPIN'S AMBITION **II**

299

## Playa Ray

I MURDER FOR THE DOUGH
By **Ambitious**
TRUE SAVAGE I II III IV V VI VII
DOPE BOY MAGIC I, II, III
MIDNIGHT CARTEL I II III
CITY OF KINGZ I II
NIGHTMARE ON SILENT AVE
By **Chris Green**
A DOPEBOY'S PRAYER
By **Eddie "Wolf" Lee**
THE KING CARTEL **I, II & III**
By **Frank Gresham**
THESE NIGGAS AIN'T LOYAL **I, II & III**
By **Nikki Tee**
GANGSTA SHYT **I II &III**
By **CATO**
THE ULTIMATE BETRAYAL
By **Phoenix**
BOSS'N UP **I , II & III**
By **Royal Nicole**
I LOVE YOU TO DEATH
By **Destiny J**
I RIDE FOR MY HITTA
I STILL RIDE FOR MY HITTA
By **Misty Holt**
LOVE & CHASIN' PAPER
By **Qay Crockett**
TO DIE IN VAIN
SINS OF A HUSTLA
By **ASAD**

300

# Kingz of the Game 6

BROOKLYN HUSTLAZ

By **Boogsy Morina**

BROOKLYN ON LOCK I & II

By **Sonovia**

GANGSTA CITY

By **Teddy Duke**

A DRUG KING AND HIS DIAMOND I & II III

A DOPEMAN'S RICHES

HER MAN, MINE'S TOO I, II

CASH MONEY HO'S

THE WIFEY I USED TO BE I II

**By Nicole Goosby**

TRAPHOUSE KING **I II & III**

KINGPIN KILLAZ I II III

STREET KINGS I II

PAID IN BLOOD **I II**

CARTEL KILLAZ I II III

DOPE GODS I II

By **Hood Rich**

LIPSTICK KILLAH **I, II, III**

CRIME OF PASSION I II & III

FRIEND OR FOE I II III

By **Mimi**

STEADY MOBBN' **I, II, III**

THE STREETS STAINED MY SOUL I II

By **Marcellus Allen**

WHO SHOT YA **I, II, III**

SON OF A DOPE FIEND I II

HEAVEN GOT A GHETTO

**Renta**

# Playa Ray

GORILLAZ IN THE BAY **I II III IV**

TEARS OF A GANGSTA I II

3X KRAZY I II

**DE'KARI**

TRIGGADALE I II III

MURDAROBER WAS THE CASE

**Elijah R. Freeman**

GOD BLESS THE TRAPPERS I, II, III

THESE SCANDALOUS STREETS I, II, III

FEAR MY GANGSTA I, II, III IV, V

THESE STREETS DON'T LOVE NOBODY I, II

BURY ME A G I, II, III, IV, V

A GANGSTA'S EMPIRE I, II, III, IV

THE DOPEMAN'S BODYGAURD I II

THE REALEST KILLAZ I II III

THE LAST OF THE OGS I II III

**Tranay Adams**

THE STREETS ARE CALLING

**Duquie Wilson**

MARRIED TO A BOSS I II III

**By Destiny Skai & Chris Green**

KINGZ OF THE GAME I II III IV V VI

**Playa Ray**

SLAUGHTER GANG I II III

RUTHLESS HEART I II III

**By Willie Slaughter**

FUK SHYT

**By Blakk Diamond**

DON'T F#CK WITH MY HEART I II

**By Linnea**

ADDICTED TO THE DRAMA I II III

IN THE ARM OF HIS BOSS II

**By Jamila**

YAYO I II III IV

A SHOOTER'S AMBITION I II

BRED IN THE GAME

**By S. Allen**

TRAP GOD I II III

RICH $AVAGE

**By Troublesome**

FOREVER GANGSTA

GLOCKS ON SATIN SHEETS I II

**By Adrian Dulan**

TOE TAGZ I II III

LEVELS TO THIS SHYT I II

**By Ah'Million**

KINGPIN DREAMS I II III

**By Paper Boi Rari**

CONFESSIONS OF A GANGSTA I II III IV

**By Nicholas Lock**

I'M NOTHING WITHOUT HIS LOVE

SINS OF A THUG

TO THE THUG I LOVED BEFORE

**By Monet Dragun**

CAUGHT UP IN THE LIFE I II III

THE STREETS NEVER LET GO

**By Robert Baptiste**

NEW TO THE GAME I II III

MONEY, MURDER & MEMORIES I II III

**By Malik D. Rice**

# Playa Ray

LIFE OF A SAVAGE I II III

A GANGSTA'S QUR'AN I II III

MURDA SEASON I II III

GANGLAND CARTEL I II III

CHI'RAQ GANGSTAS I II III

KILLERS ON ELM STREET I II III

JACK BOYZ N DA BRONX I II III

A DOPEBOY'S DREAM I II

By **Romell Tukes**

LOYALTY AIN'T PROMISED I II

**By Keith Williams**

QUIET MONEY I II III

THUG LIFE I II III

EXTENDED CLIP I II

By **Trai'Quan**

THE STREETS MADE ME I II III

By **Larry D. Wright**

THE ULTIMATE SACRIFICE I, II, III, IV, V, VI

KHADIFI

IF YOU CROSS ME ONCE

ANGEL I II

IN THE BLINK OF AN EYE

By **Anthony Fields**

THE LIFE OF A HOOD STAR

**By Ca$h & Rashia Wilson**

THE STREETS WILL NEVER CLOSE

**By K'ajji**

CREAM I II

**By Yolanda Moore**

NIGHTMARES OF A HUSTLA I II III

# Kingz of the Game 6

By King Dream
CONCRETE KILLA I II
By Kingpen
HARD AND RUTHLESS I II
MOB TOWN 251
THE BILLIONAIRE BENTLEYS
By Von Diesel
GHOST MOB
Stilloan Robinson
MOB TIES I II III IV
By SayNoMore
BODYMORE MURDERLAND I II III
By Delmont Player
FOR THE LOVE OF A BOSS
By C. D. Blue
MOBBED UP I II III IV
THE BRICK MAN
By King Rio
KILLA KOUNTY
By Khufu
MONEY GAME
By Smoove Dolla
A GANGSTA'S KARMA
By FLAME
KING OF THE TRENCHES II
by GHOST & TRANAY ADAMS
QUEEN OF THE ZOO
By Black Migo

Playa Ray

## BOOKS BY LDP'S CEO, CA$H

TRUST IN NO MAN

TRUST IN NO MAN 2

TRUST IN NO MAN 3

BONDED BY BLOOD

SHORTY GOT A THUG

THUGS CRY

THUGS CRY 2

THUGS CRY 3

TRUST NO BITCH

TRUST NO BITCH 2

TRUST NO BITCH 3

TIL MY CASKET DROPS

RESTRAINING ORDER

RESTRAINING ORDER 2

IN LOVE WITH A CONVICT

LIFE OF A HOOD STAR

# Kingz of the Game 6